Sing with Me

Bette Hawkins

Other Bella Books by Bette Hawkins

No More Pretending
Like a Book
In My Heart
Running Deep
Leading Lady

Sing with Me

Bette Hawkins

Copyright © 2025 by Bette Hawkins

Bella Books, Inc.
P.O. Box 10543
Tallahassee, FL 32302

All rights reserved. No part of this book may be used or reproduced or transmitted in any form or manner or by any means, electronic or mechanical, including photocopying, or for the purpose of training artificial intelligence technologies or systems without permission in writing from the publisher.

This is a work of fiction. Names, characters, businesses, places, events and incidents are either the products of the author's imagination or used in a fictitious manner. Any resemblance to actual persons, living or dead, or actual events is purely coincidental. The publisher does not have any control over and does not assume any responsibility for author or third-party websites or their content.

First Edition - 2025

Editor: Cath Walker
Cover Designer: SJ Hardy
Cover art credit: amoklv - Torrevieja, Spain

ISBN: 978-1-64247-675-0

PUBLISHER'S NOTE

The scanning, uploading, and distribution of this book via the Internet or via any other means without the permission of the publisher is illegal and punishable by law. Please purchase only authorized print or electronic editions, and do not participate in or encourage electronic piracy of copyrighted materials. Your support of the author's rights is appreciated.

Acknowledgment

Thanks to my editor, Cath,
and the incredible team at Bella Books.

Dedicated to my love, M.

CHAPTER ONE

Ashley Archer stood on the red carpet, trying not to think about how many cameras were pointed at her. She'd attended countless awards shows but could never grow used to it—especially the merry-go-round of appointments with stylists and beauty therapists. Her eyebrows had been tinted and plucked, her nails painted, and her platinum hair color freshened. She'd accessorized her sequined black gown with long white gloves because being styled like a 1950s movie star gave her borrowed confidence. It was overwhelming anyway, with photographers yelling at her and onlookers screaming. She patted the borrowed diamond necklace, afraid to lose it.

A TV host with dazzlingly white teeth stuck a microphone in her face. She recognized him from one of the morning shows. "Ashley, tell us who you're wearing?"

"Valentino," she replied, dutifully giving a spin with her hand on her hip.

None of this came naturally, but she was doing her best. A Vanguard Music nomination was a big deal. As the cliché said, she was grateful just to be nominated. Still, she'd prefer to be in a warm bath with a good book. She loved making music, but the rest was a circus she could do without.

"Do you think you'll be taking home a statue tonight?"

"There were a lot of excellent records this year. I'm honored to be among the nominees."

"What's it like to be up against Gigi Lark?"

Ashley stiffened at the sound of Gigi's name, even though she'd expected it. It was their first time competing against one another in a major awards category, so it was all anyone was talking about. She hoped her smile looked genuine. "She's a very talented artist. I wish her all the best."

The TV host nodded impatiently, clearly hoping for some dirt. "What did you think of her album? Everyone's saying she's the one to beat."

"I've been so busy that I haven't heard it all the way through yet, but I hear it's wonderful. Thank you so much," she lied, grateful when her publicist, Julia, finally pulled her away. She'd listened to the album and loved it, but she would never give Gigi the satisfaction of saying so.

"You're doing great. Just keep deflecting like we practiced," Julia said quietly, poised and elegant in her pantsuit.

Ashley kept the smile on her face and leaned closer to Julia's ear. "Can we please go inside now? Every question's going to be about her. I'm already over it."

"Just do a couple more. You want to project the image that it doesn't bother you, right?"

"Ha. You're so good at getting me to do what you want. Do you think I'll finally meet her tonight?"

"I hope so. I'd love to see *that* moment."

It was bizarre that even though they were on the same record label, Gigi and Ashley had never spoken to one another. Their conflict had played out through the press and social media, Internet drama at its finest. When they were both nominated for a Vanguard, Ashley assumed they'd finally come face-to-face. Instead, the category's big photoshoot was canceled, and Gigi had missed the nominee luncheon due to food poisoning. Supposedly.

Ashley went down the production line of reporters, feeling like a phony. She was grateful when she came to the section where fans hung over a barrier. She signed as many autographs as possible and posed for selfies. As she reached the end of the line, a fresh wave of screaming rose from the crowd.

Someone big had arrived.

"Gigi!" a group of teenage girls shouted.

Gigi Lark stepped out of her limo, and Ashley caught a glimpse of red hair and a shapely leg. She craned her neck to check out what she was wearing and saw Gigi's emerald dress glittering under the lights. Ashley bet she didn't have the same trouble choosing an outfit—she was always so glamorous. She was made for the pageantry in a way Ashley wasn't.

"C'mon, Ashley. Let's get you to your table," Julia said, whisking her away.

Each table in the opulent ballroom was set with place cards, bottles of Moët, and fresh flowers. She hadn't brought a date. Luckily, she'd been seated with Endless River, an Americana band performing tonight. She'd met them before, and they were nice guys. One of them had brought along his wife, Natasha, who made her husband switch seats so they could sit next to one another.

"I was so excited when I realized you'd be on our table. We saw you play at the Bowl last year. You were incredible," Natasha said.

"Thanks, that's very kind."

They'd been chatting for a few minutes when she noticed Natasha looking over her shoulder. She turned her head, and her heart lurched—Gigi was only a couple of tables away with her wife by her side. Even with their backs to her, she had to admit they made a stunning couple. Gigi had pale skin, green eyes, and a curvy figure. Hayley was petite with long, wavy black hair. They sat with their heads bent together like there was nobody else in the room. Ashley felt a strange envy at how close they seemed, though she was perfectly happy being single.

"I'm sorry. I wasn't going to bring it up, but it must be weird for you that Gigi's here on your big night. That you're competing for the same award," Natasha said.

"Sure. A little. The whole thing's really been blown out of proportion."

When had this thing even started? Clickbait articles laid out timelines, but Ashley tried to avoid those. They'd released their first records and grown famous in the same year, and the rivalry started soon afterward. She knew what the whisper campaigns said no matter how often she downplayed it. Everyone thought each was insanely jealous of the other. It annoyed her that they'd been pitted against one another from day one, as if the culture didn't have room for two successful female artists.

It was a shame that Gigi had fanned the flames, even writing a thinly veiled diss track about her. Who could blame Ashley for hitting back now and then?

The award show's host was Tom O'Leary, a stand-up comedian who'd just clinched his own late-night show. He was relentless about her and Gigi, cracking cat-fight jokes with lame meow noises. Knowing the camera would be on her the whole time, Ashley laughed and played it cool, doing her best to be a good sport. She was dying to look at the monitors to see how Gigi was handling it, but she'd have to wait until the GIFs started circulating.

The show finally moved on to awarding Best New Artist, and she headed to the restroom to collect herself, feeling eyes on her all the way. She sighed, wishing the focus could be on celebrating the music. She wasn't expecting to win but was proud of the album she'd poured so much into.

Ashley touched up her lipstick, drawing out the time until she had to return to the table. She heard flushing behind her and froze as Gigi Lark's wife approached the sink beside her. Ashley didn't look away from her reflection, blotting with a tissue.

Hayley washed her hands, their eyes finally meeting in the mirror. "That's a great shade on you."

Ashley slowly put her lipstick in her clutch, unsure how to play it. Was there a chance Gigi's wife didn't realize who she was? That was impossible. "Thank you."

"I feel duty-bound to say you shouldn't blot with tissue. You've never had a makeup artist tell you that?" she asked, her voice sweet and bubbly.

Ashley threw the tissue in the trash, smiling despite herself. Hayley was kind of charming. "Maybe they think I'm a lost cause when it comes to this stuff."

"Then lucky I'm here. Tissue will take out some of the color and leave little bits behind. Paper's better," she said, swiping a thumb over Ashley's mouth.

Ashley took a step back, trying not to make a big deal out of it. That was odd, but maybe she was one of those people who had no concept of personal space. "Thanks. I'll remember that."

"Here," Hayley said, opening her purse and taking out a paper square. "Redo your lipstick, then use this. You'll see the difference, I promise. You have beautiful lips. You want them to look perfect."

Was Gigi Lark's wife actually flirting with her? Jesus. She had to say something. "You're Hayley Doran, right? I'm Ashley Archer. I'm not sure if you recognize me."

Hayley stared at her in a way that made it clear she'd known the whole time. "Nice to meet you."

"You're Gigi Lark's wife, aren't you?"

"Georgia. I can't be caught calling her by her stage name. She's really precious about that."

"Right. Anyway, I should be getting back out there."

"Stay a while. Let's talk," Hayley said, brushing fingers along her arm. "I've always wanted to meet you. I love your music."

"That's sweet, but I really should go," she said, quickly walking past her, her face hot. As if this night wasn't awkward enough.

Endless River was about to perform, and she was grateful for the distraction. When it was finally time for her category, she'd almost forgotten the bizarre interaction. They'd chosen a pair of young actors starring in an upcoming romantic comedy to present the award. While they bantered onstage, Ashley kept her expression neutral.

As they read each artist's name and played music video clips, she clapped and smiled, trying not to turn her head again. Gigi was a magnet—the green dress and red hair pulling her in. She couldn't surrender.

And the winner is… So, this was what it felt like for your soul to leave your body. Did she accidentally move when they called Gigi's name?

She clapped harder. It was cruel to film a person while they were losing. It was especially awful to film her as she lost to the woman she'd been publicly feuding with for seven years.

Gigi went up on the stage, her hourglass figure looking heavenly in her gown. She delivered a heartfelt speech without a glance at the piece of paper in her hand. She thanked her wife first and didn't stumble over Ashley's name when she thanked her fellow nominees. She could afford to be generous. She'd just won a Vanguard.

If their rivalry was a game, Ashley had just lost in front of the whole world.

CHAPTER TWO

Two Years Later

"You want me to work with Ashley Archer? You can't be serious. How can you suggest something so ridiculous?"

Georgia's manager and publicist squirmed. They wanted her to smile and agree with the team, but she'd never been good at hiding her emotions. She looked around the conference table at the record label executives. "Am I on a hidden camera show or something?"

Cliff tented his fingers and gave her a stony look. He wore a blazer over his Metallica shirt. She'd just released her fifth album with Splash Records, and after years of meetings, she'd stopped thinking of him as the cool record label executive—the one she could relate to. Cliff had signed her and always took a special interest in her career, but they were all the same. The conference room had the same soulless quality as the people. Black leather chairs, cream carpets, and a vulgar red sofa nobody ever sat on. Framed platinum records hung on the walls. The way they were talking to her, you'd never know how many of them were hers.

"I'm not sure you're thinking about this the right way. This is a wonderful opportunity for you, Gigi," Cliff said.

"I've told you all a thousand times that I don't want you to call me that. Call me Georgia, please."

Gigi Lark wasn't as stagey as Lady Gaga or P!NK, but it wasn't her name—one of the only things she could control. The label people insisted she color her hair the same flame-red she'd worn when she first became famous. If she dared to put an extra few pounds on her tall frame, they hinted about personal trainers. Once, someone even suggested that she soften her English accent so people would think she was American. The least they could do was use the name she asked them to.

Cliff held up his hands. "I know it sounds strange at first. But we have to do something to turn this situation around. Hear us out."

The executive beside Cliff broke in. Michael peered at her over his designer spectacles. He was one of the founders of the label, and was obsessed with Splash's profile and marketing. "This album is bombing. People can't separate it from the controversy about your private life. We don't think you can come back from this."

She'd been on top of the world only one album cycle ago. She'd topped the streaming charts, headlined at Coachella, and even won a Vanguard for Album of the Year. How could that all be forgotten so quickly? She should never have rushed this album out. She should've taken more time to get it right.

"Maybe it'll be a slow burn. Or maybe it's just a miss, and I can focus on another album that'll turn things around. By myself, I mean. Not with *her*."

"You could release the best album in the world, but it might do just as badly as *All You Need*. We know how folks talk about you online. This isn't blowing over any time soon."

"No need to remind me. People tag me in their nasty comments. Surely there's something else we could do other than have me work with my arch nemesis."

The public had turned on her after a nasty divorce. Talk about being punched when you were down. The breakup with Hayley Doran was traumatic, and she wondered if she'd ever get over discovering that she'd committed herself to a stranger. As Hayley slipped that ring on her finger, Georgia had believed she was promising forever.

It lasted less than two years.

"You're not seen as likable anymore," Cliff said.

"That's what happens when her team leaks nonsense about me, and you guys don't do enough to counter it. I mean, look at all the stuff she said," Georgia said, ticking the lies off on her fingers. "That I'm horrible to everyone who works for me, that I was a cold and jealous partner. And worst of all, I stole her lyrics. Why didn't we hit out harder on that? We all know it's not true."

Sometimes, she felt like she was going crazy. Hayley's betrayal was such a mindfuck that Georgia had to remind herself none of it was true.

"We've been trying. It's not on-brand for you to engage with those negative stories," Michael said, gesturing toward her publicist, Morrison. "We agreed that responding would only give them legitimacy. So, we've done everything we can to build positive buzz instead."

"I don't get how this is where you landed. I don't even know why Ashley would agree to it. You must've offered her a good deal. She hates me."

The feeling was mutual. The rivalry started long ago and had become central to their careers. When Georgia released her debut album, it knocked Ashley's from the top of the charts. Ashley was initially gracious, but according to the lore, she pulled a face when a journalist asked about Georgia. After that, it snowballed. Over the years, they each made unkind statements about the other.

Ashley even stooped low enough to hit on her wife in the bathroom at The Vanguards. It had ruined her night and caused a huge fight with Hayley when she should've been celebrating her win. That sealed it—she'd never forgive her.

"Oh, come on. Ashley Archer doesn't hate you. She's been a Splash artist since the beginning, so we know what makes her tick. She knows how to play the game, that's all. That's what it's always been about. The beef has always kept you both on the front page," Cliff laughed.

"Right. So she's always just been using me for publicity. How comforting."

"You two haven't even met, have you? That's crazy to me. Maybe you'd like one another. You have a lot in common."

Georgia figured he meant they were both gay, and he was the kind of guy who thought all lesbians must know each other. As two of the only out female pop stars, comparisons were inevitable—but they couldn't be more different. Georgia released catchy club songs and was as famous for her looks and love life as her music. Ashley was a singer-songwriter who guarded her personal life closely and stood up for herself when journalists crossed the line. She was known for controlling every aspect of her music and image in a way that Georgia envied and resented.

"I've seen her across rooms, at events or whatever, but we've never talked. I won't play whatever little game she's trying to start. My next album will be my own work, whether people love it or hate it. I'll go it alone. I always have."

"Hey. That would make a great lyrical theme. Something about female empowerment. Let's take that down," Nicky said. She tapped a note into her iPhone, holding her hand to prevent her long pink nails from getting in the way.

Georgia loved her manager but wished she'd never told her about her writer's block. "Thank you, Nicky. All good."

"There's an angle we haven't told you about yet. This collaboration isn't our idea, or even hers," Cliff said.

Now, they were finally getting to the point. Working with Ashley made no sense, so Georgia wasn't surprised that there was a backstory. "Okay. I see. Whose idea is it, then?"

Cliff looked around the table, smirking. Everyone held their breath, but Georgia sensed they already knew. They just wanted to see how she reacted because, as usual, she was the last to find out. "It's Johnny Rail's idea."

She blinked. Now *that* was a wild card. Rail hadn't made anything for years, but he was one of the most well-respected producers in the industry. "Wait. Why would Johnny Rail be interested in me? Or Ashley?"

"He's a fan of you both. A big one, apparently."

Her eyebrows shot up. Even though she'd won major awards, she was a pop star, not a serious musician, like his usual collaborators. Did he want to do some ironic thing where she was the butt of the joke? "That seems very strange. Are you sure?"

Cliff nodded eagerly. "He wrote us a letter. Said he's been listening to both of you for years and had this revelation about how you'd sound together. He seems obsessed with the idea, actually."

People always dangled things in front of you in the music business, and she thought she was used to it, but this was a cruel trick. "This is ridiculous. He doesn't work with artists like me. I don't have that kind of prestige. Ashley's a little closer to what he likes, but I'm definitely not."

"That's exactly why you should be jumping at the chance. What the three of you could do together is unprecedented. The public will be so curious about anything you put out. It's a guaranteed hit before you even start."

Georgia swiveled toward Morrison. Her PR guy's eyes drilled into her, but he hadn't said anything, seemingly content to let the guys at the label run everything. He was supposed to work for her, and it was frustrating she had to draw him into the discussion. "What do you think of this? Don't you think I'd be making a total fool of myself if it didn't work out?"

"Not at all. The foolish thing would be turning it down. You'll never get a chance like this again."

"Agree. You need to give this serious consideration," Nicky added.

If her loyal manager had already decided, the room was stacked against her more than she'd thought. It stung when Nicky knew how much she couldn't stand Ashley—she'd ranted about her often enough, especially after The Vanguards.

"Johnny's serious about this. He has a whole plan worked out. He wants the two of you to stay at his ranch in New Mexico for a stretch so you can write and record together," Cliff said.

Georgia threw up her hands. "This is sounding crazier by the second. I've never met these people. And I'm supposed to think this is a genuine offer? That we all go live on his ranch, even though we have no idea if we'd work well together?"

Cliff smiled indulgently like she was a child. "Johnny's an eccentric man. It's part of his genius. He has a talent for figuring out how to bring the best out of every artist. You need to trust him."

"Trust him to tell me I should work with a woman who hates my guts? We've never even met. This is ridiculous. It's a hard no."

Cliff looked around the table, making eye contact with the staff Georgia had brought to the meeting. Morrison and Nicky both shifted in their chairs.

"I'm sorry to tell you this, but in that case, *All You Need* was your last record with Splash Records. We won't be renewing your contract."

CHAPTER THREE

Georgia froze. When she finally got up, Nicky and Morrison moved to follow her, but she raised her hand.

"You can stay here, Morrison," Georgia said.

She flew down the hall with Nicky close behind. The last months had been a nightmare, and she desperately wanted to wake up. She mashed the buttons in the elevator, trying to ignore her wild-looking reflection in the mirrored doors.

"Why didn't you warn me they were going to do that? I thought you were negotiating with them about my renewal, and everything was fine."

The night before, Nicky told her it would be a three-album deal and not as lucrative as her previous contract. It was the best she could hope for, given how *All You Need* was performing. She'd been happy with the offer, knowing she wasn't in a position to ask for more. She had no reason to think things wouldn't go smoothly.

Nicky twisted her diamond ring around her finger, staring at the floor. "I didn't know how the meeting would go, but they'd been talking about pulling the plug before this offer came through."

"I wish you'd told me. I wasn't ready for any of that. That was an ambush."

"I know. I'm sorry. I truly thought you'd go for it for what it's worth. It's Johnny Rail."

"This is messed up. Just because I had one album that didn't do great? I've given them so many hits. I've worked with you for years, too. You should've known better than to think I'd go for some weird collaboration I'd never have a voice in."

"Please calm down. Let's talk about this in the car."

"Fine," Georgia said, trying to pull it together so she wouldn't cry. Tears had always come easily to her, whether she was angry, sad, or both. People said she was lucky to have emotions so close to the surface because it helped her find the emotional core in every song. At times like this, however, all it did was make her feel out of control.

They got into the black town car. Putting some distance between her and the suits made her feel better. She'd been with Splash from the beginning, but they weren't the only game in town. Other labels had tried to woo her over the years. "Can you please start making a list of labels we should consider and arrange some meetings? This could be a good thing. It isn't working with Splash anymore. Maybe I could find someone who'd give me more freedom."

Nicky sighed. "You're going to make me say it, aren't you?"

"Say what?"

"I was up late making calls, trying to put together a backup plan in case something went wrong today. I'm sorry, but none of the major labels want you."

"Things can't be that bad. I know this album isn't doing great, and everyone thinks I'm horrible, thanks to Hayley, but my track record…" She trailed off. Who was she trying to convince?

"Honey, you know how this business works. You're only as good as your last big hit, and it's been too long. Some stars can get away with bad press. Right now, you're just not one of them."

"I'll do an independent release, then. Or start my own label."

Nicky sighed again. They both knew she didn't have the clout for that, that sinking her money into it would be a catastrophe. Her career was cooked without a major label behind her.

"How did things get this bad? It's *one* album."

Nicky patted her knee. "This is totally fixable. The public can have a short memory these days, and people have come back from way worse. But we've got to work within the system. You've always been good at that. You could grab this opportunity and run with it."

Georgia reeled as she tried to take it in. She'd been worried about her career lately, but surviving the industry meant dealing with ups and downs. She'd told herself everything would be okay if she put her head down, pushed through her writer's block, and created another album to make everyone remember how good she could be. She'd promised herself she'd stay single and focus on herself until all the drama with her ex-wife was forgotten.

"I wish I'd never met Hayley Doran. She's ruined my life," Georgia said quietly.

She'd started working on her last album a few months after they married and rushed the recording, throwing herself into work to distract herself from facing the mistake she'd made. It was during the period when she was beginning to understand that there was something off about their marriage. The album simply didn't work—it wasn't until later that she realized there was something limp and empty about it. It had a sad edge, even when she hadn't been trying to make it that way. She hadn't written a note since and was scared she could no longer do it. In her more dramatic moments, she could swear Hayley had cursed her.

"Oh, honey. You didn't know any of this would happen. Things are going to get better, I promise."

She stared out the window as they traveled toward her apartment. She knew how privileged she was, that it was self-indulgent to be upset. She'd invested wisely and had more money than anyone had a right to. She could sell her catalog and live off royalties from commercials and soundtracks if she wanted to. Still, she wasn't ready to let all this go. She loved writing music, and she loved being Gigi Lark. She couldn't retire at thirty-three years old.

"I can't go out like this. There's still so much good music in me. I know there is."

Nicky looked at her hopefully. "I know there is, too. And so does Johnny Rail."

Georgia drew her phone from her handbag and Googled him. "It's crazy that he's interested. I mean, look at this discography."

"I don't need to look, babe. He's famous for getting the best out of everyone he works with."

"So many of my favorite albums are on this list."

It was flattering that he was interested in her, not to mention surreal. Of course, *he* wasn't the problem. The problem was Ashley Archer. Spending time on a ranch with that woman would be crazy—she'd rather poke out an eye. Everything she knew about her told her they were like oil and water. Georgia was ruled by strong emotions, while Ashley was a cerebral artist. Ashley was classically trained, and she was a self-taught artist who couldn't read music. Georgia was the life of the party, but Ashley was famous for not even going to parties and keeping to herself.

They had nothing in common. Still, what choice did Georgia have? The days when she could call the shots had drawn to a close. If she wanted them back, she had to do something drastic.

She turned to Nicky, taking a deep breath. "I'm not promising anything, but I want to speak to her. Can you please arrange a meeting? I guess it's time I finally faced my demons."

CHAPTER FOUR

The following day, Georgia sat in the same car, traveling to meet the woman she'd been feuding with for years. She'd made an art form of staying out of Ashley's way. Once, she fled the Splash office when she discovered Ashley had a meeting the same day. At industry events, when Ashley was present, she hid on the other side of the room. When they were nominated in the same category at The Vanguards, she blew off the luncheon, pretending to be sick.

Georgia called Nicky for the third time since yesterday. "Nik, are you sure this is a good idea? Ashley isn't laying some odd trap to make me look stupid, right?"

"No, honey. I did my research before Splash raised it with you. I spoke to her manager to check things out. This is solid."

"Thanks. I was so nervous that I spent forever getting ready. Maybe I should've asked you to come with me."

"What are you wearing?"

Georgia looked down at her outfit, trying to decide if she'd achieved her goal of looking like she was making an effort but not trying *too* hard. "Chanel skirt, with a white top. And your favorite Jimmy Choos."

"Oh, nice. The black-and-white Chanel, with the thick stripes?"

"That's the one."

She heard running water in the background as if Nicky was doing the dishes. It was supposed to be her day off. Georgia had never wanted to be the needy client who leaned on their staff too much for emotional support. Poor Nicky was spending her morning reassuring her about her clothes, and Georgia realized she was acting like a total diva. She had to get it together and act like the businesswoman she was supposed to be.

This meeting was work, and that was all.

"Okay, Nicky, just one more question. Do you think I really need to do this? Maybe I can auction my Vanguard if it's about the money."

"You could sell locks of your hair. Nail clippings?"

"Why not? But I draw the line at selling underwear. Unless I can fetch a really good price," Georgia said, hanging up on Nicky's cackle.

She stepped out of the car, looking at The Chop's sign. Georgia had discovered this place with her best friend, Rachel, and since then, they'd eaten here at least once every few months. She'd grown friendly with the manager, Tom, who agreed to let them use it as a meeting space before they opened for lunch. They could've used Splash's offices, but she wanted to keep the meeting to herself until she was ready. The last thing she needed was executives breathing down her neck.

Tom let her in, telling her Ashley had already arrived. As she walked, she looked at her phone to check whether the record company had leaked anything. She wouldn't put it past them to do it to pressure her. She was still scrolling when she glanced up to find her way.

Ashley sat in the corner, reading a newspaper. Georgia's stomach dropped, remembering every passive-aggressive thing she'd ever said about her nemesis to a journalist. She put her phone in her handbag, smoothing a hand over her hair.

"Hello. Ashley?"

She set down her copy of *The Times*, eyes quickly flicking up and down over her. Georgia realized they were physical opposites, too. She was tall and curvy, but Ashley was slight. Georgia took in her thick eyebrows and soulful eyes. Her platinum-blond hair was parted down the middle and tied back, and she wore light makeup.

She stood, holding out a hand. "Hi, Georgia. Nice to finally meet you."

The sleeves of her white collared shirt were rolled up, showing off a chunky silver watch. She wore red plaid, beautifully tailored pants. Ashley looked directly into her eyes as they shook hands, making her feel even more nervous than she'd been when she walked in. What was it about her that made Georgia feel so insecure? Perhaps it was because Georgia was cotton candy in the eyes of the world, and Ashley was taken seriously. She wished people thought of her the same way, but she'd never known how to command respect like Ashley.

"Thank you for taking the time to meet with me," Georgia said stiffly.

"Of course. Thanks for finding somewhere we could meet."

"No problem. Tom and his staff are very discreet. Nobody will know we were here."

The server came to take their order, and they talked about the weather and the restaurant. Georgia waited until she had her sparkling water to dive into the reason for their meeting. "I was so surprised when the record company told me about all this. Have you known about it long?"

Ashley shook her head, taking a sip of water. "I met with Splash right before you did. I haven't spoken to Johnny himself yet."

"What's with the letters he sent Splash, anyway? Why didn't he call?"

"I've heard he doesn't like email or talking on the phone. He's old-fashioned that way."

"Right," Georgia said. She'd always assumed the stories about him were exaggerated, but she was starting to realize they weren't. He was as eccentric as they said.

"He said in his note that he wanted us to stay at his ranch. Have you heard about his place?"

"Sure, hasn't everyone?" Georgia replied.

Celio Ranch was part of the Johnny Rail legend. He'd moved from Laurel Canyon to Taos, New Mexico, in the 1980s to build a compound with a recording studio. There were so many stories about albums created there. Someone had even written a book about it, though she'd never read it. People talked as though the ranch lent magic to his music. With anyone else, she'd think the stories were bullshit, but it was easy to get drawn into the mythmaking with a body of work like his.

"It's an intriguing idea, isn't it?" Ashley asked.

"Depends on how you look at it."

Georgia hadn't meant to sound rude, but something in her tone made Ashley look down into her water. The tension made Georgia think about how utterly absurd this was. They'd never spoken, but they were enemies anyway.

She'd been in her midtwenties when she'd grown famous and thought nothing of slamming Ashley like a high school mean girl, but wasn't it all a bit embarrassing now? Like so many things about her life, Georgia wished she'd kept her thoughts private. There was no need for them to relitigate a childish feud.

There was only one thing she could never let go. She didn't want to bring it up, even though she knew she was in the right. She hated how her voice shook. "There is one thing that I've always wondered about. Why you did it, I mean."

"It's okay. You can ask me, and I'll try to be honest," Ashley replied more gently than she expected.

"My ex-wife told me you hit on her in the restrooms. At The Vanguards. Is that true?"

She didn't know Ashley, but Georgia was sure as soon as her eyes widened in disbelief. It was another thing Hayley had lied about.

"That's a complete fabrication. I met your wife in the bathroom, and we spoke briefly, but I did *not* do that."

"Okay, I see. My apologies," Georgia said quickly.

"If that nonsense is taken out of the equation, does it make any difference to you?"

"I'm just skeptical, is all. Don't you think it's a strange proposal?"

"I guess this is why he is who he is. He thinks of things that others wouldn't."

"Yeah. Maybe."

They were interrupted by the server, who stood with their meals. He set their chicken salad bowls in front of them and quickly disappeared. If he cared about who they were, he didn't show it. They ate quietly, with only the sound of their cutlery clinking against their bowls. Georgia sipped water to stop the food from sticking in her throat. This lunch was profoundly awkward, and she wished she hadn't suggested it. How embarrassing that she'd accused Ashley of doing something she hadn't. Would Hayley ever stop humiliating her?

Ashley dabbed her mouth with her napkin and pushed her bowl away. "Can we just clear the air, please? Let's talk like adults so we can move on with discussing this project. Get the rest of it off your chest. Otherwise, I'm not sure why you asked me here."

Georgia had just been telling herself she'd grown out of her grudge. In an instant, annoyance flooded back at that superior tone, the oh-so-smug expression. "I'm not sure why we're here either. Why would you want to work with someone you think can't sing? Didn't you say I was the poster child for autotune?"

That wiped the smile off her face. "I've said some stuff. So have you."

"Oh, like when you said that you didn't want to talk about who you were dating because you didn't want to market your sexuality, like someone else you wouldn't name, but everyone knew it was about me."

Ashley's eyes flashed, giving Georgia another hit of satisfaction. "I really wasn't talking about you. I was misquoted. You know how they do that. If you want to play that game, I could talk about how you said I was like if granola was a person."

They stared at one another until something strange happened—Georgia felt like she was going to laugh. The corner of Ashley's mouth twitched up.

"That *was* a pretty mean one," Georgia said.

Ashley shrugged, smiling for real now. "Like I said, we've both mouthed off a little. Now we've got that out of the way. Tell me what you really think about all this."

"I think it feels like a stunt. You and I have been rivals for years. That's how the world sees us, and why else would Johnny Rail want to put us together? I don't want to be used for publicity."

Ashley leaned back, crossing a leg over her knee. "Do you think he would need us for that? I didn't peg you for being so insecure."

Georgia's face reddened. She hadn't always been this way, but her confidence had plummeted over the last year. "That's a little personal to say to me, don't you think?"

"I don't mean to get personal. I'm saying to you, artist to artist, that you shouldn't think so little of your own work. You won Album of the Year. Doesn't that mean anything?"

Georgia crossed her arms. "Yeah, and look at me now. I'm just realistic about how I'm seen. It's easy for you to talk when people think you're talented, and I'm just lucky and good at marketing myself. I don't want to be used, is all."

Ashley held up her hands. "Okay, I'm sorry. You're right. I understand."

"Thank you."

"I'm trying to say that I think we can take this at face value," she said, speaking more slowly, carefully choosing her words. "Johnny Rail is the kind of person who sees beyond all that bullshit, like the idea that you're just lucky."

Ashley put an elbow on the table and propped her chin on her fist. Her eyes were so intense Georgia had no choice but to meet them. Their deep brown was beautiful, and Georgia realized she was letting herself be persuaded. In another life, she might be attracted to her.

"It's *Johnny Rail*. If you want to do it, I'm in. But I'm not here to convince you," Ashley said.

"I don't want you to convince me. I just want to know how you think we'd work together. Don't you prefer to work on your own? You do your own production, usually. And you usually don't have cowriters."

Georgia was trying to say it delicately—Ashley was known to be controlling. She didn't want to sign up only to be edged out. She might be an industry joke, but she wasn't desperate enough to lend her name to someone else's success.

Ashley shook her head. "It would be new territory for me. I think I could make it work. We'll never know until we try."

"Why do you think he wants both of us? Our music couldn't be more different. It doesn't make sense. I haven't even been doing that well," she said self-consciously. Ashley must have loved how poorly received her new album had been. It would have shown her how weak the competition was.

"*All You Need* was an interesting album, especially the closing track. There was a rawness to it that was beautiful."

Georgia searched her face for traces of sarcasm, but she seemed sincere. "Thanks. That's very kind of you."

"It's true."

Ashley was yielding a lot of ground, so she should make more effort. "I usually work with the same handful of people, but I could do with a change. I'm not against trying something new. I'm just not sure. Would you really be interested in this? You'd be committed if I said yes?"

Georgia didn't realize she was holding her breath until Ashley nodded. "I would."

"Okay. Would it be all right with you if we started finding out more about how Johnny wants it all to work? And then we could meet again to decide together?"

"I'd like that," she said, eyes locked on hers again.

Georgia crossed her legs, wondering why she suddenly felt so strange—like there was a spark between them. It felt like nobody had looked at her like that in a long time. Chemistry filled the air, a friction that was impossible to deny.

It must only be the weight of their past and the novelty of finally talking like this. Anything else was impossible.

CHAPTER FIVE

Ashley paced the entire length of her apartment with her hands on her head. This was so fucking weird. It was bizarre to have something this important in the hands of Gigi Lark. She'd felt like she was on her knees throughout their lunch meeting, dying for Gigi to say yes to working with Johnny Rail so that she could, too.

She loved making music, and she'd been laboring over her upcoming album for months. Her most recent release, a fourteen-track album called *Pity Party*, had done well. It was nominated for Album of the Year and was a critical and commercial success. She was confident the material she'd written lately would make for an equally successful album. Yet, she was worried that she was at risk of repeating herself. Working with Johnny Rail would be a good move for her career, but it was more important to her than that. He was a genius, and she had so much to learn from him. Her whole life was about striving to be better, and what better way to improve than to be guided by a master?

She jumped at the knock on her door. She'd asked Pam to come over for an afternoon coffee, mainly to debrief about the meeting. Everyone wanted to do Zoom meetings after Covid, even after many other things had returned to normal. She preferred to talk in person.

Pam strode in, wearing a peach-colored pantsuit with a white scarf and sunglasses pushed to the top of her head. They'd been working together for years and always got along well. Pam had grown up in New York, and like many natives of the city, she didn't tolerate bullshit from anyone. Before managing Ashley, she'd been a talent agent for Broadway stars. She looked around, her eyes coming back to rest on Ashley. "I always forget how spartan your place is."

"It's not spartan. I just don't like mess."

"Not a criticism, my dear," she said, removing her shoes and lining them up near the doorway.

Her words made Ashley look at the apartment with fresh eyes. She'd paid someone to decorate it in simple colors—black and gray with splashes of red. Having a big New York place was a luxury, and she kept it immaculate and clutter-free. It was important to her to have it like that, but if she was honest with herself, she could see that it wasn't very homely. It was a place to rest between touring and traveling.

"Take a seat. I'll get you a cup of coffee," Ashley said, gesturing toward the dining table.

The living room, kitchen, and dining area were open-plan and light-filled. Pam set herself up at the table. Swiftly, she removed the glasses from her head and took her spectacles from their case. She opened her laptop and clicked, then looked at Ashley expectantly. "So. At last, you met. Tell me everything."

Ashley sat across from her, folding her hands on the table. Where to start? She'd anticipated meeting Gigi Lark a million times. Over the years, she'd taken on a mythical status in her mind. She'd expected her to have a big personality—tick. She'd also expected the famous beauty and charisma—tick. She'd expected her to be a little mean and a bit of a phony—that part, she wasn't sure about. Ashley found a magnetic vulnerability in her. Maybe it made her want to take care of Gigi a little, and she wondered if that would've been there if her career hadn't suffered after the release of her latest album.

Pam raised her eyebrows, sipping her coffee. "Cat got your tongue, my dear? You look like you don't know what to think."

"I truly don't."

"All right. Then take me through what you discussed, at least."

"She's very unsure about working together and with Johnny, too. She seems suspicious of the whole deal."

"Why? I mean, I understand being unsure about working with you after everything. Why Johnny?"

"She just thinks it's a really weird offer."

"It is. But if anyone's instincts are perfect, it's Johnny Rail's."

Of course, Pam was preaching to the converted—they'd had this conversation before when Splash asked them both in for a meeting. When Ashley came home that day, she spent an hour online, researching Gigi all over again, reading interviews and watching videos. It was as though she were trying to find out if she'd ever said anything unforgivable about her. In the end, she decided she really did not care. It all seemed so stupid when you stacked it up against the opportunity to collaborate with Rail.

"I couldn't agree more. And she hasn't said no, she just seems noncommittal. She wants to find out more."

Pam tapped a note into her laptop. "I'll contact Splash and ask them to set up a conference call."

"I'm not sure that'd be Johnny's thing. I doubt he has a computer."

She waved a hand with her eyes trained on the screen. "Don't worry about it. We'll make it happen. We can set up someone to help him with it. I'll look into finding a New Mexico contact."

"Actually, we don't want that."

"Don't *we*?"

Ashley got it—she was surprised to hear herself use a plural pronoun that included Gigi. She pressed on, anyway. "We don't want Splash involved until we know more about it. We'll contact him ourselves."

"Okay. I know better than to stand in your way when you want something like that. Does she seem amenable to staying at the ranch, like he asked?"

"We didn't get too far into it. One thing at a time, but I suppose she knows it's part of the deal."

"Right," she said, eyes back on her screen. "I've been reviewing your schedule for the next few months. You'd need to pull out of a few things, but it was already fairly light because of the new album."

"Yeah. I figured."

"There is one thing, and that's The Vanguards. You can't miss those when you're a nominee."

A moment later, she realized she'd flinched at the name of the awards show. She'd been thrilled to receive her nomination for Album of the Year, and the predictions looked positive for her. Still, it was impossible to think about the event without remembering that thorny conversation from lunch.

Pam set aside her coffee cup. "I know you don't like these things, but as your manager, I advise you to prioritize it. If you don't go and win, it looks ungrateful. If you don't go and lose, it's even worse. It makes you look like you expected it and are acting bitter."

"I'd prefer not to go, but it's not that. I was thinking about my conversation with Gigi about the last Vanguards I went to. We talked about it at lunch today."

"Don't tell me she gloated about her win. That would be so tacky."

"No, nothing like that. There was something I never told you about that night."

Ashley hesitated, running a finger over the table and avoiding Pam's eye. She'd told a couple of friends about how Hayley had acted, but it was so off-putting and odd that she'd mainly wanted to keep it private. It felt cheap to gossip about it, and she kept telling herself that she knew nothing about their marriage or whether they were even monogamous. Gigi's reaction today told her everything she needed to know. As much as they'd always disliked one another, there was no need to twist the knife and tell Gigi the whole truth.

Pam broke their silence. "It's not like you to be like this. We've known one another long enough for you to be direct, don't you think?"

"Do we have some kind of manager-client privilege?"

"What kind of question is that? If you want something kept private, of course I will. You know that."

"I mentioned meeting Hayley Doran in the bathroom that night."

"Yes, I remember that. You said she was quite friendly toward you, and I was surprised."

"She was more than friendly. She made a pass."

Pam took her hands from her keyboard and stared over her glasses. "You're kidding."

"Nope."

She laughed, covering her mouth. "Oh, dear. You gay girls can be so messy."

"Hey! We are not. I mean, *she* clearly is. I had nothing to do with it, and neither did Gigi."

"How did she react when you told her?"

Ashley winced. "I didn't. I couldn't. Apparently, Hayley told the story that I hit on her. Complete bullshit. I was only polite, but I couldn't get away fast enough once I realized what was happening."

"And she said it was the other way around? What a snake."

"Right? So, I denied it, but I didn't tell her the rest. I didn't have the heart to."

"But they're divorced. Maybe it wouldn't matter that much."

Ashley shrugged. "I have a feeling it would. She looked super embarrassed when I told her Hayley was lying. I'm pretty sure she believed me, so that's something."

Gigi's vulnerability had stopped Ashley in her tracks. It was evident that Gigi had been badly hurt, and she didn't want to add to that pain.

"Sounds wise to not mention it, then," Pam said.

"I'll be taking that one to the grave."

"Sensible. If this all goes well, you haven't mentioned how you think you'd get along. Is it doable, as far as you're concerned?"

She shrugged again. "If Johnny wanted to work with me, and only me, I'd prefer that. But he's asked for this, so I'd do my best. The lunch was uncomfortable, mostly, but I'd put my head down and focus on the work."

Pam reached over and patted her hand. "I know you would. That's what you've always been good at. You're one of the most pragmatic clients I've ever worked with."

She went back to her computer, and Ashley smiled wryly to herself. That was one of the words people often used to describe her—pragmatic. She had a feeling nobody would ever describe Gigi that way. She seemed emotional, even romantic. They couldn't be more different, and those differences were something she'd have to learn to navigate.

She could do it. She wasn't going to let a little rivalry get in the way.

CHAPTER SIX

Georgia sat at her dining room table with her three best friends—Rachel, Rachel's partner, Eliza, and Mel. They had a lot in common, all women in their thirties and forties who worked in the music industry. Georgia met them soon after moving to New York, which she'd always dreamed about from her family's farm back in the UK's Midlands. Their friendships had transformed the city from an isolating metropolis to a home. The four of them got together as often as they could when they were all in town.

"So, let me get this straight," Mel said. She liked dressing up for poker nights—she'd slicked back her hair and wore suspenders with her black pants. "You get to work with Johnny Rail, but you can't do it unless you pair up with Ashley Archer?"

"I don't get it," Rachel said. "What put this idea into his head in the first place?"

"Nobody knows. Apparently, he's always liked our music. He's got this idea that we'd all create something interesting together," Georgia replied.

"Weird. Did your team tell Splash to forget it unless it was just the two of you? Without Ashley?"

"Splash is in on it. They said if I don't do this, I'm out. They won't renew my contract."

"God. I can't believe that. After all these years, when you've made them a fortune. There really is no loyalty in this business," Rachel said.

It was such a relief to talk about it with her friends. They'd been in the industry long enough to have seen it all. Rachel was a producer whom she'd met at a fundraiser, and she'd introduced her to the others. Eliza was a well-respected composer, and Mel was a sound engineer.

Georgia loved how much these women gave her a blueprint for her life. Georgia might continue to live alone like Mel, who had a vibrant social life. But if Georgia met someone in the distant future, she hoped her relationship would be loving and equal, like Rachel and Eliza's. It was so different than what she'd had with Hayley. They were so happy—always laughing. Rachel had blond hair and sparkly blue eyes, while Eliza was classically handsome with dark hair and eyes.

Those dark eyes now flashed with anger. "I can't believe they gave you an ultimatum. They can't make you work with someone like this, especially not a woman who's badmouthed you every chance she gets. You should drop their asses and sign with a different record company."

"I'd love to, but nobody wants to buy what I'm selling. It's this or nothing. So, I met with Ashley."

Everyone squealed, and Rachel slapped her arm. "How could you not have led with that? I can't believe you met with her without telling any of us."

"Criminal. Now, you have to tell us everything," Mel said.

Georgia fiddled with her cards. How could she explain Ashley? There were unexpected flashes of kindness, and her beauty was breathtaking. She'd been thinking about her eyes ever since. "Not as bad as you might think. We got along okay. She wants to do it."

"*Interesting.* Maybe she was putting her best foot forward because she wanted something from you. If she wants to do the album, it's in her best interests to make nice with you."

"Maybe. Who knows?"

"Does this mean you're considering it?" Rachel asked, putting her cards face down and leaning over. Georgia wished they were alone so she could confide about how confusing it was to find Ashley attractive. They were all close, but she could tell Rachel anything.

"I might be thinking about it. But I need more information, so we sent Johnny a letter from both of us, asking him loads of questions. It's the only way we can communicate with him, seeing as he's such a recluse now. Anyway, he'd want us to stay at his ranch in New Mexico while we work on the album. He has a recording studio out there."

Mel rearranged her cards. "I heard about the letter-writing thing. And how he barely leaves that ranch of his. He's quirky. But I've only heard good things about what he's like to work with."

"What about you guys?" Georgia asked Rachel and Eliza. "Heard any concerning rumors or stories? He's not a creep or anything, is he?"

"Nothing like that. No reason to think Johnny's reputation as a gentleman isn't for real. He's been married to his wife for ages, too. I bet she'll be there the whole time. Wait, what about the stuff with Hayley? At The Vanguards. I thought that'd be a deal-breaker more than anything else," Eliza said.

"I brought that up with her. I wanted to get it out there before things moved any further. I know nobody will be shocked to hear this, but it sounds like Hayley was lying about that."

"No kidding. We'll add that one to the list of her crimes. Holy shit," Rachel said with wide eyes. "Could this actually happen? Can you imagine? You could make something truly extraordinary."

Mel plucked out cards, laying them face down. "I think you should go. Even if you and Ashley end up at one another's throats, it'd be worth it. Fighting is temporary, but music is immortal."

"I don't know. It's easy to say that now, but I'd be out there with her for weeks, maybe even months. Is it worth it if she ends up being as horrible as I thought before? I'm feeling a bit trapped into this. I really don't know what to think."

Mel eyed her, then shook her head. "You've been trapped with that record company for years if you think about it that way. I say you go for it, make a killer album, then use the capital you get from having a big hit record to leave Splash and find someone better."

"She has a point," Eliza said, throwing down two cards and picking up replacements. "This could be huge. It could open you up to new audiences and give you tons of credibility. It could take you to a place in your career you haven't been."

Georgia stared off into space, allowing herself to dream. The meeting with Splash made her understand viscerally that everything she'd worked so hard for could slip through her fingers like sand. This could buy her more years of doing what she loved.

"She's right," Rachel said. "You know I loved everything you've done, honey, but Johnny Rail will make you soar. And maybe even with Ashley there, it'll be nice for you to get away for a while?"

"After everything that happened with Hayley, you deserve a break," Mel said.

"I could do with one, yeah. There are so many memories here," she replied. There were times when the apartment felt haunted—she didn't want to move, but it was challenging to be in a place where she'd created so many memories with her ex-wife.

Mel nodded, laying her cards down on the table. "I'll never forgive that woman for what she's done. But this opportunity is the best revenge, right? You'd be showing that you can pick yourself up and come back bigger and better."

"I'm excited for you. I can't wait to hear more when you get your letter back from Johnny," Rachel said, adding her cards to the table. "And I'm not worried about you working with Ashley. You can just give it right back if she gives you any trouble. She'll learn quickly that she shouldn't mess with you."

"That's right. Nobody should underestimate me," Georgia said, revealing her royal flush with a smirk.

"You damn little bluffer," Eliza said.

Georgia used both hands to pull the mound of chips toward her. It felt so good to laugh. Things had been difficult for a while now in so many ways. This could be the beginning of things turning around for her.

She grinned while her friends teased her for hustling them, feeling light as air. She hadn't been this hopeful in a long time.

CHAPTER SEVEN

As the elevator climbed floor after floor, Ashley couldn't believe she was on her way to Gigi Lark's home. It was surreal to go from avoiding one another to this. She'd worried that Georgia might not agree to a collaboration, but things were growing more promising by the day. They'd swapped phone numbers to text logistics and informed Splash and their managers they were meeting. Every time Georgia's name appeared on her phone, she held her breath.

A blonde with a pixie cut answered the door. "Hey, I'm Ivy, Georgia's assistant. Go on in. She's waiting for you."

Ashley walked down a long hall with polished hardwood floors, removing her hat and sunglasses. Georgia appeared as she rounded the corner into the living room. Ashley wasn't sure what to look at—the stunning view from the penthouse windows or Georgia. She was statuesque in blue jeans and an oversized white button-up, hair flowing over her shoulders. Her toenails were painted cherry red, and so were her full lips.

Ashley had seen her across crowded rooms and on screen for years, but distances and cameras had not captured her. It was shocking to discover how much she liked to look at Georgia.

"Hi. Thanks for coming around. Do you think anyone saw you?"

She'd slipped into the building by going around the back and taking the service elevator. They'd gotten lucky that day they met at The Chop, with nobody realizing they'd entered the restaurant around the same time. They'd agreed not to take any more chances. "No, I don't think so. You have the letter?"

Georgia nodded. "It's in the living room."

"And you haven't opened it yet?"

"Of course not. A deal's a deal," Georgia said as she walked backward, leading them into the kitchen. "Can I offer you something to drink while we read it?"

Ashley absently pulled her bag from her shoulder to rest it on the counter. She was eager to read that letter but was distracted by her surroundings: double island counters decorated with a fruit bowl and flowers, a wide oven, and a massive stainless-steel fridge. What she liked most about the kitchen was how well-used it felt—it smelled of something freshly baked.

"Are you checking out my kitchen? I like to cook. I baked us some cookies. I thought we could eat them while we read the letter."

Ashley could feel eyes on her as she stared around. "This place is amazing. Maybe we can make the album here instead of the ranch."

"Thanks," Georgia said, bemused. "So, do you want that drink?"

"Not right now, if that's okay? And I appreciate the cookies, but I'm too wired to eat right now. I'm so ready to look at this thing. Aren't you?"

"Okay. Let's go to the living room and put you out of your misery."

Georgia led her up a spiral staircase to the living area, talking as they went. "I meant to tell you, I asked my friends if they'd heard anything about Johnny. Everyone says he's got a reputation as a good guy."

"I've asked around, too. I've been hearing the same thing," Ashley said, settling onto one of the luxurious sofas when Georgia gestured toward it.

She watched Georgia fidget, then run her fingers through her hair. She'd been acting cool since Ashley arrived but was clearly just as nervous. The letter was on the coffee table, propped against a vase. They'd agreed to communicate with Johnny as a team and tossed a coin to see whose address to put as the return one on the envelope. Georgia lived in Central Park West, so Ashley came up from the Village in an Uber, keeping her face turned away from the driver as much as possible.

Georgia grabbed the envelope and passed it to her. "Let's do it."

"Okay," Ashley said, slipping a finger under the envelope's glue. She couldn't remember the last time she'd opened an actual letter. It was written on yellow legal paper and folded into thirds.

"Wow. Looks like a few pages, huh?"

They sat quietly and read the first few paragraphs together. Johnny introduced himself in a neat hand, listing some of his favorite albums he'd worked on.

Georgia laughed. "Does he think we don't know who he is?"

Ashley shrugged. She'd been thinking the same thing. Next, he wrote a couple of paragraphs about how he'd been watching tapes of music videos, and their songs came on one after the other.

Something about watching the clips in a row was so interesting that I spent hours alternating your songs. You have such different voices, but I grew sure you would complement one another perfectly. You are both excellent lyricists and composers.

"Wow," Ashley said. "I've never heard us compared favorably like that before. Have you?"

She shook her head. After that, he addressed them separately. Rail described how he'd connected with their music, drawing on examples from their catalogs. He gave them equal praise, taking care not to single either of them out.

"Everything he says is so specific. That's nice of him," Georgia said.

Turning the pages, Ashley realized how closely they were sitting. She tried to focus, but Georgia's thigh almost touched her own, and her hair smelled lovely. There it was again—the odd, way-too-strong twist of desire, the same one she'd felt the first time she saw Georgia at the restaurant. She'd been trying to forget about it, and when she was not with Georgia, she almost could.

Ashley handed the papers to her and leaned back on the sofa. "Sorry. It's all making me too nervous. Can you please read the next part aloud?"

Georgia looked at her curiously. Her accent was beautiful, and Ashley could listen to her read all day. "'I want a real collaboration with everything cowritten. Let's not create a version of me watching those alternating clips. I'd want to blend your outlooks and voices and sounds.'"

They made eye contact, Georgia smiling softly at her. Ashley forced herself to focus on Johnny's words, looking away from her and out the window.

"'I want to create the conditions for you to do your best work together. I'd be there to guide and draw out what is already in you. I don't want too much influence. I'm an old man who has said most of what he wants to say.'"

Georgia broke off again, quietly rereading the last part. "He makes it sound awfully attractive, doesn't he? He's making me believe in his idea. I didn't expect that."

"Yeah. Is there more?"

She turned the page. "'I know it may be difficult to imagine coming to live at my ranch for as long as it takes to complete this project. You may think it's asking a lot. I don't have an Internet connection. Though I'd never be so arrogant to ask you not to bring your cell phones, I would ask you to limit their use in my presence. I hope you'll forgive an old man for his grumpiness. I promise that aside from this, I'm quite pleasant company. That's all I have to say for now. If you'd like to visit me, my door is open.'"

Georgia turned the page and searched, even though he'd signed off. "That's all. I guess he answered all our questions, right? We wanted to know why us and why us together. I'm satisfied with those answers. Are you?"

Ashley chewed a thumbnail. The truth was, she didn't need a lot of convincing. When she first heard about this idea, she was apprehensive about working with Georgia, but not as much as Georgia seemed reluctant to work with her. Maybe it had something to do with her reputation as being a little pedantic. Still, there wasn't much she wouldn't do to collaborate with her hero. Georgia's inclusion was an inconvenience, like eating her vegetables so she could have dessert.

Now that Georgia was in front of her and she understood more about the process, she couldn't afford to think that way. They couldn't write separately or downplay Georgia's role, not if she wanted this to be a success. She'd have to learn to share.

"I'm satisfied," Ashley said, holding out a hand for the letter. "But would you mind if I read it over again? There's a lot to consider."

She was distracted by Georgia's eyes on her but quickly became absorbed. Ever since she was a teenager and read that book about Johnny Rail and his ranch, she'd dreamed about visiting. She'd never even imagined that he might want her to become part of the legend built up around him.

Throughout her career, she'd done as much as possible independently. It wasn't that she thought other people had nothing to offer her—she just had such strong tastes and opinions that it was easier to execute her vision alone. The idea of working with Johnny changed all that because she trusted his ideas. He was a better producer than her, and she had everything to learn from him. She needed to know that she could do everything he asked. She'd never forgive herself if this failed or she let him down.

As she finished her reread, she looked up and into Georgia's eyes. Georgia quickly looked away as though she'd been caught at something. What had she been thinking about?

Abruptly, Georgia jumped up from the sofa. "C'mon, let's go back to the kitchen. I'm making a pot of tea. I can't make such a big life decision without tea."

Ashley rose, thinking how funny it was to discover that Georgia's sunny disposition and big energy weren't just a part of her image. She was really like this.

She rose and followed her, smiling to herself. She was charmed, and who wouldn't be?

CHAPTER EIGHT

Georgia pushed the plate of cookies across the countertop, and Ashley couldn't take her eyes off her pale, delicate-looking hands. Her fingers were long, she didn't wear any rings, and her painted nails were short and neat.

Ashley picked up a cookie and took a bite. "How did you get this so soft and chewy?"

Georgia smiled at her like she didn't want to give up her secrets. "Practice."

With oddly deep concentration, Georgia rotated her teapot. It was decorated with yellow flowers. Maybe it was because Ashley had never met anyone—at least anyone her age—with a fine bone china tea set, but it was adorable. Locks of red hair caught the sun as she poured each of them a cup.

"Why did you turn it around like that?"

Georgia sat across the counter from her. "I don't know. It's what my mother always does, turn it three times. This used to be her tea set. It makes me feel close to home when I make it."

"Where are you from? Exactly, I mean?"

"A place called Hereford, in the Midlands. I moved to London to start my career and played the clubs for a while, but my goal was always to move to the States. Why are we talking about a boring thing like where I'm from when we could be talking about that letter? What did you think?"

Ashley sipped her tea. She wasn't sure how to express herself and couldn't understand why Georgia wasn't jumping at this chance. She told herself to be patient. Maybe it was because she'd lost a sibling early, but Ashley had always had a strong sense of her mortality. Everything was about building a legacy, ensuring she built a life that would be remembered. Nobody would talk about her indie-pop records in fifty years, no matter how proud she was of them. However, she was convinced that Rail would help her create music that would live on when she was gone. That was all she wanted.

She couldn't say all that to Georgia, not when they barely knew one another. "I like how he's laid things out. He sounds sincere about making sure he doesn't overshadow us."

"Yeah. I've wondered about that. But between what we've both been hearing and that letter, I feel like we'd be in safe hands. His wife, Judy, lives there, too, right? That's comforting."

Ashley smiled. They were a legend as a couple. He wrote songs about her, and she created famous portraits of him. They'd been together for over forty years and were often mentioned in the same breath.

"I love her work. I'd be excited to meet her, too. What do you think about all the technology stuff he talked about? It's a little controlling, but if I had to leave my phone in my room while we worked, I wouldn't see that as such a bad thing."

"Same. It'll probably be good to have a digital detox. I hate how much time I spend scrolling."

"I don't think I'd die if I couldn't play Candy Crush for a few weeks or if I couldn't see what they think I've done wrong lately on Twitter. I mean X, whatever," Ashley said.

Georgia laughed, then quickly grew serious, making Ashley wonder if she was thinking about the trouble they'd gotten themselves into online. Ashley was embarrassed to think about all the times she'd done childish things, like unfollowing someone who posted a picture with Georgia. Social media could bring out her worst impulses. It really would be good to have a break.

"I guess posting anything from his place would be out of the question anyway. Because if we do this, I'd like to keep this all a secret until we're done, wouldn't you? It's a big swing, and it would draw so much attention," Georgia said.

"I'd feel terrible if the whole media circus showed up in that small town. We'd have to give this one the full cloak-and-dagger treatment."

"We wouldn't know how this was going to go. It would be too much pressure to have everyone knowing."

"I'm completely on the same page."

Georgia set down her teacup. "Really, though, can you imagine how much people are going to lose it when they find out we're collaborating? Nobody would ever see that coming. It'd be worth it for that alone."

Ashley's heart leaped with hope. She didn't want to leave here today without knowing whether they were going ahead. She'd already spent sleepless nights trying to work out if Georgia would say yes. "Going to? You just sounded like you were agreeing to all this."

Georgia toyed with her cup, turning it like she'd done with the teapot. "Can I talk to you about something kind of private?"

"Of course," Ashley said. The sadness in Georgia's eyes made her want to lean over and touch her hand, but that would be too intimate. "Whatever it is, go ahead."

"You won't say anything to anyone? Not even your team, or a friend, or anything? I wouldn't want anyone to get the idea I'm not up to this, even if…I don't know," she said, pushing hair behind her ear.

Now Ashley touched her hand, just for a moment. She wanted to show that she was serious about being taken into her confidence. "Absolutely. What we talk about right now is between you and me."

"Have you ever had writer's block? Because I haven't written a word since my last album."

"Oh. I'm sorry it's been like that for you. That sounds rough, but I don't think writer's block has to be a long-term problem, does it? The well goes dry sometimes, especially when you've been through a lot like you have. But it always comes back."

"I don't know about that. I used to come up with ideas all the time. I have a keyboard in my bedroom, and I'd get up in the morning and sit there for hours tinkering away. Now I sit there, and there's nothing. Or, I'll think of an opening line and realize it's too close to some other piece of music, and I can't use it. It's driving me crazy."

"That happens to me sometimes, too. At least you recognize it."

"You probably heard what my ex said about me. That I stole her ideas."

Ashley scoffed. She'd always been quick to believe the worst about Georgia, but even she knew that was a joke. Georgia had a large body of work behind her, while Hayley had only released one EP with no writing credits. "I don't know how to say this nicely, but nobody seriously believes that. No offense, but your ex comes off as unhinged."

Georgia laughed, covering her mouth.

"Sorry, too far?" Ashley asked.

"No. I needed that."

"She's not to be taken seriously. So if you think I'm worried about that in the least, I'm not."

"Thank you for saying that."

"You wrote or cowrote everything on *All You Need*, right? I'm remembering that correctly?" Ashley asked, pretending she hadn't checked at the time of the release. She'd always followed Georgia's career like a hawk, telling herself it was important to check out the competition.

"Yeah."

"Then it hasn't been that long. You'll find your feet again. This is perfect. You might just need to get into a new environment and work with new people."

"What if it doesn't work? I'm trying to say, what if we get out there, and I can't get it back? I'd be mortified if I let you or Johnny down."

"I'd help you in whatever way I can. I know he would, too. C'mon, you can't let that stop you."

"It really doesn't worry you?"

"Honestly, no. You've written four albums. That doesn't just go away overnight," Ashley said, trying to cover her eagerness to move on.

She knew of people who only had one or two good albums in them, but there was no point mentioning that. If anyone could help Georgia start writing again, it was Johnny. And if she had to carry more of the load herself once they were at the ranch, she didn't care. That was how she was more comfortable, anyway. She only wanted to get them there—they could worry about everything else later.

"And what about us?" Georgia said, meeting her eye gamely. "Is this a truce, or are we done with the whole war?"

So many thoughts ran through Ashley's mind. She could say that it wasn't only up to her—did Georgia promise to stop, too? Were the sweetness and sincerity genuine or part of an act? Did any of it even matter? Once the album was done, they could go back to fighting, not that she was interested in that anymore.

"I think we've outgrown all that. Don't you?" Ashley said.

Georgia nodded. "Well, I've told you at least. If we get out there and it doesn't work, I'll know I tried. A lot is riding on this for me. If I don't do this, it's all over for me, anyway."

Ashley had heard the rumors about Georgia's contract hanging in the balance. She didn't like to think of Georgia being coerced, but she couldn't do anything about that. "I hope it winds up being more than that for you. I mean, that it's not just something you have to do. I promise I'll do everything possible to make it a positive experience."

Georgia finally locked eyes with her. "I want us to get along. I know we might never be friends or anything. I don't mean that. But you're different than I thought. Getting along seems like it could be nice. Does that sound totally lame?"

The honesty was disarming. Ashley knew it was meant in a friendly way, but it still gave her tingles. "It doesn't sound lame. We haven't known each other long, but I trust you. That's not in my head, right? I can do that with you."

"You can. Let's toast to it."

Georgia picked up her teacup, holding it over to her. Ashley's heart hammered a steady beat because this moment felt so charged. Like they were making a sacred promise to one another.

Georgia's next words made Ashley feel like she'd read her mind. "How about a good old-fashioned oath? To seal that, we're going to put all our history aside."

Ashley picked up her cup. "I'm in. I swear that I'd never do anything to screw you over."

"Me too. I promise."

They clinked their teacups with twin smiles.

"Maybe we should go to Splash together about this? I don't trust them not to play us off against one another in negotiations. We split everything down the middle," Ashley said.

Georgia nodded, and they clinked again.

This was happening. Oh my God, this was really happening.

CHAPTER NINE

Georgia and Ashley waited for the elevator in the Splash Records lobby, Georgia bouncing on the balls of her feet. She hadn't seen anyone from the label since that disastrous meeting when they'd threatened to drop her. They'd been asking her to come in to discuss Johnny's offer further, but she'd managed to avoid it until now.

"So, here we are. Where the magic happens. It'll be nice to get away from this place for a while when we get to New Mexico," Ashley said.

Georgia was distracted by how gorgeous Ashley looked in her dark-blue jeans, white shirt, and checked blazer. She had an excellent eye for putting an outfit together, and those jeans hugged her thighs in a most delicious way.

"Sure, *magic*. Corporate bullshit magic, where they make your money disappear," Georgia said.

She liked the way Ashley looked at her when she made her laugh. She liked having Ashley by her side, period. It meant a lot to her that Ashley suggested they negotiate with Splash as a team.

Ashley was coming from a stronger position, and they both knew it—*Pity Party* had outstripped Georgia's latest album by a mile. Everyone said she was at her peak, but they had no idea what was coming next. Thinking that way about Ashley's career—as something exciting rather than threatening—was a strange new feeling.

The doors opened with a *ping*, and Ryan Worth stood in black leather pants and a golden mesh top, flanked by his entourage. Georgia grinned. The timing was perfect for the larger-than-life pop star to make a grand entrance into the foyer.

"Georgia, babe. Nice to see you," Ryan said in his thick Irish accent, leaning in to trade air-kisses.

"Lovely to see you, too, Ryan. Have you met Ashley?"

"I haven't yet had the pleasure, but I'm always happy to meet another Splash victim. I hope they're not rounding up all the Splash gays to run us out of town. Nice to meet you, love," Ryan said, kissing her cheek.

"Nice to meet you, too."

"Wait, are you two friendly? I thought you were in that big catfight. Was that media spin or something? Don't tell me these bastards made that up."

"It wasn't fake, but we buried the hatchet a while ago. We've moved on from all that, and we just happened to run into one another down here," Georgia said smoothly.

"Congratulations on the new album. You really pushed the envelope this time," Ashley said.

"Thanks, sweetheart. The guys upstairs tried to tell me it was too gay, but I showed them. My video's breaking YouTube."

"I loved your video. Great cameos."

"Cheers," he said, looking back and forth between them, putting a finger on his chin. "You know what, girls? You'd make an extremely hot couple. One of those couples that just…you know. All that old tension. You should do a video together or something. That'd go viral in a heartbeat. Anyway, I've got to run, I have interviews downtown."

Ryan winked at Georgia as he passed. The women giggled as they got into the elevator. Georgia noticed Ashley blushing and wondered if she looked the same way.

"I can't believe he wears those pants in his daily life. I thought they were just for the cameras," Ashley said.

"I don't think I've ever seen him when he's *not* wearing those pants. He probably wears them to bed."

They entered the conference room, where everyone was already gathered. Nicky grinned at them, and so did Ashley's manager, Pam. The energy in the room was so different from the last time—relaxed and happy. They knew Ashley and Georgia wouldn't come together without good news. Everyone smelled dollar signs, that much was clear.

Cliff threw out his arms. "Ladies, sit down. I'm so happy we're meeting with you together. Never thought I'd see the day."

They sat beside one another, Ashley angling her body toward her in her chair. Nicky often tried to protect Georgia, but after she'd sided with the record label at their last meeting, it made her feel like she could rely only on herself. It was another entirely new feeling to have Ashley in her corner.

"Well, let's hear it, ladies. What's going on?" Cliff said.

They started talking at the same time, tripping over one another's words. Georgia waved a hand at Ashley. "You go, please."

"One of you go. We're dying to hear what you two have been talking about."

Ashley looked at her again, checking in. "We've met a couple of times and talked things through. We agree. We want to do the album with Johnny."

Nicky pumped her fist, and Cliff started a round of clapping that made Georgia cringe. These people thought nothing of threatening her career, telling her they were dropping her like a hot potato. Now, they'd gotten what they wanted from her. They all had big smiles pasted on their faces, but when she looked to the side, she realized that Ashley wasn't joining in either.

"This is fantastic. And you've already told Johnny?"

"We've sent him a letter. We're waiting to hear back from him about when he'd like us to come to New Mexico," Georgia said.

"I'll postpone the release of my next album," Ashley said.

She'd explained to Georgia that she'd been preparing to record. Still, she was happy to shelve the project for as long as necessary.

She'd been planning on producing it herself, and Splash would prefer her to go ahead with this album, anyway. They hoped to start as soon as possible—neither had a tour scheduled, so the timing was right.

"I'll start preparing a press release," Morrison said, turning to Ashley's publicist, Julia. "We'll draft a joint statement."

"No, thank you," Georgia replied. "We've already agreed we don't want that kind of thing. We'd like to keep this project a secret until after we're done."

"I'm confused. Why wouldn't you want to capitalize on the excellent publicity this would bring?"

"We don't want the pressure, and we don't want to bring so many people to Johnny's door. The press would hound us, and so would fans. He's a private man. We all know that."

Cliff stepped in with a smug smile. "We understand, but Johnny hasn't said anything about keeping it quiet. We could arrange for security to stay nearby and keep the paps away from his place. So we could get some buzz going and boost sales for your back catalogs. It'd be a smart move."

Under the table, Ashley lightly rested a hand on Georgia's knee, making her jump. They hadn't discussed it, but the meaning of her touch was unmistakable. Ashley was telling her to keep going and that she was still with her. "Thanks, but we insist," Georgia continued. "No statement and no leaks, please. We'll pull out if this gets out before we're ready."

Cliff rubbed his chin, confused. "Okay I guess."

Ashley took her hand away, and Georgia shifted in her chair, surprised at how much the touch had affected her. Georgia sensed the change in the room—nobody had expected their united front. Cliff was usually aggressive, and she liked that they'd thrown him off his game.

"There's another thing. We know you guys have been in contact with Johnny's lawyers. We want anything that's already been discussed thrown out so we can go back to the drawing board."

Nicky sat forward anxiously, and Georgia almost felt bad about not keeping her in the loop. "You don't have to worry about that," Nicky said. "We've been working hard to get you both a good deal. You'll be happy."

Georgia didn't answer. Instead, she used the same signal, reaching for Ashley's knee. She caught a smirk before Ashley spoke. "We don't want this to be one of those things where you all go off and work out the terms, and neither of us knows what the other is getting. We'd like full transparency and ask that everything be split down the middle."

Ashley's manager, Pam, gave them a cool stare. "Ashley, can I speak to you privately for a moment?"

Ashley looked back calmly. Georgia bet neither of them ever raised their voice like she and Nicky did. "I'll say it one more time. We don't want separate negotiations. We're asking for everything to be split equally. Anything you want to talk to me about has to be done with Georgia there."

Pam's nostrils flared. "I advise against this."

"Noted. So, that's clear? We're doing fifty-fifty all the way down. That's how Johnny wants it to work creatively, so we'd like the business side to reflect that."

"Wait. What if Georgia contributes more during the songwriting sessions? I don't think this is fair. We should wait until after the songs are finished," Nicky said earnestly.

"Nicky. Seriously?" Georgia said. She felt like a teenager, being embarrassed by her parents. "Ashley and I have already agreed on this."

Everyone in the room exchanged baffled eye contact, but nobody said anything. Ashley quietly waited, so Georgia followed her lead. The seconds ticked by until Ashley grazed her knee with her fingers again. *Hold steady.*

If this was going to be their new way of communicating, Georgia was all for it. She tried not to squirm in her chair, wishing Ashley would slide her hand higher to her thigh.

"So, I guess that's it unless anyone has any questions?" Ashley said.

"Okay," Cliff said, picking up his water glass. They watched as he drained it, then stared around the room as though waiting for someone to save this meeting. "No questions."

"We'll let you know when we find out our start date," Georgia said.

They walked slowly down the hall and away from the meeting room, then faster so nobody could hear their laughter. Ashley grabbed her arm and pulled her into a small conference room, closing the door behind them.

"That was so good!" Georgia said. "They didn't know what to do. I've never seen Cliff go quiet like that. He seriously had no idea how to react."

"I know. I hope you didn't mind me touching your leg like that. I should've asked first."

Georgia looked at her mouth, thinking she wouldn't mind if Ashley did more than that. "That's okay. It was so awkward a couple of times that I might've cracked if you hadn't done it."

"Oh, good," Ashley said, blowing out a breath. "I learned that way back. If you stay quiet, they have nothing to argue with. Plus, it freaks them out."

"It certainly does."

"They really weren't happy about the secrecy thing. I guess it takes them all out of the loop, and they hate that."

"Do you think we'll manage to keep it quiet?"

"We can do it. We'll throw out the usual playbook. For one thing, I don't think we should fly to the ranch. I'd like to have my car while we're there, so I'll drive. It'll take me a few days, but I don't mind. What about you?"

"Why do you even have a car? You live in New York."

When Ashley smiled, her cheek dimpled. Georgia hadn't noticed that before.

"I love driving. I go on road trips all the time. You blend in more when you do stuff like that. I dress down, wear a hat, and nobody ever recognizes me."

"Sounds nice."

"You could come with me if you wanted. Nobody would ever expect us to be traveling together, stopping at diners and stuff. We'd totally get away with it."

They were getting along well now, but the thought of sitting in a car for days on end with someone who'd recently been an enemy? That seemed crazy. It seemed like a waste of time to spend days driving when you didn't need to, either. "Oh, thanks, but I'll just fly into somewhere nearby and hire a car to get out there."

"Sounds good. So, you'll let me know when the next letter arrives?"

"Immediately."

"Great, well, we should go separately so nobody sees us leaving the building at the same time," Ashley said, pointing at the leather satchel slung over her shoulder. "I've got a book in here. I'll sit and read. You can go first."

"If you're sure?"

"Absolutely, go ahead."

Georgia closed the door behind her. Why didn't she want to leave? She hated this place but could've stayed in that meeting room and talked to Ashley all day.

CHAPTER TEN

It was Georgia's last chance to catch up with her friends before leaving town. A letter from Johnny Rail had arrived the day before, and she'd called Ashley to read it to her. Together, they learned they'd be going to Celio Ranch in a week. Full of fear but excited as hell, Georgia had no idea what to expect. She'd invited Rachel, Eliza, and Mel over as soon as she found out, eager to spend time with them. There was a lot to process.

As soon as they sat down, Mel unhooked her bra and pulled it out through her sleeve, making them all laugh. They played cards sitting cross-legged on the living room floor and ordered pizza from their favorite place across the street. Georgia was already in her pajamas, and everyone else was in sweats. Eliza copied Mel's earlier move, twirling her bra around in the air before flinging it across the room.

"Okay, maybe we're getting too comfortable with one another," Rachel said.

"You and I both know there's nothing better than taking your bra off after a long day. Anyway, I still can't believe you'll be working with Ashley Archer. It's so wild," Mel said.

"Yep. It's pretty crazy. I still can't believe it."

"Does this mean I can finally listen to her music without feeling guilty?"

"Did I ever say you couldn't listen to her?" Georgia asked.

"It was strongly implied. Hey, why don't we watch a few of her music videos? I've seen some of them before, but it'll be fun to watch and think about what you two might sound like together."

They crowded onto the sofas to watch YouTube on her TV, Mel grabbing the remote to search. "We have to do these in order, of course. I want to see her stuff from the beginning."

Eliza slid on her glasses. "Let's try and figure out what she's stolen from you as we go."

Georgia didn't tell the others, but it wasn't the first time she'd had an Ashley Archer marathon. In the past, she told herself it was to check that Ashley wasn't outshining her. Lately, she'd been watching her videos to see her face. Ashley's videos were simpler than her own, and of course, Ashley directed them herself. They weren't big-budget or high-concept, but they always had beautiful cinematography. Lots of shots of Ashley with her guitar and close-ups of her lips. Georgia sank into the couch, trying to hide how it affected her.

They'd been watching and analyzing for half an hour when Mel stretched her arms over her head. "This is so fun, but I should really get home for some sleep."

Georgia walked her to the door, hugging her goodbye. Mel squeezed her tight. "I can't wait to see what happens next. Go off and do something amazing."

"I'll try. I'll miss you."

"We'll be doing this again before you know it."

Georgia found Rachel and Eliza in the kitchen, making hot chocolate. They returned to the living room, relaxing with blankets wrapped around them.

"How's the renovation?" Georgia asked.

Eliza inherited their nearby apartment from her grandparents a decade ago when she and Rachel were a new couple. They were updating the kitchen and bathroom, and Georgia had been listening to months of complaints about how long it took.

"Now that we've knocked that wall down, Eliza convinced me we need a bigger dining room table," Rachel said.

Eliza put her hands in the prayer position. "At last, she agreed. We can have proper dinner parties."

"Shame I'll miss your first one. I'll be halfway across the country," Georgia said.

"That's okay, sweetie. We'll throw you a big party when you get home."

"Do you really think I can trust her?"

Rachel and Eliza shared one of their private looks, understanding flowing between them effortlessly. Georgia had never had that kind of coupley shorthand with anyone. "What?"

Eliza raised her eyebrows. "Do you realize you've talked about Ashley all night? Even before we binged her music videos?"

Georgia looked at Rachel, whose stare was sympathetic. She hoped they weren't about to tell her they'd changed their minds and thought this was a horrible idea. Her faith in her decision-making was so fragile. "Sorry. I didn't mean to go on about it. It's a pretty big deal for me, that's all."

"Of course, it is. It's just that you're talking about *Ashley*, not so much the project," Eliza said.

"Well, she's a big part of all this. Why shouldn't I talk about her?"

Georgia wasn't ready to let on how much she'd come to care about Ashley so quickly. They'd been spending lots of time together, meeting to iron out details. Ashley was leaving before her, and they'd agreed she'd pick Georgia up in Dallas to take her the rest of the way to New Mexico. She'd been so against traveling together at first, yet all Ashley had to ask was, "Are you sure you don't want to come?"

Her resolve had melted like snow in the sun.

Rachel reached over and patted her knee. "Nobody's saying you shouldn't talk about her, sweetheart. Eliza's trying to say you seem preoccupied with her."

"I'm not preoccupied with her. I didn't suggest watching all those videos. It was Mel, remember?"

Eliza and Rachel looked at one another again. It was starting to get on her nerves. Eliza rose, picking up her hot chocolate from the coffee table. "I just remembered I have to call someone. I'll go to the kitchen."

"Could you be any more obvious?" Georgia joked.

Rachel turned to her. "Now it's just us. You can tell me what's going on."

"Like I said, it's a big deal for me. I'll stop talking about it so much if it's a problem."

"Of course, it's not a problem. It's just that I can tell when you like someone. I thought you might need to talk about it."

Georgia rested her mug on the coffee table, her mouth dry. Why was she so scared to discuss this? Rachel had been there through every hook-up, every crush, and the disaster with Hayley. She'd never made Georgia feel judged for being a little girl crazy. She needed to feel big feelings, which got her into trouble sometimes. Rachel always accepted that about her, even celebrated it.

Still, Georgia denied it. "I don't like her like *that*. She's just very different than I expected. I'm getting to know her as a person, that's all. I'm adjusting."

"Bullshit."

They stared at one another like they were still playing poker, Rachel narrowing her eyes and calling her bluff.

Finally, Georgia gave in. "Okay, fine. I might have some feelings."

"I knew it. Tell me everything."

"It feels so weird to talk about it. I can't believe I'm saying this stuff about Ashley Archer."

"You're not saying anything yet, and I'm dying to know. I haven't seen you like this for a while."

"All these years, I thought she was one thing, but she's the opposite."

"You always said she was boring. It doesn't seem like you're finding her boring now that you've gotten to know her, right?"

"Not at all. I thought that just because she's never been like me. No big costumes or choreography, just her and her guitar. Turns out, that's more than enough. She's one of the most interesting people I've ever met."

"Is there chemistry between you?"

Georgia considered all the little touches and the looks. She might think it meant something with anyone else, but Ashley having any interest in her felt so unlikely. Ashley hadn't publicly dated many women, and the ones she had were nothing like Georgia. A theater director of Off-Broadway plays, a Columbia professor—Georgia had always wondered how she met these women. They were all so sophisticated.

"I don't know if I can say. Sometimes I wonder, but then I worry she might be keeping me close because she wants the album to work out."

"I can't see you making this up in your head. You have good instincts. If you think she's into you, I'm sure she is. And if you like her, she must be worth it."

Georgia scoffed. After marrying a woman like Hayley, how could anyone say she had good instincts about women? She tried not to put all the blame on her ex—she hated it when people did that—but she'd come to believe Hayley was really not a good person. After they married, Hayley had turned cold, freezing her out when Georgia tried to talk through their issues. She always made things up, not just after they'd broken up. "I didn't have a radar for my ex-wife turning out to be a bad idea, did I?"

"Maybe Ashley's different. Anyway, I did not see this one coming at all."

"There's probably nothing to see except for me being foolish. I'll have to make myself get over it. Otherwise, it'll be a long few months."

Even as she said it, she didn't want to stop feeling this way. She'd missed the electricity from the touch of a hand on her skin. Things had gotten so ugly with Hayley, and those simple, sensual feelings were over long before their relationship ended.

"It's hard to switch attraction off. Especially when someone is as hot as Ashley."

Georgia stared at her for a moment before cracking up. "Didn't think she was your type."

"Well, I'm very happy with Eliza, you know that. But of course, she's hot. I still have eyes. I've thought that for years."

"For years? Seriously?"

"I couldn't tell you that, not when you were so mad at her for so long. You would've lost it."

"You're probably right. I don't know what it is about her. She's so delicate-looking but strong and pretty."

"That sounds about right. Those brown eyes are to die for, too."

"Right? And you really think she seems okay?"

"I never had anything personal against her. I was always only being protective of you. So if you're putting down your weapons, I don't see why I'd hold a grudge."

Georgia slumped against the back of the sofa. "What have I gotten myself into? I'll be sitting in a car with her for hours, and that's before we even get there. I don't know if that's wise. It might make it worse."

"What's that about, by the way? I thought you'd decided you didn't know her well enough to take a road trip together."

"We thought it'd be a good idea. Dallas means I could be on my way anywhere. People might start speculating if I'm seen getting off a plane in Albuquerque. Not that anyone would think of this, but you never know. That's what she said, anyway, and it turns out I find her very convincing."

"Oh, I just bet you do."

"Stop it."

Rachel smiled softly at her. "It's really nice to see you with a crush again. Love shouldn't be painful like it's been for you lately. I hated seeing what Hayley did to you."

"Don't go talking about love. I'm perfectly happy as a single woman, and that's how I'll stay. I like being on my own."

"Liar."

"Okay, maybe I just want to like it, but it's still what I need to do. Isn't that what the therapist you made me see thinks?" Georgia said.

After the divorce, she'd felt so low that her friends were worried about her. If she'd ever thought about divorce in the past, she'd assumed it couldn't be that different from any other breakup. How wrong she'd been. The end of a marriage felt impossible to accept, the sense of betrayal shattering. Georgia and Hayley had made vows that turned out to mean nothing, and she wondered if she could ever believe another promise again.

Rachel suggested she see a therapist to begin coming to terms with the loss, so Georgia had had a few sessions. Dr. Lewin picked up on it quickly—Georgia had a history of jumping from relationship to relationship. She'd rarely been single during her adult life, and Dr. Lewin suggested she spend time on her own to explore herself and the kind of woman she might want to be with. It had been almost a year, and she'd enjoyed spending more time with her friends.

"I didn't *make* you see her," Rachel pointed out. "And you said she really helped."

"Yeah, I did, and she was right. It's been a special time for me in lots of ways. I'm not ready for it to end."

"I can understand that. So, then, you can just enjoy having a crush. It can be fun if you don't have to worry about the outcome, right? Spend time with her and take it one step at a time."

"Exactly. Now that you've got it out of me, let's go and get some ice cream, shall we?"

Georgia tried to put the whole situation out of her mind. She had to set her feelings aside and focus on the work. This thing with Ashley and Johnny Rail had become a runaway train, and she had no choice but to jump on and enjoy the ride.

CHAPTER ELEVEN

Even though she was eager to get to Johnny's place, Ashley wanted to soak up New York before she left. The city's noise and pace drove her crazy, but she'd miss it anyway. She loved the wit and world-weariness of New Yorkers, the history on every corner, its cafés and museums and galleries.

More than anything, she'd miss her friends, especially her best buddy, Aaron. She traveled a lot for work, and it was always hard to say goodbye. They met in Central Park at their favorite park bench overlooking Harlem Meer. The water and surrounding trees never failed to relax her, no matter what else was happening.

"Thanks for meeting me," Ashley said.

"Of course. Wouldn't miss it."

Aaron was still in his uniform, a ball cap and polo shirt with the Enid's Deli logo on the pocket. He'd turned the cap backward, stuffing his long hair underneath to keep it off his face. They'd met years before she broke into the music business when they worked together at a burger place, and he'd kept her grounded ever since. They'd explored every corner of the city together, spending hours walking around this park, picnicking, and watching free concerts.

"Here you go," Aaron said, handing her a sandwich and unwrapping the foil from his own.

"Thanks. What have you brought me?" Ashley asked excitedly as she opened it. "You make the best sandwiches, for real."

"Truffled mushroom with pesto and cheese," he said, taking a big bite.

"Yum. This has got to be one of your best."

"Thanks. I'm gonna pitch it to the boss next week. So, what's the latest?"

"I've been getting ready to go. I'm nearly packed," Ashley said, leaving out that she'd unpacked and repacked her case several times. What did you wear at a ranch you'd always dreamed of? How could you prepare to spend time with a woman like Georgia?

"I still can't believe you'll be working with Johnny Rail. The man is my hero."

"I know. It's like a dream. I have all these ideas, but I'll have to wait until we're together before I can do anything with them."

"I can't wait to see what you come up with."

Ashley took another bite of her sandwich. She wondered what the food would be like at Johnny's and where they'd sleep. She'd pored over photos of the ranch from back in the day, but things might have changed since then. There was no way to know because Johnny and his wife had stopped letting photographers in years ago.

"And how are things going with the pop princess? I still can't get over you two teaming up. Who would've thought?" Aaron asked.

"I know. Pretty crazy," she replied, though her relationship with Georgia had changed so much in the last couple of weeks that it didn't feel crazy anymore.

What *was* crazy was how much she looked forward to spending more time together. She had amazing friends, but few were musicians, and they hadn't reached the same fame she had. She knew she had to be careful about that. Nobody wanted to hear about your struggles with celebrity when they were hustling to support themselves. It would be selfish and obnoxious, so being able to talk to Georgia was unique. She could understand her experiences firsthand, which made it okay for her to be honest.

"You didn't answer my question. How's it going with Gigi?"

"It's good. We've been working well when it comes to dealing with the record company and all that. Whether we'll write well together is another story, but we'll just have to wait and see."

"Do you think that stuff about her stealing music from Hayley Doran is true?" he said, wiping his fingers on a napkin.

"Dude. I didn't know you followed that kind of gossip."

He shrugged. "I don't, but I follow you. The algorithms always push articles about her to me."

"I don't think she stole her ex's music, no. She's a talented songwriter. Her ex isn't."

"Sure. I don't like her stuff, but it's okay as far as that kind of thing goes."

"Why don't you like it?" she asked, not realizing she'd snapped until he held up his hands.

"Whoa. You don't like her either, remember?"

Ashley finished her sandwich and balled up the wrapper. She didn't know why she felt so defensive when they'd roasted Georgia and her music countless times. "Sorry. I guess I've been listening to her through a different lens lately. Makes me realize I've been too harsh because I didn't like her personally. I listened to that last album again before meeting with her, and it's good. Maybe not as good as her earlier stuff, but it's not as awful as people said."

"Okay, sure. I've never listened to it. I'll give it a try."

Ashley wondered if she should talk about how much her feelings toward Georgia were messing with her head. In the early days of their friendship, she and Aaron were just work buddies who loved listening to music. It had changed when Aaron broke up with his long-term girlfriend. Ashley held him while he cried, his guilt about hurting his ex hard for him to bear. Since then, they were always real with one another.

Ashley turned toward him. "I've got to tell you something."

"Of course. What's up?"

"My feelings toward Georgia have changed a lot. I genuinely like hanging out with her."

"Fair enough. You're allowed to change your mind after seeing another side of her. I'll stop talking shit about her, I promise."

"It's a bit more than that," she said, closing her eyes like she was about to dive into deep water. "I mean, I like her."

"*Like*, like?" he said, wide-eyed.

Ashley held her finger and thumb an inch apart. "Just a tiny bit."

He put an arm around her shoulder, grinning down at her. "Don't downplay it. It's okay."

"It's so weird, I know. I was attracted to her straight away, and I never thought I'd look at her like that. It came out of nowhere."

That first meeting—and each time she'd seen Georgia since—were so powerful they knocked the breath from her. The long legs, wavy red hair, and how Georgia carried herself made an irresistible combination. It didn't make sense, but she couldn't remember when she'd ever felt this attracted to someone.

Aaron squeezed her shoulder. "It's not that weird. Does all the stuff between you really matter at the end of the day?"

"I'm not sure. It's been a big part of my life for such a long time."

"It's nothing to be feeling all guilty about."

"It's not? After years of treating one another like shit? It's pretty weird."

"It is, but this is not a normal situation. You can't apply normal rules. When you think about it, how can you genuinely dislike someone you never met? You didn't like Gigi Lark, but you like Georgia."

She liked how he'd put that. There was something so sensitive and theatrical about Georgia, but she was miles apart from the prima donna Ashley had believed she was. The more she discovered the real person beneath the glitter and makeup, the pizzazz, the more intrigued she became. "Maybe I shouldn't have offered to pick her up from Dallas. Spending time alone with her could be a bad idea."

"Why try so hard not to feel it? You're both single, and you both like women. There's no good reason you couldn't date. Why not just see where it leads?"

"Because neither of us can act like normal people. There are too many eyes on us," Ashley replied.

"Do you think she could be into you, as well?"

"There could be something there. But maybe I'm getting it all wrong."

It was a question she'd asked herself a thousand times since they'd met. She'd wondered if she was misinterpreting what seemed like sexual tension between them. Was it only the novelty of getting to know one another, with all their history? Was the electricity she felt when she touched Georgia's leg under the table nothing more than the thrill of the taboo? Georgia was the last person she should be feeling this way about.

She watched leaves move in the breeze in the trees overhead, thinking about what Aaron said. Technically, he was right, and nothing stood in the way of them having a relationship. Except for that one major, intractable problem—they'd fought with one another through the press for years. They were getting along well now, but their history was so complicated.

She valued what little privacy she could cling to. If anything happened between them, they wouldn't be left alone for a minute. It was easy to imagine things getting messy, especially if they dated and things didn't work out.

She couldn't take a risk like that. It wasn't in her nature. "Anyway. I'm sure this will pass. It's just a fleeting thing. Doesn't mean anything."

His blue eyes stared into hers, telegraphing compassion, but he didn't say another word.

He didn't have to. They both knew she was lying.

CHAPTER TWELVE

They met at a gas station on the outskirts of town, a lonely building with a single pump. Georgia looked around one last time to check, but nobody had clocked her. A couple of skinny teenage boys stood outside the store chugging energy drinks, and they hadn't spared her a glance. She walked toward the car, her shoulders hunched, shrinking herself like she'd been doing the whole way.

She wasn't wearing any makeup, and her thick hair was pulled into a ponytail. When she paired the look with baggy jeans and a plain pink shirt, she found that what Ashley said was true. People looked at her less, and she didn't notice stares or whispering. Nobody pointed their phone at her to take photos like she wouldn't notice. Blissful anonymity—she'd forgotten what it felt like.

Ashley leaned against the car in black linen pants and a short-sleeved top, platinum hair peeking out from under a black ball cap. Georgia hadn't realized she had so many tattoos on her biceps, which were lean and muscled. She looked more rock than pop star, especially with those black Ray-Ban sunglasses. In fact, she looked like a dream, and Georgia's stomach fluttered as she drew nearer.

Ashley waved and stepped forward, pushing off the car. Over a week had passed since they'd seen one another, and the days were long. Ashley texted her photos from the road of the hotels where she'd rested and the beautiful landscape along the way. Georgia loved being in such close contact, but it wasn't enough. Seeing her face was the only thing that could scratch that itch, and she drank in the sight of her pretty pink lips.

Ashley reached for one of her cases, but Georgia shook her head. "Thanks, but I'm delicately balanced. If I hand you anything, I'll drop it all."

Smirking, Ashley popped open the trunk. In contrast to Georgia's Gucci luggage set, Ashley had one case. They packed it all in, then slid into the front seat of Ashley's black Subaru Forester. Georgia stared at Ashley's blindingly pretty profile and toned arms as she put the car in drive. Her tattoos were black-and-gray renderings of flowers, an arrow, and a clock. Georgia wondered what it all meant to her. There was so much about Ashley that she didn't know, and she couldn't wait to learn more.

They didn't speak until they were on the road, with a Tom Petty song playing softly in the background.

"Ten hours to go," Ashley said. "I've enjoyed the drive, but I can't wait to get there."

"I bet. Let me know when you want to switch so you can take a break."

"Thanks. Maybe after we stop for lunch."

Ashley drummed her fingers on the steering wheel. Georgia had anticipated this moment so keenly that she didn't know where to start—it felt too big for small talk. Maybe Ashley felt the same way, but they had to start somewhere.

"I think we're getting away with it. Nobody noticed me on the plane, and my Uber driver barely looked at me," Georgia said.

"Glad to hear it. Pretty sure I've slid under the radar, too."

The awkward silence that followed made Georgia think it might be a long day. Messages had felt easy when she could craft each response, trying to make herself sound witty and thoughtful. Being together in person was so different.

"Do you ever wish you never got famous?" Georgia blurted out the first thing that came into her mind.

Ashley gave her a sideways glance and a half-smile. "All the time. It'll always be a hassle to get stared at in restaurants. Or have paps chasing you."

"Exactly, or on planes. I love my fans, but some people can be downright rude. Especially the photographers, like you said. I hate it when they say mean things to try and get a reaction."

"Yep. We can't complain about that in public, though, can we? We're supposed to *like* getting chased by photographers. We want the attention. Otherwise, why would we have gotten into this business?"

"What would you have been if you hadn't?"

"I'm not sure. It's not very adventurous, but I'd probably still work in the music industry, just behind the scenes. I've always loved producing. And if I couldn't get into that, I would've been a music teacher. What about you?"

"A vet, definitely. Not for domestic animals though, for farm animals, like cows and sheep. A livestock vet. Not that farmers like calling vets because they want to fix everything themselves, but sometimes they have no choice."

"Really? That's not what I expected you to say," she laughed, glancing over at Georgia. God, she had a beautiful smile.

"I grew up on a farm, remember? I was always around animals, and I love them. Plus, if animals get sick on a farm, it can impact livelihood a lot. Vets do a lot of good."

"I know. Maybe I expected something more glamorous, is all."

"I haven't always been Gigi Lark. I don't mind getting my hands dirty."

With the ice broken, the hours flew until they stopped for a lunch break. They pulled off the interstate into a Cracker Barrel, where they walked through the shop and sat across from one another on the familiar wooden seats. Ashley rolled her neck and rubbed her shoulder before she picked up the menu. Her arms looked so amazing in her sleeveless top that Georgia wished she could reach across and touch them.

"It's nice to stop and have a hot lunch," Ashley said.

"What are you having?" Georgia asked as she scanned the menu. "There are so many choices at these places."

Ashley smiled slyly at her. "You sound excited. Are you a big fan?"

"Sure. Even after all these years, these American chains still feel like a novelty. It reminds me of watching American TV shows and movies as a kid back in England. I'd see things like diners and wish I could go to them. Everything seemed magical."

"That's cute. I never thought of someone from overseas seeing it that way. I was thinking of steak and eggs. You?"

"I'll have the same," she said, putting aside the menu. "But I'll let you order, in case they notice my accent."

The server who took their order had frizzy blond hair and a kind smile. Before she walked away, she searched Ashley's face. "Anyone ever told you that you look like that singer? Ashley Archer. Dead ringer."

Ashley smiled back at her. "Someone told me I looked like her once. I think it's just my hair color."

The waitress nodded like that settled it. Georgia chuckled after she walked away. "Looks like the student has become the teacher. I'm blending in more than you. She barely looked in my direction."

"I don't know how she missed you with that red hair," Ashley said, tipping her chin up toward it.

She tucked a stray lock behind her ear. "It's just hair like anyone else's, nothing special. Plus, I made myself look a little dowdy today."

"I don't think you could look dowdy even if you tried."

Their eye contact suddenly felt intense. Georgia could drown in those brown eyes, and she loved having them on her. She wondered how she could've ever thought Ashley was anything but a genuinely kind person—it was all in her gaze. Georgia told herself to slow down and look away. It was too soon to feel this way.

The server returned with their coffee. Ashley sipped and looked out the window, and when she turned back, it was like that moment of intimacy had never happened. "Have you ever been out to New Mexico?"

"I've played a gig in Santa Fe but never spent any time there outside the tour bus. Same for you?"

"Yeah. As a kid, I lived in Colorado for a while, so I've visited as a tourist, but that's it."

The server placed their meals before them and refilled their coffee cups. When she was gone, Georgia laid her napkin on her lap and started cutting up her steak. "You said you lived there for a while. Did you live somewhere else, too?"

"Yeah. We moved away when I was twelve and went to New Jersey. We lived there until I was old enough to move to the city."

"Did you have family there?"

"No. We moved for my mom's job."

"What job?"

"She's a doctor."

"Do you have any brothers and sisters?"

Ashley shook her head, clearing her throat. Georgia wasn't sure what she'd said wrong. Ashley was a private person, but Georgia didn't consider her questions personal. She liked learning about family because it was so significant in shaping people. As an only child, Georgia had relied on fantasy to guard against loneliness, and it had helped make her independent and ambitious. She'd wished often for brothers and sisters but had a theory that if she'd had them, she might never have become Gigi Lark.

"I don't have siblings, either. Growing up, I had some imaginary friends, and I truly thought the animals were my friends. We had working dogs, and my father would make them babysit me, so you can see why I'd think that," Georgia said, talking too much to fill the awkward silence.

Ashley made eye contact with her again, smiling. "He didn't. You're making that up."

"No, it's true. When Dad was minding me at the farm, he'd just put me on the ground, and the dogs would circle me. He knew they'd run over to him if anything seemed wrong. Mom hit the roof when she found out, but I always felt safe. My favorite was Dirk Bogarde."

Ashley laughed. "You had a working dog called Dirk Bogarde as a babysitter? Now I've heard everything."

"It's all true. Dad loves movies, especially British ones. All our dogs are named after famous Brits. He has Michael Caine and Helen Mirren these days."

"Your dad sounds like a cool guy."

"Yes and no. My parents are rather traditional. The coming out as a lesbian thing was a challenge, then me announcing I was moving to London to try to get into the music business…That was so foreign to them. Moving to America was, of course, even worse. They thought I'd gone quite mad."

Ashley leaned across the table like she wanted to hear more. "I bet. And I bet they're proud of you."

"They are. But then I added thirty-three-year-old divorcée to the list of my accomplishments. They're not so happy about that one."

"And you can't help that. I'm sorry," Ashley said, with so much feeling Georgia wanted to reach across and take her hand. She was touched that Ashley wouldn't let her get away with playing her divorce off as a joke.

"They don't understand why we had to get married when we hadn't been together very long. But I wouldn't have done it if I didn't think it would last."

"Of course not."

"They'd like me to be all settled down, preferably with children. My life is very different from theirs. I try to remember that when I'm feeling judged."

"Mine too, with my parents, I mean. Mom's very career-orientated, just like me. She went back to school and became a doctor when I was a kid. I thought she was a superhero for doing that."

"She *is* a superhero. That's amazing," Georgia replied, tucking the detail away. Insights into Ashley's life were precious, breadcrumbs she had to pick up to find her way to her. "Does she still practice?"

"Oh, yeah. Mom won't retire until she absolutely has to. Dad works part-time as a mechanic and stays on top of everything at home. My parents aren't very traditional like yours, but they'd love me to settle down, too. They want me to have what they do, I guess."

Georgia had been dying for an opening to ask about her love life, and she grabbed it. "Are you seeing anyone? You're so good at keeping that stuff private. When I'm ready to date again, I'll take a leaf out of your book."

"Nope. I haven't dated anyone seriously for a while. I'm happy to focus on work, especially with an opportunity like this."

"Exactly, me too."

They ate the rest of their meals in comfortable silence, Georgia trying to hide her happiness. She shouldn't care so much that Ashley didn't have a girlfriend, but she couldn't help it. She would've been crushed to find out otherwise, and she didn't want to think about what that said about her.

CHAPTER THIRTEEN

When they'd settled the check, Ashley slid the car keys across the table, raising her eyebrows. "Looks like it's your turn to drive. Take good care of my baby."

"You sure you're okay with me driving your car? Are you aware that we drive on the other side of the road back home?"

"I can keep going now that I've had a rest," Ashley said, reaching doubtfully for the keys.

Georgia stood and scooped them up. "I'm joking, I've driven in America before, many times. I'm a good driver, I promise."

"Okay, well, I'll take my chances so I can have a break. When I close my eyes at night, all I can see is the road. It'll be nice to be a passenger," Ashley said, holding the restaurant door open.

Georgia bit her lip as she passed, their bodies almost touching. Her skin was hot, and her mind rushed with desire. Again, she wondered why the feeling was so powerful. They could joke around one minute, and the air between them was charged the next. During the time apart, there'd been moments when she'd wondered if it would dissipate as quickly as it had come on.

She was wrong. The days of not seeing one another made the attraction even stronger than before.

Georgia got into the driver's seat, wishing she'd agreed to make the whole trip from New York together when Ashley suggested it. Traveling with Ashley made Georgia feel free—like they were on a grand adventure together. She loved having Ashley all to herself, and she'd cheated herself out of having this for longer. Who knew what it would be like at Johnny Rail's? Maybe they wouldn't get to spend much time alone.

Before starting the car, Georgia adjusted the side mirrors, squinting into the sun. She pulled down the shade. "I should've bought sunglasses back at that gas station. I forgot mine."

Ashley took off her Ray-Bans and passed them across, their hands touching. "Here. Take mine."

"Are you sure? What about you?"

"Driver gets dibs on sunglasses. Rule of the road."

"Thanks," Georgia said, putting them on and checking the mirror.

Ashley laughed. "Don't worry, they look good on you."

"I wasn't looking at myself. I was adjusting the mirror," she said, scanning radio stations until she found a Lady Gaga track.

"Excuse me, nobody said that you could change stations."

"The driver chooses the music. Rule of the road. What have you got against Lady Gaga, anyway?"

"Nothing, I think she's great. I've always liked her music."

Georgia guided them smoothly back onto the interstate. It was a few years since she'd been behind the wheel, and it felt good. She loved seeing the road stretching ahead, knowing Ashley was beside her.

"Hey. There's something I've been wondering about since I met you."

Ashley had her arm out the window, trailing her hand in the wind. "We've got about seven hours until we get there, so go ahead. Ask me anything."

Questions had been on the tip of her tongue for weeks, and they'd been brought to the surface again. Maybe she was a hypocrite, but hearing Ashley talk about liking another artist made her jealous. "Why has it been so bad between us? You can appreciate someone like Lady Gaga. Why didn't you like me?"

As soon as the words left her mouth, she hated how whiny she sounded, like a kid who'd asked why someone didn't want to play with her. Ashley kept looking out the window, taking a while to answer. "I could ask you the same question."

"I was only reacting to how you were with me."

"We're getting into this now, huh?"

"Like you said, we've got hours to talk. I'd like to go into this situation knowing we've worked a few things out, wouldn't you?" Georgia asked, gripping the steering wheel, worried she was pushing it too far. They were getting along, so why drag up the past? She couldn't let it go, that was why.

When Georgia glanced over again, Ashley leaned against the seat, her knee drawn up, staring at her. She looked so beautiful that she had to remind herself to concentrate. She wished they were talking in a different setting so she could keep looking, but it was the first time she'd felt brave enough.

"I can't even remember how it began. All I knew was that you rubbed me the wrong way," Ashley said.

"Do I still do that? Do you really want to do this with me or are you just putting up with me for the sake of Johnny Rail?" she asked, holding her breath as she waited for an answer.

"No."

There was so much feeling put in that one word. If Ashley didn't mean it, she was an excellent liar. "Good. I don't feel like that anymore about you, either."

A long silence followed. Georgia desperately wanted the conversation to continue, for Ashley to open up even a little. She bit her tongue, trying to give her space to talk.

"I don't know why I always felt so competitive with you," Ashley said.

"Was that all it was? Competition?"

"Unhealthy competition, sure. Our styles are so different, but right from the start, people were comparing us."

"I felt like that too," Georgia said. "And those differences between us made me feel so inadequate. I still remember the first time you were asked about me in an interview and refused to answer. Your silence spoke volumes. I liked your stuff, and I wanted you to like mine."

"See, I never would have known that. You never said anything nice about my music, nothing that sounded genuine, anyway. And I barely remember that interview, but you know what journalists are like. They would've made such a big deal out of that question when it was a tiny part of the interview."

"True. It's funny how things snowball."

"It might not have snowballed so much if you hadn't avoided me like I was the plague," Ashley replied. "All it might've taken was a hello. We could've started with that."

"I didn't avoid you," Georgia said reflexively.

"Oh, come on. You didn't even come to that nominee lunch for The Vanguards. You were always running away. I only saw the back of your head for years."

At the same time, they started laughing.

"That's fair," Georgia said. "I was nervous about seeing you. And the longer it went on, the more afraid I was to meet."

"One of the things I always hated was how I heard everything through the record company. It was like when you weren't swiping at me through the media, I'd go to Splash and find out you'd said my new album was shit or that the dress I'd worn to an event was ugly. And then I'd get all fired up and find myself saying stuff about you I didn't mean, and I'd feel bad about myself."

Georgia's mouth hung open. "I *never* talked to the record company about you, not like that. I knew they knew all about it, of course. How could they not? But I never brought it up. In fact, they'd do the same thing to me. Tell me you'd come in for a meeting and spent a lot of time trashing me. I figured you must dislike me so much to make business meetings about me."

From the corner of her eye, she saw Ashley sit up straighter. "I can't believe it. Actually, what am I saying? I can *absolutely* believe it."

"Why would they do that? It's so weird."

"Why do you think?" Ashley said impatiently. "It's served them to have us competing with one another. Think about it. How many times did they talk you into something by using me?"

Georgia searched her memory, quickly coming up with examples. They'd drop Ashley's name in contract negotiations, when she was trying to go in a new direction with her music, and even when she wanted to change how she dressed. Cliff said that if she cut her hair or wore suits, people would think she'd stolen Ashley's style. Ashley was the edgy, cool one, and she should stay in her lane. They knew how afraid she was of being compared to Ashley. It worked every time. "They did it a lot."

They were both quiet, letting the revelations sink in. Georgia slapped her hands on the wheel. "Those jerks. They got me to host SNL last year by saying they'd give it to you if I didn't take the slot."

"Oh no, they didn't! I'd never host, by the way. That's far too scary. I'm not funny."

"I'm not funny, either. I didn't do that great."

"That's a lie, I saw it. You were good," Ashley said.

"Thanks."

"And then they push us together as soon as they think it'll be lucrative."

"The worst part is, we let them do that to us. Doesn't that make you feel awful? It does for me," Georgia said, looking across at Ashley again.

The touch on Georgia's arm was featherlight, making her shiver. "It's all right. It's over now. We won't let them do that anymore, will we?"

Georgia's heart skipped a beat. She wanted to put her hand over the top and keep it there, but it was over as quickly as it had begun. "Of course not. I'm so glad we're going away from all that."

The road unfurled before them, taking them somewhere exciting and unknown. Georgia could feel her excitement rising again. She didn't know how long this project would take—though they'd both cleared as much as they could for the next few months—but it felt like the world had been cracked wide open. They'd wake up under the same roof and have weeks and weeks to get to know one another. She was so relieved they'd talked about all this. Maybe now, they'd finally be able to put all the rancor behind them.

Ashley turned away from the window again. "I feel stupid, you know. I'm a feminist, and I'd like to be the kind of woman who doesn't get into petty squabbles with other women. I feel horrible that I let all those executives keep it going. I should never have listened to them."

"It's okay. This is a tough business. You don't always know who to trust or believe."

"True, but still. I'm sorry I never reached out to you or did anything to patch things up."

"Nah. I was running away, remember? I don't know if you would've been able to catch me," Georgia said, smiling.

Her heart was swelling so much that words didn't feel like enough. Georgia put out her hand until Ashley took it. She squeezed gently, wishing she never had to let go.

CHAPTER FOURTEEN

Darkness fell, and they shared one of their new, companionable silences. They hadn't spoken much since stopping for gas and coffee a couple of hours ago. Ashley didn't want this drive to end so they could be alone for longer, even if her excitement about the project was at a fever pitch. She loved listening to Georgia's voice, clear and sweet. Loved looking at her, too, how her red hair framed her face while she smirked at Ashley from behind her sunglasses. All she'd done while she drove alone earlier in the week was think about seeing Georgia, and it was living up to her expectations.

The talk earlier had felt so freeing because all her resentment was turning to forgiveness. Ashley hadn't realized how much their troubled history had weighed on her, and she appreciated the chance to apologize.

Georgia made one more turn, and the voice on the navigation app announced they were arriving. Ashley couldn't believe it. At last, they were *here*. They pulled over at the side of the road, the compound's high fences illuminated by the headlights.

Georgia yawned behind her hand. "I just want to take a second to breathe and wake up before we go inside."

"I know what you mean. It feels like a big moment."

"Yep, and God, I'm tired. It reminds me of taking road trips as a kid when Dad would carry me inside after a long day."

"I'm not carrying you in," Ashley joked.

"I don't think you could. I'm a little heavier than you—a lot, actually. You're so slight, and I'm just not. One of the things people like to attack me about."

"People are assholes." Ashley frowned. She'd always hated that. She'd seen people talking about it online and wanted to step in and tell them to stop. The only reason she didn't was because she worried about calling further attention to it. "They should never criticize someone's weight, and your body's perfect, anyway."

"I'm curvy. I always have been."

"Like I said, perfect," Ashley said, her face coloring. She did her best not to stare, but she was only human. "Should we go in?"

"Sure," Georgia said, driving closer to the gate until she reached the intercom. A woman's voice answered, and the gates swung open.

They pulled into a driveway lined with oaks and lantern-style lights. The one-story house was lit up, its façade marked by curved windows, red tiles, and more lanterns. Bushes and succulents dotted the gardens out front. As they exited the car, Judy Rail walked toward them in a long skirt and peasant top, strings of beads around her neck and wrists. She was barefoot, and her hair reached past her waist. Ashley was almost as excited to meet her as she was Johnny.

"Welcome. I'm so happy you're here," Judy said.

She hugged Georgia, then wrapped her arms around Ashley. It felt gentle and maternal, soothing her nerves. "I'm so glad to meet you."

"You too, both of you. Come inside, please. We need to talk about something."

Georgia shot her a look as they followed Judy inside. Ashley was sure she was wondering the same thing—where was Johnny? He might be reclusive, but his letters had sounded so friendly. It was hard to imagine him avoiding them when he'd been so eager for their arrival. As Judy closed the front door behind them, a big dog came bounding up to them. Ashley crouched, patting the golden retriever.

"This is Willa. She's fairly new to us, a rescue. She's been here for less than a year."

"She's gorgeous," Georgia said, ruffling the fur on Willa's head.

Ashley stood, hoping to see Johnny any minute. The room had a fire crackling in the stone fireplace in the corner. A rug lay between two white sofas in the center of the room. "You have a beautiful home."

"Thank you. We hope you'll be comfortable here. I'll show you to your rooms in a moment, but first, I must pass on Johnny's apologies. He's had to leave, and I'll join him tonight."

"I beg your pardon?" Georgia asked.

Judy took her by the shoulders, smiling kindly. "I know this is a surprise, but everything will be all right."

"What's going on?"

"Johnny's older sister had a fall. She's quite elderly and frail and lives over in Santa Fe. His brother came by to tell us."

"God, I'm so sorry," Ashley said.

"Thanks, sweetie, but she's going to be okay. She didn't break anything. Pretty banged up, though, and scared. He really wanted to visit her after he heard, and so do I. So, I stayed behind to let you know. I'll go and meet him tonight."

Ashley's heart sank, their plans crumbling to dust. She was grateful when Georgia took the lead. "Okay, well, no problem. I hope she recovers well. We'll find a hotel for the night and head home in the morning."

Judy shook her head. "No, no, please. We're both sorry this happened, but Johnny wanted me to say he'd love you to stay. He promises he'll be back by Saturday or Sunday at the latest. In the meantime, you can treat this place as your own. He even left Willa here to keep you company instead of taking her along like usual. The kitchen's fully stocked, and your rooms are ready. Rest until he gets back. Enjoy yourselves."

"Are you sure?" Ashley asked, looking around the room uncertainly.

"Absolutely," Judy said, patting her shoulder. "My car's all packed. I was only waiting for you to get here. I'm sorry we couldn't call you. The phone will only call 911, and there was no time to send you a letter. It's been one of those times I wish we lived a little more in the twenty-first century, but what can you do? Anyway, Johnny left you a note on the kitchen counter. Let me show you around, and then I'd better hit the road. Sorry, but I want to get there before it gets too late."

"Of course," Ashley said.

Judy bustled around, showing them their rooms and encouraging them to use the pool and hot tub and explore the recording studio. Ashley stood helplessly as Judy hugged them both again, bent down to let the dog lick her face, and then turned away. It all happened so fast.

"Have a relaxing few days, and we'll be back before you know it. See you soon," Judy said, closing the door behind her.

They stood next to one another, staring at the door, with Willa sitting between them. The sound of a car door slamming followed.

"Um…" Georgia said. "What?"

"I think we're house-sitting for Judy and Johnny Rail and looking after their dog. That's what just happened, right? That wasn't a dream?"

"That's what happened. I guess we should get our stuff out of the car?"

They walked back out together, hearing the gate closing. What a start to their project. Ashley was so tired from the long drive it was hard to keep perspective. It wasn't Johnny's fault he'd had to leave, but she was so disappointed she felt like crying. She'd waited so long to meet him that he felt like a ghost, and now the moment had slipped from her grasp. They silently gathered their things from the car and brought them inside, the dog at their heels.

"Which room would you like?" Georgia said, looking comically weighed down by her fancy luggage set.

"I don't mind. They were both nice."

The bedrooms were down the hall from the main living room. They'd only had a moment to look, but both spaces had queen-sized beds, oak dressers, and Judy's art hanging from the walls. They'd been identical, as far as she could tell.

"Okay. I don't mind either."

When they reached the first door, Georgia paused. "I guess I'll take this one?"

Ashley nodded and continued to the next room, dropping her suitcase and backpack on the bed. She felt suddenly, desperately homesick. The room was lovely but smelled unfamiliar, like incense or something. She wished she was sleeping in her own bed.

"Ashley? Do you want to come and look around the house with me?"

Georgia stood in the hallway, and it made her smile just to see her. "Thanks, but I'm pretty beat. Maybe we can check it out first thing? I'd love to take a look at Johnny's note, though. Should we read it together?"

Georgia's eyes lit up. "I'd already forgotten about that. Let's go."

A notebook sat on the counter next to a vase of daisies. Ashley recognized Johnny's handwriting from his letters. They read the note with their heads bent close.

To Ashley and Georgia. I'm sorry this happened, but please enjoy settling in at our home. All the instruments in the recording studio are yours to use. I humbly suggest you spend this time going for walks, talking, and resting. Refresh your energy—it can be all part of the process. All my respect and love, Johnny.

"It doesn't sound like a bad way to spend a few days," Georgia said.

"You're right. Being here without them makes me feel weird, but he still sounds eager to get going."

"Totally. Let's do what they say, huh? Try and enjoy it a little."

"That sounds good to me," Ashley replied.

They read another note on the counter from Judy—a list of instructions for what to feed Willa and how often to walk her, directions for using the espresso machine, and more encouragement to eat and drink whatever they liked. It said they didn't need to worry about the other animals on the ranch—a young man from town came in daily to feed and water the horses and muck out their stalls.

"I don't even feel like dinner," Ashley said. "It's getting late, and I guess all those car snacks did the trick."

"Same," Georgia said, stretching her arms over her head.

Ashley's gaze ran over her body. It made her stomach flutter, and she had the crazy thought that she'd like to ask to come and sleep in the same bed with her. It would feel like heaven to lie against her body, just to have her near when she felt homesick like this. She tried to shake it off. "I really need to get some sleep."

"No worries. I'll put Willa to bed and lock up. Good night."

Georgia reached for a hug, and Ashley froze. She tried to relax, knowing it didn't mean anything. She seemed like one of those tactile people who were affectionate with everyone. Still, Ashley found having those soft arms around her overwhelming, mainly because of the scent of Georgia's perfume and shampoo. Her body had such a natural sensuality that it felt like the beginning of something when she was sure it was the furthest thing from Georgia's mind.

"Good night," Ashley said, stepping back quickly.

She walked toward her room with every inch of her still buzzing.

CHAPTER FIFTEEN

When Ashley awoke in the morning, it took a moment to remember where she was. Instead of car noises or sirens, she could hear birdsong. The room had heavy curtains and a small strip of light coming in around the corners. She put on her robe, stretched, and padded out to the kitchen. A strong coffee aroma wafted toward her, and Georgia stood with her hair in cute plaits, looking out the glass door.

Willa was sitting beside her but ran over to Ashley, the sound making Georgia realize she was there. She turned and said, "Good morning."

Ashley had assumed Georgia would have fancy pajamas, but she wore a blue shirt and striped boxer shorts. Her legs were a work of art—long, toned, and perfectly shaped from foot to thigh. She did her best to keep her eyes on Georgia's face. "Morning. Have you been up for long?"

Georgia held up her coffee. "Second cup. Plenty there for you, too."

Ashley joined her at the door overlooking the backyard. A low fence separated the yard from the rest of the ranch, and beautiful gardens and statues filled the space. The back patio stretched toward a pool, with comfortable-looking chairs and a hot tub nearby.

"It's all so nice, but I feel so strange being here without them. Do you?" Georgia asked.

"A little. It was a letdown last night, but I feel better about it after getting some sleep," Ashley said, sipping her coffee. She couldn't remember the last time she started her morning slowly like this, just talking. Back in the city, she'd been prepping for her new album, and there was always somewhere she had to be. She usually squeezed in a run before she went to work or dealt with her emails.

"Me too. I can't wait to explore this place. God, look at it."

"I know. It's amazing."

"Should we take Johnny's advice and go for a walk after breakfast?"

Willa's tail wagged as she looked up at them. Ashley patted her, talking in a baby voice. "What a smart girl. Someone recognizes that word."

"You're one of those dog weirdos. You'll get a dog and call it your fur baby, right?"

Ashley bumped her with her elbow, but she couldn't stop smiling. She was so happy to be here with Georgia. "Maybe. What can I say? She's an extremely good girl."

"I've been checking out the kitchen. Want me to make you eggs?"

"Sure. I won't say no," Ashley replied.

They took their breakfast to the dining room, which adjoined the kitchen. It had a long table with comfortable upholstered chairs. Framed photos were lined up along the wall, and Ashley kept getting up to examine them.

"Look at this one. Johnny's standing between Neil Young and Joni Mitchell, and I think they're in this room!"

"Amazing."

"Sorry. I hope you don't think I'm not enjoying the food. It's delicious, by the way," Ashley said, returning to her seat and eating a forkful of scrambled eggs. Georgia had served them with green chili and cheese.

"I like watching how happy this is all making you. Don't worry about me or my food."

After breakfast, they went to their rooms to shower and change, then met in the living room. Georgia had kept the cute plaits but changed into running shorts with stripes down the side. She gestured around the room. "Now, we're going to check this place out from top to bottom."

"I don't know about that. What if they're watching us or something? They might have cameras."

Georgia put a hand on her hip. "Would you like to think that through a little more? The man doesn't even have a cell phone."

"You have a point."

"Seeing as he's left us here and said we can do whatever we want, I'd like to give ourselves a grand tour. You looked desperate to check it all out when we were in the dining room."

Ashley laughed. "You've got me. Of course, I want to check out every glorious inch of this place."

They went room by room, exclaiming over canvases, ornaments, and Johnny's room full of vinyl records. They were neatly lined up and alphabetized, so Ashley searched for Georgia's name. She held up *All You Need*, grinning. "He was for real. He really is a fan."

"Has to be if he has that one," Georgia scoffed.

They left the recording space until last, and it didn't disappoint. It had dark wood floorboards, sofas with throw rugs, and artfully arranged instruments. Johnny had left the string of fairy lights around the ceiling on, casting a soft glow over the space and making it look even more magical.

Georgia immediately sat down at the white, baby grand piano with a row of candles along the top. "This looks like something Stevie Nicks would have in her house," she said, running her fingers along the keys.

"Stevie's probably played that thing," Ashley said, reverently picking up a vintage Fender guitar.

They spent an hour checking out different instruments and deciding on their favorites. Willa sat on a dog bed in the corner and watched curiously as they went around the room.

Georgia grew quiet as she settled back at the piano, playing a Linda Ronstadt song and humming along. It seemed like it wasn't only the bittersweet song making her blue—it was obvious she'd been through a bad time these last few months. Ashley hoped being here and working on this album would help.

"C'mon," she said when Georgia played the opening notes of a Leonard Cohen tune. "We can't have you here playing every depressing song you can think of. It's a beautiful day. We've done the inside. Now it's time to check out the outside."

"Okay. Sounds good."

It was warm out, the sky clear over their heads. Ashley breathed in the fresh air and sighed. "Do you ever go somewhere and immediately wish you lived there? This place is like that for me."

"All the time. As much as I love New York."

"It's special, isn't it? It's like the sky is a different blue here. It's so clear and bright."

Ashley scanned the bushes when they walked away from the house and into the gardens. "There's a path through these. I've read about it. They have a sculpture garden, all pieces of Judy's. She's never shown it anywhere else. It's not open to the public, but people always talk about walking through when they visit."

"You know a lot about this place."

"I've read a bit about it."

"It's so beautiful. I wonder if their eyes ever get tired of the beauty."

"What do you mean?"

Georgia pointed to a stone at the base of a bush. A plaque was affixed to it, with a quote that she read aloud. "'The destination cannot be described. You will know very little until you get there. You will journey blind.' T.S. Eliot. It's got to be here, right?"

"Good find," Ashley said, and they started along a path, Willa sniffing the ground beside them. She was still thinking about Georgia's words and trying to figure out what she meant. "What were you saying about the beauty?"

"Oh, I always think that when I'm in a beautiful place, especially with mountains or water. I wonder if waking up here becomes normal. Like, you just stop seeing it as special? Your eyes tire of the beauty, and it's just another place."

"Huh. I suppose a person can adjust to anything. Like the noise in New York and how tightly packed people are, especially in Midtown. It has a crazy rhythm, and you get into it and forget it's there. We'll have to ask Johnny if he ever feels that way."

They came to the first sculpture. It was a woman's body, boldly naked and pointing to the sun. They stood quietly, taking it in. Ashley studied the clean, curving lines and observed how the light played over them. She wished she could take a picture, but it would feel wrong. As far as she knew, there were no published pictures of this art. She couldn't believe she was seeing it with her own eyes.

After a while, they walked on. The next sculpture was a mountain range, a perfect replica of the one seen in the distance. They sat together on the bench across from it, Willa curling up on the ground nearby. Ashley felt so peaceful, but Georgia jogged her leg like she wanted to get moving again.

"How are you feeling about being here?"

Georgia smiled at her, but it didn't quite reach her eyes. "It's beautiful."

"I meant, how are *you* doing?"

Georgia turned back toward the sculpture, shrugging. "I'll be all right. Sorry if I'm being a drag. I don't mean to be."

"You're not being a drag. I was just wondering what was on your mind. Whether it's about this project."

"I wish I was more excited about it, like you. But having Johnny away like this means even more time to worry that I'm not up to this. When I played the piano before, I could only think that I hadn't written anything for months."

"That must be scary," Ashley said. She'd been writing songs since her early teens, and there was always something to work with. When she sat down to write, she always produced something. It might only be fragments she could tuck away for later, but she'd never worried about it. She couldn't imagine feeling like her ability to write had abandoned her. It meant so much to her, a right and natural thing. The thing she was born to do.

"It is. It's all tied up with Hayley. I hate that I've let her get to me so much."

Ashley turned to face her. "It's so normal to be depressed after what you've been through. I can't imagine. But a lot of great stuff could come out of that pain. I'm not trying to reduce it to just like, fuel for music, but it's not just about what you create. It's also a great way to heal."

"How do I start doing that?"

"You just…start," Ashley said, fumbling for the right words. She wanted to instill Georgia with confidence, but you couldn't make someone feel confident. It needed to come from within, and she could see that Georgia had stopped knowing how to be kind to herself.

"Thanks, that's so helpful," Georgia said, and they laughed. "I'm sorry. I know you're trying to help. I just keep hearing Hayley's words in my head. She thought I had no talent. That my best work was behind me, and I can't help thinking that's true."

She was blurting it out before she could think about it. "How long can you let her dictate your worth? Who says that to somebody they love, even in an argument? It's not okay. She has no business telling you who you are or what you're capable of."

Georgia stared at her. "I know."

Ashley was so angry her hands shook. She couldn't stop thinking about how Hayley had lied about their meeting in the bathroom—she would never pursue a married woman. More than that, she couldn't understand how someone could treat Georgia that way. Calling her talentless was cruel. Still, it wasn't her place to trash Georgia's ex. "Sorry. I shouldn't have said all that."

"No, it's okay. I've been in a black hole since we ended things. Maybe I need to hear it. You can keep going."

"Are you sure about that? I already feel like I've said too much."

Georgia held her arms open. "Go on. Hit me."

"Okay, but only because you asked. There's so much I don't know about your relationship. I also know it's not my business, but what you've said tells me a few things. Hayley was trying to make you feel bad about yourself, and you've got to take her power away. You'll never move on if you keep thinking about her and what she said. I know it can feel like the hardest thing in the world to let go of that pain, but it's a choice you have to make every day. It's the same with any kind of grief. I'm sorry you're going through it, and it takes work."

"Sounds like you're speaking from experience."

"Maybe," she replied. She didn't want to talk about herself—this was about Georgia.

"So, what are you suggesting I do? I hear you think I should stop thinking about her, but I would if I could. If only it were that easy."

"Here's what I'm saying you should do. We take the rest of today to explore this place and relax, but tomorrow, we get to work."

"Johnny's not back until the weekend. How do we know he wouldn't just scrap whatever we do? He told us to relax, anyway. I don't think he wants us to do that."

"Nope, it's not about creating something to go on this album. I agree. We shouldn't touch on this project until we talk to him in person."

"So, what is it about?"

"It's about you believing in your own voice again. Sit down tomorrow and write a bad song. Write the meanest song about Hayley Doran if that's what you want. Write about that sculpture. Write about this conversation. Just write something. Get it out of your system so that when Johnny gets back, you're ready to at least try."

"Yes, ma'am," Georgia said, saluting her.

They laughed again, Ashley playfully pushing her. "I know I'm being blunt, but you have to do what I say. I'm trying to help you."

Georgia sobered, locking eyes with her. "Okay. I'll write a bad song. But I don't have to play it for you. It'll be for my eyes only."

"Deal."

They shook hands, Ashley's heart beating like a drum at the feeling of Georgia's skin on hers.

CHAPTER SIXTEEN

Georgia rose soon after dawn, filled with a sense of purpose for the first time in months. She'd never imagined that being given an assignment would help—wouldn't that be too much pressure? It turned out that Ashley's direction was motivating. Georgia had wanted to write something worthwhile and brilliant to prove to herself and everyone else that Hayley was wrong. It was a paralyzing place from which to try.

This was just one song, and she had permission for it to be less than perfect.

Willa slept on a fuzzy blanket in the living room. She ran over to Georgia, who scratched her behind the ears. "Would you like to help me write a song? That's right, we're going to write a song together."

She brewed coffee and sat at the island counter with her notepad, buoyed by the morning sun spilling in. Her songwriting was often sparked by a hook or a melody popping into her head, but she couldn't count on that anymore. Today, she would work on lyrics as though she were writing a poem. To make herself smile, she titled it "Ashley Made Me Do This." The sensation of the pen moving across the paper felt good. Very good.

She rhymed *who are you* with Ashley's *Subaru*. Next, she added a couple of lines about the road trip. *You picked me up at the gas station/ I knew this would be no vacation.*

She was pouring another coffee when Willa ran toward the door at Ashley's approach. She wore a black tank top with her pajama bottoms, and the sight of those shoulders made Georgia's mouth dry. Her skin looked smooth and soft, and her shoulders were muscular and lean. And those tattoos—Jesus

Ashley rubbed her eyes. "You're up early. Are you writing already?"

Georgia ran over and snatched up the paper from the counter. "Don't look. It's no good. I'm just messing around."

Ashley laughed, shaking her head. "Good, that was the point. Don't worry, you're not getting graded, remember? Have fun. I'll take this back to bed."

Georgia watched her go, eyes drawn back to her arms. She doodled, then wrote a line about platinum hair and gorgeous brown eyes. Before she knew it, she'd completed a full verse. She took a break to eat a quick breakfast, then carried another cup of coffee and her notebook to the pool. Writing for herself was much easier when she wasn't trying to anticipate what the record company or the public would think. She'd stopped writing for fun years ago. Why did she let that happen?

She stared at the water and hummed until it became a chorus. Again, it wasn't that good, but she was creating *something*. It was like setting a match to kindling, a fire that burned brighter as she fed it. She slowly filled the page. When she had something, she stood up and stretched.

Ashley was in the studio, strumming her guitar. She looked up, giving Georgia a heart-melting smile. "How's it going, you?"

"It's kind of working? At least I don't feel terrible when I try like usual. The lyrics are done," she said, waving her sheet of paper.

"I knew you could do it. There's no such thing as writer's block, not long-term. The muse always comes back."

"I'm not sure I agree, but being here helps."

"Want to set it to music together?"

"No way. This one is just for me, and then this paper will be trash."

"Okay," she replied, placing the guitar on its stand. "Have fun. I'll take Willa for a walk."

When Ashley stepped out of the room, Georgia sat at the piano, trying to tell herself this was no big deal. Nobody was there to see if she failed, and she could lie to Ashley if she couldn't make this work. No, she could never do that. They were working hard to build trust, and she'd rather embarrass herself than break it.

She took a deep breath and experimented with chords until she'd chosen a progression. She fiddled around, smiling at her silly lyrics. She worked at it over and over until it sounded like a song. She played it through one last time, amazed. She always felt a click when something was finished—even now, with a song like this.

She couldn't believe that she'd done it after all this time. She'd only needed to try without counting herself out before she'd even begun. She'd try again tomorrow until she wrote something good enough to show Ashley.

She ripped up the paper, went to the kitchen, and put it in the trash. There was no need to cling to the practice song or worry over how silly it was. She'd completed the assignment, and that was all that mattered.

The wall clock told her it was eleven, and she could hear splashing outside. When she crossed to the window over the sink, she could see Ashley in the pool, floating on her back and looking up at the sky. Georgia rushed to her room to change, then returned to the kitchen and poured two glasses of sparkling water. She went outside, setting them on the small table between deck chairs. Ashley swam over to the edge, pushing her hair back from her face.

"Got you something to drink," she said, trying not to stare as Ashley pushed up and out of the water. Her striped bathing suit showed strong arms, lean legs, and beautiful thighs. She seemed so unselfconscious—beautifully at ease in her skin.

"Thanks," Ashley said, reaching for the glass. "I always get so thirsty when I've been swimming. Don't you?"

"It's been so long, I barely remember. I'll get in soon."

"Well, don't leave me hanging. How did you do?"

Georgia sipped her water and nodded. "I wrote a song. Nobody would say it was a good song, but it was something."

"And you definitely won't even give me a little bit? Just a line or two?"

"Hell, no. You said you wouldn't make me play it for you."

"Just putting it out there. It must be awful. Congratulations," Ashley said, raising her hand for a high five. They grasped hands for a moment, beaming at one another, Georgia's palm tingling.

Ashley lay back on her deck chair and closed her eyes. Georgia looked her up and down, watching the water glistening on her skin. She looked like one of Judy's statues. Her body was perfect, and Georgia wanted to run her hand along her side. They were alone out here, and with them being thrown together like this, it felt like anything could happen.

"I've got a long way to go, but it's a start."

Ashley opened her eyes. Georgia realized how mortified she'd be if she ever guessed what she'd been thinking. They were here to work, and this project was essential to Ashley. She promised herself that she'd put everything into her writing. She wouldn't let this opportunity pass her by—not only to work with a master like Johnny Rail but to impress Ashley Archer.

"I'm happy for you. You deserve to feel good about your work. I know it hasn't been easy for you. Thanks for humoring me."

"Thanks for pushing me a little. I guess I needed it."

Ashley shrugged. "No problem. I know how good you are, that's all. If I'm ever being too much, let me know."

"You're not. Keep encouraging me. It helps."

"I've always been a bossy boots. That's what everyone tells me. Too driven for my own good sometimes."

"Yeah? I bet you were an excellent student at school, weren't you?"

"I was a nerd. My parents have strong work ethics, and they taught me that. I was all about pleasing them. Wanted to do what I could to make them happy."

"That sounds like a lot for a kid," she said gently. Every time she got a glimpse of Ashley's past, she sensed an undercurrent of sadness. What was that about?

Ashley waved a hand. "They're great parents. I'm glad I've got this crazy drive. It's what got me to where I am."

It didn't look like she'd be finding out, not any time soon. She decided to drop it—for now. "Of course. What about the rest of the day? What do you want to do?"

"I want to relax like I've never relaxed before," she said sleepily, rolling onto her stomach. "I feel like I'm in heaven."

Georgia's gaze traveled over Ashley's back, admiring her lean figure and how the muscles shifted under her skin as she moved. She could watch her all day. "Relaxing sounds good to me."

"Might as well take it easy before he gets back. I think it'll take a while to relax when we meet him, you know? Doesn't matter how nice he is, he's still Johnny Rail."

They'd only been there for two nights, but it was already jarring for Georgia to think about Johnny and Judy's return. It was their home, of course, but she felt so safe when it was only the two of them. She wished they could stay in their little bubble, getting to know one another.

Georgia lay down and daydreamed about the woman dozing at her side, feeling a contentment she hadn't known for so long.

CHAPTER SEVENTEEN

Ashley watched Georgia as she opened and closed cupboards in the kitchen, gathering tools and ingredients. She grabbed a red apron hanging on the back of the pantry door and tied it around her waist. "Hey, look, it goes well with my dress."

"I agree. You should always wear that while you cook from now on," Ashley said.

She bumped the pantry shut with her hip, a movement Ashley followed with her eyes appreciatively. The pink shirt dress stopped just above the knee, showing off her gorgeous legs. Ashley loved how playful she was—she'd seemed much lighter this afternoon since writing that song. And Ashley had never known she found that sort of thing sexy, but Georgia in an apron was everything. Her hair was tied loosely back from her face, soft red tendrils accentuating her jawline.

Ashley still wore her bathers, a towel wrapped around her waist and a shirt over the top. She was mainly dry, and her skin was still warm from the afternoon sun. She was having the time of her life just hanging out at the ranch. She already regretted that she'd have to leave to attend The Vanguards, but she pushed the thought away. She'd only be gone for a little while, and then she'd be back in this paradise.

"What are you making us?" she asked as Georgia lined up packages and spice jars on the counter.

"Rice, beans, and asada. Marinated beef. I started preparing that this morning," she said, pointing at a bowl she'd taken from the fridge. "Do you want to find us something to drink? I'm not a big drinker, but I love having a glass of wine while cooking."

"Sure," Ashley said, jumping up from her stool. In the pantry, she found a couple of bottles of wine with Post-it notes that said, "Help yourselves." She selected a bottle of cabernet sauvignon. She put the glass of wine in front of Georgia and stood beside her at the counter, watching her measure spices with one of Johnny's carved wooden spoons.

It was still light out, the sun casting its spell over the mountains. She loved the homely feel of the kitchen and the soft music from a local station playing on the radio on the counter. Georgia's voice was sweet as she passed over a can of beans and asked her to open it. Was this what it would be like to be with someone like her? Everything felt so easy yet thrilling.

"What should we do after dinner?" Georgia asked.

"Hadn't thought about it. Have you got any ideas?"

"I'd like to watch a movie. Did you notice that big TV in the living room and all those DVDs?"

"I'm glad he has DVDs, seeing as we can't get streaming here."

"It's a good collection, too. They have *Funny Girl*, one of my all-time favorites. I'm a huge Barbra Streisand fan."

"I've never seen that," Ashley confessed.

"You've never seen *Funny Girl*? We have to watch it tonight. For 'Don't Rain on My Parade' alone. I think it's one of the best musical moments in cinema."

"I'm not much of a musicals person, but I'm open to trying it. I know the song."

Georgia tilted her head and squinted. "Let me guess, you're more of a documentary person. And you love art house and foreign films."

She'd probably mentioned that in an interview at some point. It was one of the burdens of fame that people wanted to know everything about you, regardless of whether that information was genuinely interesting. "Did you read that somewhere?"

Georgia's eyes twinkled like she was trying not to laugh. "No, Ms. Serious, I guessed."

Ashley laughed. She hadn't known she was so predictable. "I'm not *that* serious."

"Yes, you are. But I like that about you," she said, and Ashley smiled.

When Georgia belted the opening lines of "Don't Rain on My Parade," it sent a shiver down Ashley's spine. She'd never heard her sing live in person, and her voice was smooth as velvet but powerful. When she trailed off, Ashley couldn't hide her disappointment. "Your voice is so beautiful. You're a great singer."

Georgia grabbed the dish towel over her shoulder and flicked it at her legs. "Stop, you'll make me blush."

"I know you think I don't appreciate your talents, but I do. A lot."

"Thank you," Georgia said, ducking her head.

She reached for a red pepper and chopped it, separating those annoying little seeds and getting them out of the way with the knife. Ashley wondered where she'd learned how to do that, whether her folks taught her how to cook. Ashley's mom was a good cook but always busy, so she'd grown up on microwave food and casseroles.

"How did an English girl learn to cook Southwestern food?" Ashley asked.

"I never learned. I'm just trying it out. We'll decide if it's good in an hour or so."

"It'll be good, I can tell."

"All cooking's the same, just taste and experimenting. You don't like it?"

"I've never really learned," said Ashley.

"Does someone come in to cook for you?"

"Nope. I go out a lot or bring home stuff from the hot bar at Whole Foods. I guess I'm always too busy. It never feels worth it…All that trouble just for me, usually."

"Good food is always worth it. When we're back in New York, you'll come to my place for dinner."

Georgia turned away to get something from the pantry, and Ashley stared after her. It was the first time Georgia had made it clear that this friendship—if they could call it that—would extend past their time at the ranch. She hoped she meant it and wasn't just saying it out of politeness.

Georgia returned with an onion and handed it to her. "This is for the rice. Would you mind chopping it finely, please?"

Ashley passed the onion back. "I think that's more of a job for you. Unless you mind it being roughly chopped, possibly with part of my finger in there."

"You've never chopped an onion?"

"I mean...Probably at some point in my life? Not regularly enough for me to remember."

"I'm happy to do it myself, but I can teach you if you want."

"All right. I'll try it."

Standing so close, Georgia put the onion on the wooden chopping board. "We've got to peel it first. You slice the ends off like this. Then, you can get your fingers in there and peel off the outer layer. Go ahead."

Georgia's perfume overwhelmed her senses, sensual tones of jasmine and vanilla. It was strange to do something as mundane as chopping an onion with Georgia close enough to reach out and touch. She pictured putting an arm around her waist, resting it on the cotton over her hip. The woman who got to touch her any time she wanted would be so lucky.

Georgia traced a line with her finger. "Now cut it in half this way."

"Like this?"

"Yep, perfect. Then hold it like this while you're slicing. It'll make it easier," Georgia said, motioning.

"Like how?"

Georgia got even closer to her. She demonstrated, holding the onion in place, then put her hand over Ashley's on the knife's handle. Ashley shivered inside. Georgia's voice was low, and Ashley wondered if she knew what she was doing. "Remember, thinly. Make the cuts close together."

Ashley cut into the onion, but Georgia didn't move, watching her hands. "Keep holding it like that, but go the other way."

Ashley wanted to make a joke to ease the tension, but she couldn't think of anything to say. Her only thoughts were of Georgia's body so near that she could almost feel it. All she would have to do was move an inch, and she'd know that softness. She'd know what those curves felt like against her back instead of what was in her feeble imagination. She moved on to the other half of the onion, wondering why she could still concentrate while vibrating with longing.

What was going on with her? How could she go from finding Georgia insufferable from a distance to *this*? She'd always been so sensible about love and sex, especially since she'd grown famous. She didn't do anything to court controversy—if she was honest with herself, she saw herself as being above all this.

Ashley just hadn't met Georgia yet. She'd throw all her careful planning away, maybe even her career, for only a kiss right now.

She inhaled shakily, picturing putting down the knife and putting her fists in Georgia's hair. She wanted to taste the lips she'd started to dream about. She imagined Georgia pressing her hips into her from behind, kissing her neck, her hot breath in her ear.

At last, she thought of something to say. It was stupid, but she was finished with the onion, and Georgia still hadn't moved. "Surprised you trust me with a knife after everything."

"I don't know, you seem pretty good with your hands."

That was it. Ashley wasn't thinking about whether it was right or wrong anymore. If they didn't kiss, she might explode. She stepped back into empty air. She turned, but Georgia was over at the counter, grabbing her wineglass with a blush creeping up her neck.

"I'm so sorry, I didn't mean that to sound so, I don't know… anyway," Georgia said. She opened a cupboard, rattling around in there until she found the pot she wanted.

Ashley was still frozen. What Georgia said had sounded suggestive, but it had all been that way—the touching, the standing practically on top of her. Still, she wasn't about to force a conversation about it. She reached for her wineglass, and the room's atmosphere felt normal again, the sexual charge draining away.

"Do you mind if I go take a shower before dinner? I'm still a bit wet," she said, and she wished the floor would open up and swallow her. "I mean, I'm still in my bathers. I should get out of them."

Georgia turned toward her briefly, her face so red it almost matched her hair color. "Of course. I'm good here."

"Thanks," she said, clearing her throat. She had a feeling that when she returned, they'd both act like nothing had happened, which was fine with her. Was she losing her mind, wanting Georgia this much?

None of it made sense, but one thing was clear. This couldn't happen. They had to be more careful.

CHAPTER EIGHTEEN

After a cold shower and a stern talking to herself, Ashley returned to the kitchen, where Georgia was putting the finishing touches to their meals. She'd shed the apron, and her pink dress outlined just enough of her body to make Ashley's stomach flip again. Ashley had changed into a gray shirt and loose black jeans. Georgia stared at her arms when she came in, and she figured she must be checking out her tattoos. Once she got her first, she'd become a little addicted to decorating herself.

A mouth-watering meal was plated up on the counter. The aromatic beef sat next to beans, rice, avocado, and sliced radishes. Ashley couldn't believe how quickly she'd put everything together.

"Wow. This looks amazing. Thank you. You didn't have to do all this, but I appreciate it."

"I love cooking." She shrugged.

"You don't have to do all the work. At least let me take care of the dishes after."

"No need. Already done, mainly. I'm a clean-as-I-go cook. I was thinking we could eat out on the deck?"

"Thank you, and yes, that sounds wonderful."

Georgia had already turned on the fairy lights, though it wasn't quite dark yet. They sat on the outdoor lounges and wrapped themselves in fuzzy blankets.

"I'd heard it gets cold here fast," Ashley said, taking her first mouthful of delicious asada. "Everything's so different out here."

"I love how warm it is during the day and then fresh like this."

Ashley took another bite of her meat. It was well-seasoned and tender, melting in her mouth. "Well, it's confirmed. A Brit *can* cook Southwestern food."

"We can do a lot of things when we put our minds to it. A British person invented the toothbrush, you know."

"Really? What's with the stereotype that you all have bad teeth?" Ashley said, and Georgia guffawed.

Georgia was known for her loud laugh, and before they met, Ashley assumed it was an affectation. In person, it was genuine, like everything else about her.

Ashley cleared and rinsed their plates, then rushed to return to the deck. The sunset was awe-inspiring, and she promised herself she'd watch the sky painted all those gorgeous colors as often as possible. They watched quietly, but Ashley felt so connected to Georgia in the silence. Georgia's toes were sticking out from the end of the blanket, and Ashley kept eyeing the red toenail polish and her fine-boned feet. Everything about her was pretty.

They stayed in place when the sun was down, Ashley drawing her blanket in more tightly against the cold. Willa sat between them on the ground, and it felt so warm and sweet to all be together. She was grateful they weren't avoiding one another after that stuff in the kitchen—it could so easily get weird. She didn't want it to. She just wanted to be around Georgia as much as possible.

"This is so lovely. What would you be doing if you were in the city?" Ashley asked.

"Hmmm. Probably sitting in my apartment feeling sorry for myself about the state of my career after being dropped by Splash."

"For what it's worth, I don't think they really would've dropped you. They're not nice people, but surely even they must've known you would've turned things around."

"I'm not sure about that, but it's nice of you to say. Anyway, this is much better than whatever I would've been doing back home. What about you? What would you be doing on a night like this?"

"Working on my new album and getting stressed out about making sure everything was perfect. That all feels so far away. I'm glad I'm here."

"Me too," Georgia said quietly.

If she could bottle this feeling and take it home, she'd never be sad again. It was the kind of night that felt made for talking, and she wanted to know everything. "There's something I've wanted to know for a while. Can I ask you a personal question?"

Georgia stretched her arms over her head. "Not a natural redhead, no. I'm a mousy brown under all this. Next?"

"Ha, ha."

"No, really, go ahead. Ask me anything."

"I've been thinking about how our careers have been so different but the same in many ways. Like, we are probably the two most successful female artists, now anyway, who are publicly gay. Ten years ago, nobody could've seen that coming. It's such a big deal."

"It is a big deal. Things have changed so fast. The generations before us never could've imagined it."

"Yeah. One of the things I'm most excited about with this album is showing everyone that we don't need to fight because the world is big enough for two gay women, gay artists. Know what I mean?"

"I do. They'll be able to see us supporting one another like it always should've been. But you said you wanted to ask me something. What was it?" Georgia said.

"I wondered if you ever thought about keeping it a secret. Staying in the closet, like so many successful singers and actors."

Georgia rolled onto her side, facing her. "Would you think less of me if I said yes?"

"Not at all. I considered it. Everyone told me I was crazy to be open about it. The record label and my team said I'd never get to where I wanted to go. I kept giving them examples of women who'd reached the top…You know, like Melissa Etheridge. They said my style of music was different, and it wouldn't work."

"What made you refuse to do what they were all saying?"

It all felt so long ago, and she'd been more afraid they were right than she could ever admit. The memories had faded now that she couldn't imagine her life any other way, but it had been challenging. Even her parents wanted her to keep it to herself to protect her. How had she found the courage?

"I don't know if I can say that I refused. I simply couldn't do it. I thought about all the things they ask people to do, like have fake boyfriends…Taking a date to awards shows."

She'd talked to Aaron about that. They'd joked about him being her beard or merkin or whatever they called it. Once, he'd taken her by the shoulders and told her he'd pretend to be her boyfriend if that was what she wanted. Better him than some jerk who might be unpredictable or expect something in return. She told him no, not under any circumstances. Authenticity was everything to her.

Georgia shook her head. "I don't judge anyone who does all that, but wouldn't it be hard?"

"I don't judge them either, especially when people have their reasons. Sometimes very good ones, like families who wouldn't accept them. But yeah, I think it'd be hard. Anyway, we're talking about me too much. I wanted to know more about your journey with it all," she said, chancing a foot on Georgia's chair. If they were a couple, she'd pull her chair closer and tangle their feet together. The thought of it made her hot all the way through.

"Funny you should ask because you were quite a big part of it all."

"Huh? How?"

"I was under a lot of pressure from Splash. I had no leverage because I hadn't made my name yet, but my album's release was scheduled. They wanted me to be seen around town with some actor—they had it all lined up. But your first single was out, and it had a lot of buzz."

"And you could tell them I was marketable, so you could be too?"

"Bingo," Georgia said, pointing a finger gun at her.

Ashley threw her head back and laughed. She could picture the executives earnestly trying to tell Georgia that being closeted was for her own good. They'd tried it with her often enough. "I bet they *hated* that. And it means I got to stick it to them twice, me coming out and then you. That's fun for me to know."

"Glad I could help."

"No, no. I'm glad *I* could help *you*."

It was Georgia's turn to kick at Ashley's deck chair. "Don't be smug, it's unbecoming."

"Sorry. I always thought I must've paved the way for you a little, even though we started around the same time, but it's nice to hear you admit it."

"You did make it easier for me. But honestly, it wasn't that much of a decision. I don't think I ever would've fooled anyone if I'd tried to act straight."

"Really? I think you'd pass as straight. Easily."

"Not talking about how I look or anything like that. I try to imagine writing songs that would sound like they were about men, and I can't."

"You wouldn't do the vague thing or just switch out the pronouns?"

"No, I don't think so. I knew I was a lesbian from a very young age and could never pretend I liked boys. Did you?"

"Oh, sure. I had posters of men on my walls even though I wasn't interested in them at all. I'd have crushes on all these girl musicians and actors. Coming out was such a relief. Even though it's so long ago, I don't think about it much anymore."

"I understand what you mean about the crushes. As soon as I hit my teens, I got this hormonal rush. Like bam," Georgia said, clapping her hands together.

Ashley laughed. "Really?"

"Yep. I knew I liked women, and it just got stronger. I'm still like that a little, maybe. I love everything about them. Their hair, the way they smell. Everything about their bodies. Anyway, sorry, I go on a little too much sometimes," she said, sipping her wine.

"You're not going on. That's okay," Ashley said, her stomach fluttering. Georgia hadn't said anything graphic, but she liked hearing her talk like that, even if she wished it was about *her* specifically.

"God. Don't you wish we'd been friendly so much earlier?" Georgia said. "We have so much to talk about. We could've been teaming up against Splash forever."

"Better late than never, right?"

"Sure. So, it's been a good second day. What will we do tomorrow? I want to write more, but we have all day."

"I don't know. We have a lot of great options. Eat some more great food, for one. Let's decide when we get up?"

"Sounds good."

Ashley breathed in the crisp air and gazed at the mountains in the distance. The starry sky above her gave her the awed feeling of being small in the universe, which she loved. The wine tasted sweet on her tongue, and Willa was curled up on the ground between them. She could hear Georgia's breath.

She always tried to hold on to these moments. They were rare and precious, and you couldn't take them for granted.

It didn't get better than this. Georgia made everything feel right.

CHAPTER NINETEEN

Ashley woke up with an urge to explore. She looked up local tourist attractions and read about the Rio Grande Gorge Bridge, which was only a few miles from the ranch. Visiting a place like that was out of the question when she was on tour. There were so many places she'd only viewed through tour-bus windows, and all cities felt alike when she only saw dressing rooms and arenas.

Even the short drive gave her the sense of adventure she craved. The view of the surrounding mountains from the car was breathtaking. It was a warm but not-too-hot day, the powder-blue sky stretching overhead. They were each in leggings and T-shirts, ready for a hike.

"Are you sure this is a good idea? Don't you think we'll get recognized?" Georgia asked from the passenger seat.

"We'll be fine. We managed to drive all the way here from Dallas without anyone knowing, remember?"

"Yeah, but the stakes are higher when we're not just passing through town. People around here know where Johnny lives. They could put two and two together."

"It's okay if you don't want to, but I'd love to see this place while we're here," Ashley said, wondering if she should turn around. They'd been through it all earlier that morning when she suggested the hike. She couldn't imagine how anyone would ever figure out what they were doing here, especially when Johnny wasn't even in town. She didn't want to live like a prisoner, but she didn't want to make Georgia uncomfortable, either. Georgia kept saying she knew she was being paranoid, but she couldn't seem to switch it off.

"Don't be silly, of course I want to come. I'm just fretting for no reason. We should probably have a cover story if anyone tries to talk to us. It was a close call with that waitress at Cracker Barrel. She almost recognized you."

"You're my ex-husband's new wife, and I'm trying to get to know you so things can be amicable. My husband wants us all to spend Christmas together," Ashley said quickly.

Her heart soared when Georgia looked at her with a big smile. "Weirdo, you came up with that way too fast. No, we're sisters, and our parents run a local bed-and-breakfast."

"Who'd believe we're sisters? Your accent, for one thing."

"Maybe I grew up here but got sent away to boarding school in England. An all-girls one, of course. That's how I wound up such an unrepentant lesbian."

"I see. That's how you catch it. I always wondered," Ashley laughed.

"Or what if I talk in an American accent like this?"

"Hey, that's pretty good. You sound so different. Your name's Joanne, and I'm Christine."

"Where did you get those names?"

"I don't know, they just popped into my head. And even with that accent, we look way too different to be sisters. You're my long-distance girlfriend, and we're meeting for the weekend."

Ashley said it playfully but liked the sound of it far too much. Georgia's smile gave away how much she liked it, too. They pulled into the busy car park near stalls where people sold jewelry and art. They shrugged on their backpacks and walked toward the white bridge.

Ashley took a three-sixty turn, soaking up the view. The scope of it was otherworldly, the canyon surrounded by the red mountains against the New Mexico sky. It was a painting brought to life. She'd never seen anything so beautiful.

They crossed over to stand on one of the small lookouts, leaning over to see the river far below. An eagle soared against the backdrop of the mountains like it was showing off just for them.

"Look at that. Isn't he special?"

"I'm so glad we came," Ashley said, pulling her phone from her pocket. She took a photo of Georgia leaning against the railing, then stood next to her for a selfie. Their smiles radiated in the phone's camera, their faces close together.

"Can you imagine if you posted that? Out of nowhere, with no explanation?" Georgia said.

"It'd break the Internet, for sure."

An older, short-haired woman stood nearby in cargo shorts and a Cardinals jersey, taking photos with a long-lens camera. She paused and let it hang around her neck by the strap, smiling at them in a friendly way. "Would you ladies like to have a photo with the two of you in the shot?"

They looked at one another to check, and Georgia nodded. "Thanks, that's kind of you."

Ashley handed her the phone and put an arm around Georgia's shoulder. Georgia surprised her by slipping an arm around her waist and leaning closer. Ashley could smell that delicious perfume again. The tourist was a serious photographer, zooming in and out and testing different angles. Finally, she handed the phone back to Ashley.

"Think I got some good ones in there."

"Thank you. It was kind of you to offer," Ashley replied. Over the years, she had developed a finely honed radar for being clocked as a celebrity. It was hard to put your finger on it, but she could tell when someone pretended not to know her out of politeness or because they thought it would get them further in a conversation.

This woman was sweet, and she didn't have a clue. "You girls visiting from out of town?"

"That's right. I'm from LA, and she's from New York," Ashley said smoothly. "Where are you from?"

"Arizona. This place isn't so impressive when you've seen the Grand Canyon, but it's still nice," she said, chuckling.

"I'll bet. Thanks again for the photo."

"No problem. You make a lovely couple," she said, lifting the camera and returning to her view. "Enjoy your trip."

"You too," Ashley said.

They stood for a while longer, just looking. It was so special to spend time sightseeing anonymously, and she loved sharing it with Georgia. Out here, their carefully curated professional images didn't matter. They were shorn of their personas—just two ordinary people hanging out.

Georgia leaned over, speaking in a low voice. "Acting like a couple is the perfect disguise. Nobody would believe it was us, even if we told them."

Ashley grabbed the excuse to lean closer, Georgia's eyes widening subtly, staring at Ashley's mouth as she said, "That's right, Christine. It's an excellent cover."

"You said I was Joanne. You're supposed to be Christine," Georgia said.

"Oh, of course."

"You'd never make it if you tried to go undercover."

If she leaned over and kissed her lips, would Georgia pull away like she had the night before? Ashley had no idea how to interpret what was going on between them. She'd been in a handful of long-term relationships and enjoyed dating when the woman was right for her. Still, Ashley had always been reluctant to get involved. She only invested when she was sure she wasn't wasting her time, so she'd always been picky, weighing her options thoroughly before she dove in.

This felt so different. Ashley had no idea if there was potential for Georgia to be serious about her and had barely taken time to consider the future. The pull of this attraction was so intense that she didn't want to think. For once, she was happy to rely only on how she felt.

They were still standing so close together, but the moment was slipping away. Ashley could feel it. Georgia nodded toward the other side. "Let's cross over."

They walked to the other side, then back toward the car park. They were passing a fence when Ashley froze, noticing a shape next to a cluster of rocks. She'd sensed something unusual before she knew what it was.

"Shit," she said, putting an arm out so that Georgia would stop walking. "Bighorn sheep."

"Whoa," Georgia whispered.

Three sheep rested near the rocks, their large horns curling around their faces. They looked over at Georgia and Ashley but didn't move.

"They're kind of beautiful, aren't they?" Georgia said, softly.

"Yeah. I wouldn't want to get too close to them, though."

The woman with the camera appeared next to them, taking photos of the sheep. "Look at those big guys."

"I know. I've never seen one before."

Georgia didn't look at her, but she took Ashley's hand. The gentle pressure felt so good—warm and exciting at once. They stepped back, moving together toward the car park. As they walked hand in hand, it felt so natural. Nobody knew who Georgia was, but Ashley felt proud to be seen on her arm. On the other side of the car park, they came across the sign for a trailhead. Ashley wanted to stay close, but Georgia dropped her hand as soon as they were away from all the people clustered around the stalls.

They made their way quietly along the winding dirt path. Ashley kept glancing back at the bridge and could still see the eagle gliding around. She felt locked inside her mind, unable to make small talk with Georgia when she could only think about holding her hand.

Finally, Georgia broke the silence. "Do you think the penny will drop for that woman with the camera one day? She'll hear about our album and realize who she was talking to back there?"

"Maybe she'll never know who we are."

"Maybe. But if she does, I hope it makes her happy to think about it."

"Me too."

"I was just wondering. How do your friends feel about you doing this with me?" Georgia asked.

Ashley shrugged. "I've mainly spoken to my friend Aaron about it. He's supportive, of course. And he loves Johnny Rail. He's excited about it all. What about you?"

"They were surprised but excited for me as well. From the moment I mentioned it to her, my friend Mel told me I should do it. You'll meet them all one day. I mainly hang out with Mel and a couple called Rachel and Eliza."

"Sounds good. I'd love to meet them one day."

Georgia kept hinting at the future like that, and Ashley didn't know what it meant. They stopped walking because a flag was sticking out of the ground before them. It had a peace sign on it, and nearby was a spiral pathway of stones that led to a circle. Objects were piled up in the middle.

"I want to get a closer look at that stuff," Georgia said and started following the pattern of stones.

"You can just walk right to that stuff, you know."

"Where's the fun in that?" she replied, so Ashley followed.

It seemed like a random collection of things left behind—cards, coins, sticks, and stones. "What do you think it's for?"

Georgia opened her backpack, rummaged, and then put a receipt from her purse in the pile. "Whatever it is, we have to leave something."

Ashley checked her pockets and found a black guitar pick. She added it and closed her eyes, making a wish. When she opened them, Georgia stared at her. "You were just making a wish, weren't you?"

"Maybe."

"What did you wish for?"

Ashley only smiled. "If I tell you, it won't come true. C'mon, let's go back to the car park?"

This time, she reached for Georgia's hand first.

CHAPTER TWENTY

It was their fourth day in New Mexico, and Ashley loved how quickly they'd fallen into a morning routine. Aside from their trip to the bridge, they'd spent all their time at the ranch, which felt more like home each day. Georgia prepared breakfast while Ashley made the coffee. Afterward, they ambled around the grounds with Willa and talked.

Today, they visited the horses in the paddocks to the left of the house. Georgia wore a black-and-white striped dress with sandals and her hair in a braid—it all made her look pretty and relaxed. They stood by the fence until a white horse approached, big brown eyes staring at them. Ashley patted his nose, completely in love. "He's so sweet. I wish I knew what his name was."

"He looks like a Benedict or Hugh."

"Are you trying to name him after English actors like your father would?"

"Maybe. My point still stands. Definitely a Benedict."

They continued, passing a pair of chestnut horses grazing. One turned his head to look at them, showing off the white diamond shape on his nose. Ashley waved. "It must have been amazing growing up around so many animals."

"Did you have any pets?"

"Never, aside from goldfish."

"I loved growing up on a farm. It gives you a different perspective on life. You get introduced to death early. You understand where your food comes from…All different kinds of things."

"Tell me more about the food thing. Did you get to milk cows?"

"We didn't have a dairy farm, but one of my uncles did, and he showed me how once. But they don't do it by hand, of course. Anyway, one of my earliest memories is of sitting down to dinner for a pork roast and Dad telling me we were eating Vanessa. Our pig."

"Oh, no. Were you upset?" she asked, wanting to hear every detail, good and bad. She loved hearing Georgia's voice and how she grew animated when describing her family. In the back of her mind, Ashley wondered if she'd get to meet them all one day.

"I cried, and then I got in big trouble. Dad said we were lucky to have fresh food when other kids go hungry. His dad and all his brothers were farmers, too, so he didn't have much patience for that kind of thing."

"Would you ever want to live on a big property like this?"

"Sure. I can imagine that. Maybe after I retire, I'll move away from the city. So, that's how I learned about life and death and all that. What about you? What are your earliest memories of all that stuff?"

"Wow. Going right into the existential questions, huh?"

Georgia shook her head. "I'm sorry. Bad habit. My friends always tell me I ask too many questions. Let's talk about something else."

Ashley's heart pounded because her instinct was to deflect, but she knew she would tell Georgia the truth. She rarely talked about her childhood, keeping it safely tucked away where nobody could touch it. Her parents didn't start talking about her brother until she was old enough to understand what they'd lost. Did she ever understand it? Could anyone? It was confusing to look back on, but she didn't blame them. It was just how they were—they did what they needed to do to survive.

"I had a brother. Brandon. He died of leukemia when he was ten."

Georgia's breath caught. "Oh, my God. I'm so sorry."

"Thank you. It's a long time ago."

"I can't imagine what that must've been like for you and your family."

Ashley hesitated, trying to describe the indescribable. For years, her parents were hollowed out by grief. They'd been to a place not many could understand—living through years of hospital visits and treatments while she was a toddler, knowing what might be coming. She still remembered how scared she was when she came across her mother sobbing in the living room. It was one of her earliest memories. Ashley could feel Georgia's presence as she walked quietly beside her. Suddenly, she realized she didn't need to sugarcoat anything. Some people couldn't take the sadness, and she couldn't blame them. But Georgia was so comfortable with her emotions that Ashley wasn't scared to talk about anything.

"I don't remember much, to be honest. I look at photos of us as a family, and I can't believe it's me in there with them all. I always looked at his picture, trying to make myself remember more. It's strange to think that little boy is my big brother."

"That's heartbreaking."

"I wish they would have talked about him more when I was growing up, but I understand why they couldn't."

"Did they think they were protecting you?"

This was the kind of thing she'd spoken to a therapist about in her early twenties as she began coming to terms with the tough aspects of her childhood. There was so much to process, and she never felt she could discuss it directly with her parents. "I guess that was part of it, but I also think they've never talked to *each other* about it that much. I mean…I'm sure it doesn't mean they still don't think about him every day. And they love one another and everything. They have a great relationship."

"You don't have to explain that. Nobody should judge them, though it must've been hard for you. Losing a kid is devastating," Georgia said softly, obviously picking up on Ashley's defensiveness about people thinking it was strange. An ex-girlfriend had told Ashley her parents were emotionally repressed, and they'd made her repressed too, and she'd been so angry. It meant a lot that Georgia got it.

"It is devastating. I wish I knew what my parents were like before it happened. They're wonderful people, but they always seem a little sad. And it's weird how sometimes I don't feel like part of it because of how much I don't remember."

They walked toward the sculpture garden. Georgia was so easy to talk to, and she took her arm, making Ashley feel cared for. Nobody else was around, and the affection was just for her.

"That makes sense. They've lost a lot. I wish none of you had gone through that," Georgia said.

That was what Ashley wished, too. Still, her folks had done the best they could with what they had, and her mother had found purpose in becoming a doctor. She loved her career. Ashley had even found gratitude for how her early exposure to grief helped her understand the value of life. She grew very sad sometimes, but it was a sadness she'd learned to live with. "Thank you," she said, a lump in her throat.

Georgia squeezed her arm. "Thanks for talking to me about it. I guess it's something you've wanted to keep private. I've never read anything about it."

"You're right, that's very deliberate. Of course, lots of people know I lost a big brother, but thankfully, nobody has been tacky enough to go public with it. When I started getting famous, my parents didn't need to ask me not to talk about it. I knew what they'd want."

"I wouldn't want the press to know about something like that, either. Unfortunately, you can't trust everyone to be sensitive."

"You sure can't," Ashley said.

Georgia was being so supportive, but Ashley was starting to feel the weird shame that always seeped in when she thought she'd overshared. "Anyway, enough about my childhood trauma. Should we go back to the house?"

They'd come to the same bench seat they'd rested on when they first arrived. Georgia pointed to it. "Let's stay for a minute. We don't have to keep talking. I want to honor what you just told me."

They sat facing the mountains. Ashley wished they were still walking so Georgia would hold her again. A moment later, she put an arm around her shoulders as though she knew exactly what Ashley needed. "I just realized something. Your song, 'Remember' is about your brother, isn't it?"

"Good catch. Not many people know that, but yeah."

"I know it is a beautiful song, but now I think that even more. Now I understand why you were talking about how writing is healing."

"Thanks. And thanks for listening. You're a good listener. Has anyone ever told you that?"

"I like asking the questions, but I do like listening to the answers. I love people. What can I say?"

"It comes across. You love music, too, don't you?"

Ashley watched Georgia looking out at the mountains, her brow furrowed. She was so cute. "It's everything. I don't know why, it just is."

"I feel the same way. I don't know what I'd do without it. Not just writing and then playing it like I did with 'Remember,' but listening to it, as well. It can capture things beyond words. I've always been fascinated with how that works, like how you can listen to a minor chord, and your whole body feels sad. You know what I mean?"

"I do. But let's not forget that you're so good with words."

Ashley lightly pushed her shoulder. As easy as it was to talk about more profound things with Georgia, the lightness was a relief. "You're such a flatterer."

"I mean it. Your lyrics are poetry."

"So are yours."

"I'm dying to see what we come up with, aren't you?" Georgia said, talking with her hands. "It's so nice to go from being scared to write to believing there's something we can do here."

"I can't wait to see what we come up with either."

They were both smiling, the sadness of a few minutes ago forgotten. Their closeness made Ashley's body tingle with excitement. She wasn't sure she ever wanted to finish this album, even though they hadn't even started.

She never wanted to leave this place.

CHAPTER TWENTY-ONE

They chatted about music in the garden for an hour, and then it was time to return to the house for their writing time. They worked separately because Georgia still wanted privacy while she got back on her feet. Ashley liked to picture her nearby, her beautiful hands on the piano keys, or writing in her notebook. Today, it was Georgia's turn to use the studio first. Ashley sat in the living room, working on lyrics. She had a file of ideas—phrases and words she saved in case she wanted to use them later—and she worked through it to determine if anything was worth expanding.

Hungry, she went to the studio and rapped on the door. "Is it time for lunch?"

Georgia tossed a salad with cherry tomatoes, black beans, quinoa, and corn, giving Ashley instructions for the dressing. After eating, they changed and headed outside. They sat in the bubbling hot tub, Georgia leaning her head back on the edge. The water had darkened her hair, and the skin of her throat was so white. The bubbles covered her swimsuit, and Ashley couldn't stop herself from trying to catch a glimpse of her cleavage under the water.

She looked away, thumbing through a book of poetry she'd found on the living room shelf. Turning a few pages, she put it far away on the ledge where it couldn't get wet and sighed. "I shouldn't read poetry. It's not good to envy other people's words when you're trying to write."

"I told you, you're a great poet. But I know exactly what you mean. Nobody ever picks up on it, but I used to get inspired by Romantic poets a lot. I'd try put these little nods into my silly pop songs, just for my own enjoyment, really."

"I'd noticed. I bet you like Coleridge, right?"

Georgia splashed water at her. "You're so clever. It makes me sick."

"Thanks. How did your writing time go this morning?"

A soft smile crossed Georgia's face. "It was better than yesterday's. Each day, it gets a little better, so that's something to be grateful for. Hey, you know what? I'm getting warm. Time to move back in the pool."

They stood up and dove back into the cool water. Ashley loved how they could do this all afternoon—go back and forth, lie around in between. All her usual restlessness and tension were gone, as if she'd shed weight she didn't even know she was carrying. For once, she didn't feel the need to do anything. She could just *be*.

Georgia swam a couple of laps and returned, standing by her side in the water.

"So, what you were saying before about the writing...It sounds like you're getting somewhere, right? Anything you'd be willing to share?" Ashley said.

"Not yet, but I'm *working*. I didn't think I would be able to say that, especially not this quickly. It makes me feel like myself again," Georgia said, lying on her back to stare at the sky.

Ashley stayed in place, treading water and eying Georgia's body as she floated. It should be illegal to look that good. Her emerald-green swimsuit was as modest as a swimsuit could be, but it wasn't easy to see her getting around in that thing. Ashley knew she'd go to bed tonight hopelessly frustrated, thoughts full of Georgia's curves and skin. It had been like that every night. She dove under the water, and Georgia stood facing her again when she came up for air.

"I have to thank you," Georgia said.

"What for?"

"You know what. For pushing me, just the right amount."

Ashley grinned and splashed her. "You're the one who's doing the work. All I did was nag you."

Georgia slapped her hand into the water, splashing her back. "You need to learn how to accept a thank-you graciously. I think the words you're looking for are you're welcome."

Ashley cupped her hands in the water and threw it at her. Her desire for Georgia made her want to crawl out of her skin. How long could they be this close without one of them making a move? Maybe that was why she acted the way she was—a little silly—but Georgia seemed to be in the same mood. They splashed and squealed like kids until Georgia launched forward, grabbed her by the shoulders, and dunked her under.

Ashley pushed to the surface, gasping for breath.

"Sorry. Did I take things too far?"

"I'm fine," Ashley said, knowing that her tone would make Georgia come closer.

"Are you okay?"

Ashley threw herself into Georgia when she was near enough, taking her revenge. She managed to get her under the water. They struggled, and somehow, they ended up with Ashley's legs wrapped around Georgia and Georgia's arms around her middle.

They slid against one another in the water. The laughter died as they stared into each other's eyes. Ashley was breathing hard, and in a glance, she took in the way Georgia's chest rose and fell just as quickly. Georgia smiled nervously, her mouth looking so soft and inviting.

With a tenderness that took Ashley's breath away, Georgia brushed the wet hair from Ashley's face. She could feel Georgia's breath on her lips and knew that this was the moment the tension would break. Georgia would kiss her under that clear blue sky, and she'd never wanted anything so much. All at once, she didn't care about their history, that they were supposed to be preparing to work together, or that Georgia's recent divorce might have made her vulnerable.

Ashley wanted what she wanted, and she was about to take it.

She put her hand on Georgia's face, staring at her full lips again.

The moment stretched long enough for her thoughts to circle. They were hesitating as though daring the other to make the first move. Ashley's doubts flooded back in. If they kissed right now, would she be taking advantage of the situation? Did Georgia feel sorry for her after what she'd confided about her brother? Would it be awkward afterward? They'd spent the last days trying to get themselves into the right frame of mind to work, and a kiss could blow it all up.

There was still time to reverse course and pretend she hadn't thought about Georgia that way. They were only being friendly the last few days. None of the hand-holding or arms around one another meant anything more significant.

Before she could make a mistake, she drew back. "Okay, you won that water fight. I'm no match for you. You're too tall."

Georgia's face showed what might have been disappointment—or relief—Ashley wished she knew which.

"Time to get back in the hot tub."

She was shaky as she sank back into the water. She wanted Georgia to join her, but instead, she swam lengths of the pool, then toweled off and lay on one of the lounges.

Ashley's heart still raced, and she tried to calm herself down. It should be easy to pretend nothing had happened. Nobody could blame her for thoughts she hadn't acted on. As casually as possible, she exited the hot tub and lay on the lounge beside Georgia's.

She needn't have worried. Georgia was as determined as she was to act like nothing was going on. They were both getting pretty good at it. "I've been having a lot of ideas about what I'd like to work on with Johnny."

"You are? That's exciting," Ashley responded.

"You're dying to know what it is, right?"

Ashley thought they were done flirting for now, but they weren't. Georgia's voice was sexy enough to send shivers down her spine. "It sounds like you're dying to tell me."

"Oh, no, we're not discussing any specifics about the work until he arrives. That was the rule."

Ashley sat up, squinting into the sun. "If you don't tell me, I'll throw you in the pool."

"Okay, okay. I'll tell you. But you're not allowed to laugh if you think it's stupid."

"When have I ever given you the idea that I'd laugh at you? C'mon, please. I want to hear it."

"Right, here it is. All anybody's going to be talking about is the rivalry. So, why don't we lean into the mythology?"

"How would we do that?"

"Why don't we make the album *about* us, in some way? Like a concept album where we tell a story? We're the main characters in the songs."

Ashley took a moment to consider it. Concept albums were a risk. They'd already be accused of being gimmicky, and she wanted the album to be taken seriously. She couldn't imagine how this would work but didn't want to dismiss it. "That's interesting. Tell me more."

"You don't like it," Georgia said matter-of-factly.

"Let me catch up. Tell me more about what you're thinking. Would it be satirical or straight down the line?"

"No, no," Georgia said, sitting up. They faced one another on the lounges, and Ashley admired how her eyes sparkled as she talked. Her excitement was infectious. "Definitely not satirical, but not straightforward, either. Each song tells a story, so we're exploring different emotions and ideas, and the audience is left wondering what's true and what isn't."

"That's kind of cool. That's very cool, actually."

"Do you want to work on it, maybe?"

"Definitely," Ashley said. What Georgia said was true—why turn away from the controversy? It was a part of them whether they liked it or not. They could do something interesting and unique with that.

"Good, because I'm really excited about the idea."

"Let's pitch it to Johnny."

Already, she wanted to run to the studio and make notes. She couldn't think of any other album like that, especially one created by two women. They could have a lot of fun threading the truth with lies. They could create a whole narrative to intrigue and confuse. Nobody needed to know which parts were genuine, and it could even be an opportunity for them to laugh at themselves a little. Ashley liked the idea of poking fun at her serious persona. Georgia made her more playful.

"Do we have a deal?" Georgia said, scooting closer to the edge of her chair and extending her hand.

"Sure. I'm interested in this idea."

Ashley shook Georgia's hand, wondering if what she hoped was true—that Georgia had started looking for any excuse to touch her. That's how *she* was beginning to feel. She wanted to wrap herself up in Georgia and never let go.

She hadn't planned to do it, but when Ashley stared down at Georgia's hand, she couldn't resist. Her skin was so soft, her fingers long and elegant. She raised Georgia's hand to her lips and kissed the back of it. She squeezed her hand and dropped it, then rested back on her lounge, her stomach fluttering.

She couldn't meet Georgia's eye after that, but she wasn't sorry she'd done it. Not even a little.

CHAPTER TWENTY-TWO

It was the middle of the night, and Georgia was wide awake. She'd slept heavily the last few nights, lulled by the quiet and warmth of her room, but tonight was different. She was hyper-aware of every creak and the sound of Willa pacing around the house. She could even hear Ashley tossing and turning in her room down the hall, though she knew that couldn't be possible.

Before leaving New York, she'd asked Ivy to get her a KSafe for her phone to help her respect Johnny's wishes. She'd locked her phone up most of the day, only taking it out to check her texts in the evening. She hadn't bothered to set it this morning because, with Ashley here to talk to, she'd barely been tempted to look at it. She opened the lid, retrieved her phone, and tiptoed down the hall.

When she got to the living room, Willa was already up and waiting for her. Georgia grabbed a folded blanket from the sofa and draped it around her shoulders, went to the back deck, and closed the sliding door behind them. The night stars and cool air instantly helped clear her mind. So quickly, this place had become a cocoon, sealing them off from the rest of the world. She desperately needed some outside perspective.

She walked deep into the yard, far away from the house so there was no chance of being overheard and texted Rachel. *Are you awake?*

The cell immediately rang, and Rachel spoke breathlessly. "Of course, I'm awake. You know a New Yorker couldn't be in bed this early. We've barely finished dinner."

Georgia laughed. "You're exaggerating. You're always saying you two are getting old."

"Okay, you're right. Eliza's in bed, but I was watching TV. Anyway, I'm dying to know how everything's going. It's wild that Johnny's not there. I couldn't believe it when I got that text."

"I know, it's crazy. But it's been kind of nice. It's meant I've had time to adjust to being here."

"What's it like out there?"

Georgia spun slowly, looking up at the sky. "It's magical. I've never seen a sky this clear. It gets cold at night, but it's lovely and warm during the day."

"And the house and grounds? Does the famous ranch live up to the legend?"

"Absolutely. There is so much history everywhere you look, great photos and stuff. We've been getting to look at Judy's art. There are lots of pieces you can't see anywhere else."

"Now we've got that out of the way, tell me everything. How are things with Ashley?"

Georgia looked up again as though searching the night sky for answers. "I'm not sure where to start. I think something almost happened between us today. It's not the first time."

"Wow. You girls work fast. What happened?"

"We keep having these little moments. The other night, I was showing her how to chop an onion, and I think we came close to kissing."

"Huh? How did chopping an onion get all sexy?"

Georgia laughed. "I don't know. And we were messing around in the pool this afternoon, and I think she was about to kiss me again. That's what it felt like, anyway."

"So why didn't it happen either time?"

"I don't know. I pulled away, she pulled away. But then, she kissed my hand."

There was a long silence before she answered. "What do you mean she kissed your hand?"

"We were talking and shook hands, but then she literally kissed my hand."

Rachel squealed. "She kissed you. Even if it was only on the hand, that's so intimate."

"I know. But then, she just broke off and lay down like nothing was happening."

"It sounds like she was testing the waters. She wanted to see what you'd do and was trying to find out if you'd reject her. You should've gone for it. That's what she wanted you to do."

Georgia lay down on the deck chair, thinking it happened here—she'd been lying on this chair when Ashley kissed her hand. She rubbed her feet together, her skin tingling. "I guess I got scared. I keep thinking that I don't know exactly what this is. She seems curious about me, and I'm definitely curious about her, but what if we mess everything up?"

"That's a risk any time you start anything new."

"Don't be obtuse. You know what I mean. If anything happened between us, we'd start out with the whole world's eyes on us."

"Again, that's not new to you, sweetie. People already watch everything you do. So, why not enjoy yourself? You're just two people. Whatever happens between you is about *you*."

Georgia sighed. She wanted to believe that. "You know what's still exactly the same, even if I weren't famous?"

"What's that?"

"I'd still be a divorcée in my early thirties who has no idea about love."

There was a pause before Rachel's voice came down the line again. "That's a cruel way to look at yourself. Don't say that."

"It's true. That's me."

"Subtract all of that. If you could get out of your head and leave that all aside, what would you do right now?"

She bit her lip. They were best friends who shared a lot, but she still didn't want to say some things to Rachel. If she could do anything she wanted, she'd go to Ashley's room. She'd go right to her bed, get on top of her, and kiss her senseless. She'd touch that perfect body and take Ashley's hands to put them in the places Ashley couldn't stop staring at. The thoughts set Georgia's body alight.

"I'd go for it."

"I truly think you should. It all sounds very romantic. You should at least talk to her. Tell her how you feel. Do you trust her enough to do that?"

Georgia pictured Ashley's kind eyes. How could she not trust her even with everything that had passed between them? How could she not be drawn to someone so supportive and encouraging toward her, especially since they'd arrived? Ashley believed in her when she needed it most. She made her feel special. "I hope I'm not being naïve, but yes. I trust her."

"Then, what will you tell me during our next call?"

Georgia took a deep breath. "That I got up the courage to say something. And see if she wants to kiss me for real."

"That's a little more PG-13 than I would've said, but well done."

"I'll do it tomorrow. Johnny and Judy should be back on the weekend, so it's probably my only chance for a while. Besides, I don't think I can go on much longer like this."

After they signed off, Georgia managed to get a few hours of sleep. Rachel was only being pushy with her because she knew that Georgia truly wanted this. It would be incredibly awkward if Ashley rejected her. Still, she was full of hope. There'd been something between them since that first day at The Chop. The way Ashley looked at her meant something—she knew it like she knew her own heart. No matter what happened, they had to talk about it and clear the air. Such a quick, intense intimacy had sprung up between them over the last few days. It was easy to imagine them working this out together.

When she woke, she pressed a hand to her stomach, feeling scared but excited. After breakfast, she'd suggest they take Willa for a walk through the gardens, and she'd force herself to be brave.

Since the split with Hayley, she'd been jaded about love. It was funny to think that only a short time ago, she'd felt so broken she couldn't imagine feeling this way about anyone again. She thought about Dr. Lewin, who'd worked hard to get her to a place where she thought being alone was best for her. She'd truly believed that for a while. She'd never imagined meeting someone like Ashley, whom she could not resist. Didn't want to. It meant that the rules simply did not apply.

Georgia rose, stretched, and threw on some clothes. Feeling optimistic that she might finally kiss Ashley, she brushed her teeth. She went to the kitchen, knowing Ashley would be making their coffee by now.

The person standing there had her back to Georgia, and the first thing she noticed was that she was taller than Ashley. Her gray hair hung loose, and she wore a patterned prairie skirt with a white top.

Georgia's heart sank. "Judy. Good morning."

Judy turned around, water glass in hand. "Good morning, sweetheart. Hope we didn't wake you up last night. Or, perhaps I should say this morning. It was after midnight when we got in."

"No, not at all. We thought you'd be home tomorrow or Sunday."

It was their house, so why did she feel intruded upon? She wasn't ready to let go of their bubble yet. She thought she'd have more time to prepare.

"Johnny got itchy feet. We crept in, but I still thought you might've heard Willa. She was so excited to see us. His sister's doing okay, thankfully. I'll look in on her in another week or two."

"That's great news. I'm glad to hear that," Georgia said, trying to catch up. Would she have the opportunity to talk to Ashley alone? Now that Johnny was here, should she stick to her plan and lay it all on the table? It changed everything.

"We're happy to be home. I've been wondering how you two girls were getting on."

"We've been good, enjoying ourselves. Thank you for opening your lovely home to us. Is Johnny still in bed?"

"No, he's already started on breakfast," Judy said, pointing to a warmer with a lid on top. "He can't wait to meet you in person, so he was up just after dawn. He made tamales, then took Willa out for a walk. He asked if I'd finish things up and serve out on the patio. We thought having our first breakfast together outdoors would be nice. What do you think?"

"That does sound lovely. Is there anything I can do?"

"Thanks, but it's all under control. You put your feet up and relax. Oh, hi, dear."

Georgia turned to see Ashley, still in her pajamas. She looked just as surprised as she was to find Judy in the kitchen. She stepped forward. "Good morning. Wow, you guys are home. That's wonderful."

"We couldn't be happier. I hope you're hungry. Breakfast is almost ready. I was just telling Georgia that Johnny's out walking the dog. He'll be back soon."

"Wonderful," Ashley repeated.

She walked over to the bench to pour coffee, silently holding up a cup, and Georgia nodded. Judy was at the sink rinsing something with her back turned, and Ashley brought her coffee over. She looked into Georgia's eyes gravely as she handed it to her. Perhaps they were having the same thought.

They'd been waiting for this moment all week, but neither wanted it to arrive. They weren't ready.

CHAPTER TWENTY-THREE

Georgia went to her room and sat on her bed, her head in her hands. Her anxiety about meeting Johnny the night they arrived was back in full force. So much had changed in a few short days. She'd regained some confidence, and learned how much she cared about Ashley. The stakes had always felt high, but they were even more so now. If this didn't work out, or if she didn't impress Johnny—she didn't want to think what might happen.

After she'd changed, she took a deep breath and brushed her hair in front of the mirror. Dr. Lewin had been teaching her about positive self-talk. She usually felt stupid about doing it aloud but was willing to do anything to stop the room spinning. "Okay. I'm strong and in control. I'm confident. I am enough. I will go out there and try to be in the moment. Just talk to him. I'll take this one little baby step at a time."

As she left her bedroom, she ran into Ashley in the hall. She'd changed from her pajamas and dressed in a collared shirt and black pants. She'd neatly tied back her hair and wore dangling silver earrings. Georgia grabbed her arm. "Oh, good, you're here. It'd be like walking into a really scary party by yourself."

"Are you that nervous?"

"Aren't you?"

"C'mon, it's just breakfast. I'll be there with you," Ashley said, taking her hand and smiling at her warmly. It was like magic, making her feel calmer.

Ashley dropped her hand just before they reached the sliding door that led out onto the deck, and Georgia felt a little dizzy as she opened it for them. Johnny stood with his hand on his heart, wearing a black button-up tucked into black jeans. His tan belt had a large silver buckle. He removed his cowboy hat and laid it on the table. He was smaller than she'd imagined and older than she'd realized, his skin tanned and heavily lined. His smile was gracious and hopeful, like this moment was as important to him as it was to them.

Ashley was closer, so he shook her hand first. Then, he took Georgia's, putting his other hand over it. His palms were rough, like someone who worked a lot with them. "I can't tell you how happy I am to meet you both. Thank you for being here."

"It's wonderful to meet you," Georgia said, finally finding her voice.

"Please, sit. I'm sorry about the start we got off to. I felt terrible about having to take off like that, but you know how it is with family."

"Of course. Judy said your sister's doing all right? Sorry about her troubles," Ashley said, while Georgia nodded along.

"Thanks. I'll tell you, it's not fun getting old and watching everyone around you do the same. We all start to fall apart. Part of why it will be wonderful having some young people around the ranch for a while."

He gestured to the food platters on the table, which held chicken tamales, cut grapefruit, yogurt, scrambled eggs, and tortillas. "Please, help yourselves."

They filled their plates while Judy walked around the table, her multiple bracelets clinking. She poured water from a silver jug. "This is all so wonderful. Johnny hasn't had anyone out here to stay for a long time. I've missed it, having other creative people around."

"It's an absolute honor," Ashley said.

As they ate, Johnny asked them questions in his soft, easygoing way. What did they think of the ranch? Had they an opportunity to walk through the sculpture garden? Which of the horses was their favorite? Had Willa behaved for them? When he asked the next question, his eyes twinkled. "What do you think of the recording studio?"

"It's gorgeous," Ashley said. "That vintage Fender guitar is a dream. That's the main thing I've been playing. Would you mind if I played it as lead on the album?"

He put a hand on his heart again. "That's one of my favorites, too. I'd love for you to play it. And you, Georgia? What's your favorite instrument? Have you found anything you particularly enjoy?"

There was no contest. She thought of those velvety tones and how they made every note sound better. "The piano."

"Ah, the Steinway. Ain't she a beauty? I've had her since the 1980s. She's been played by many hands over the years. I love that you love her."

"I'm very grateful to have the chance to play it."

Johnny pushed back from the table, sipping his coffee with a leg crossed over his knee. "Ashley, Georgia, I have a problem. See, I want us to take our time. I don't want to come here bombarding you with questions, especially over this nice breakfast, but I'm finding it difficult."

They made eye contact, and Ashley spoke first. "It's okay. If you have things you want to ask, I'm sure we're both happy to try and answer them."

Judy stood with her plate and patted Johnny's knee. "The man's beside himself. I haven't seen him this excited in a good long while."

"Let us help you clean up," Georgia said, eager to be the perfect guest.

"Thanks, but it'll only take me a moment, and you all should talk. You've waited long enough," Judy said firmly, stacking plates.

"What did you want to ask us?" Ashley said when she was gone. If Georgia hadn't started to get to know her so well, she might not have noticed the tremble in her voice.

Georgia jumped in, her own anxiety forgotten. "We want you to know that any petty stuff between us has been put to the side. You won't see any of that now that we're here."

Johnny nodded. "Thank you for putting that out there. I have to say, though, I wasn't particularly worried about it."

"Oh. Good."

He waved a hand. "I know how it all goes. I didn't ask you to pair up because of any of that. I figured the rivalry was overblown if you agreed to come here together. People thought the same about me and Peter Coleman, but it was exaggerated. Besides, even people who don't get along that well can still create great music. Look at Fleetwood Mac or The Beatles."

He chuckled, and Georgia glanced at Ashley, raising her eyebrows. She knew he wasn't comparing them, but hearing him say the names of those bands was surreal when he'd met some of them. They'd seen the photos.

"Okay, that's good to hear," Georgia said. "We can put all that behind us."

"Indeed. What I wanted to ask was how things have been going here? I wondered whether anything had risen to the surface—if you developed a process when I was away."

Ashley shook her head. "We didn't want to do too much until you arrived. We've both been spending a little time in the mornings writing and then the afternoons relaxing. But we were only writing to get warmed up, not to have things to show you. I hope that was okay."

"Of course, it's okay. I'm not the boss. I'm your collaborator. Tell me more about it, please."

"I've been finding it useful to do it the way we have. I've been writing silly little things—disposable, to get the juices flowing. To be honest, I'd been having a little trouble with my writing," Georgia said.

"Happens to the best of us," he said, smiling at her.

Why had she been so worried about this? Johnny was easier to talk to than she'd imagined. Anyone who'd lived a creative life understood that it didn't always come easily. From the outside, you could listen to albums or watch movies and not know how much blood and sweat went into them. All creation was work, and she'd forgotten that she only needed to work harder.

"Where do we go from here?" Georgia asked. She was so ready for this, and it was strange to think she'd been doubting it only an hour ago. She'd been too focused on her relationship with Ashley, whatever it was. Seeing Johnny made her realize how much she had to get her head in the game.

Johnny held out his hands like it was simple. "If that's working for you, then we keep going with it. Mornings will be time to play around with the music for a little while. Afternoons, we do whatever we want. How have you been working, together or separately?"

"Separately, for now," Ashley replied.

"There are no rules here. When you're ready, we can all start getting into a room together. I think the best thing for everyone is to keep living. I never wanted us to just hole up here and grind it out. Let's take our time if neither of you is rushing to leave."

"I'm certainly not in a rush. I love it here." Georgia smiled.

"I have to leave in a few weeks for The Vanguards. It's the one commitment I couldn't get out of, but I only need to go for a few days. Then I'll come back."

"Fantastic. Judy and I have a lot of friends around here who are discreet. People think I don't head out much, but I just keep things low-key with folks I know. If we need to get off the ranch and find inspiration, we can do that. What do you think?"

"That sounds great. We went out to the gorge bridge the other day. It was spectacular."

"I'm glad to hear it."

Georgia hesitated, wondering if she was ready to share her news. What if it wasn't good? Maybe she should take more time to polish the song—or even shelve it for now. She felt a hand on hers under the table and smiled. Ashley knew she wanted to say something and was encouraging her.

The day after she'd written that first silly song, she woke up in the morning and started humming before she got out of bed. It was still in her head when she got in the shower, and the tune felt so ready-made she assumed it was someone else's song. Only when she sat at the piano and tinkered with it, did she grow sure it was coming from inside her. She was so excited she almost leaped up from the piano stool, but instead, she patiently worked until she had something that matched the sound in her head.

She played it every time she could be alone at the piano. It was different than anything she'd written before—joyful but subtle. It was so catchy, but she had no idea what it was about. When Ashley asked how things were going, she downplayed her discovery, not ready to expose herself.

Ashley squeezed her hand again, and it gave her courage. "I'd like this morning to work on it some more, but I think I have something I'd like to play for you both. This afternoon or tomorrow morning."

Georgia thought she might melt when Ashley grazed her knee with her fingers and gently touched her thigh. She could truly understand how much this meant. "I can't wait to hear it, but only when you're ready."

Johnny rubbed his hands together. "Well. What a great start this is."

When Ashley took her hand away, Georgia felt the loss acutely. These moments felt like much more than an excellent start to their music—like they could be the start of something far more significant.

CHAPTER TWENTY-FOUR

Georgia sat at the piano the following day, wondering if she was about to make a fool of herself. She felt compelled to play it for Ashley and Johnny, but she'd never been this nervous about performing a new song. It was unlike any of her previous work. Once, she'd known something was good without needing anyone to tell her, but her recent self-doubt was confusing. It would be easier if she could play it to a lower-stakes audience like Rachel first.

She tried to summon some courage.

The best thing about sitting at the piano was that Johnny and Ashley were behind her, so she didn't have to see their faces. She looked back over her shoulder. They sat in the nearby armchairs, armed with coffee, Ashley leaning in toward her. Her hair was pulled back, showing off her beautiful jawline and sculpted cheekbones. Her white-blond hair stood out against her dark clothes.

"It's just a kernel of an idea. Maybe you can do something with it," Georgia said, running her fingers over the keys. At least this piano would make the song sound better than it was.

Ashley smiled, her eyes so compassionate. As much as she admired Johnny, Georgia wished they were alone, although maybe that would be even scarier. "It's okay if it's not perfect or amazing. Let's see what happens."

Johnny nodded, gesturing toward the piano. "Go ahead, please. This is only the beginning. First step."

Georgia took a deep breath, heart bolting. Her nerves began to lift when she put her hands in position and played. It was one of those songs that felt right. She'd never learned music theory—when something worked, she didn't know why. All she had was her ear and an instinct for sounds that fit together well. With this song, the chords were unexpected, so there was a kind of a rub, something one's ear caught onto.

When she'd finished, she paused with her fingers still on the keys. She wanted to live in this moment a little longer while the song remained untouched. If they didn't like it, she didn't know it yet. No sound came from behind her, not the clapping she hoped for. When she finally turned, what she saw was better. They stared at her, stunned, but she immediately knew it was a good surprise.

Johnny came over and put his hand on her shoulder. "Thank you. That was beautiful."

He stood back, and Ashley moved to sit at her side. When she looked into Georgia's eyes, it made her stomach flip. "Will you play it for me again?"

"I'll excuse myself," Johnny said, bowing. "I think this time should just be for you two."

"You don't have to do that. We can start talking about ideas," Georgia replied.

"We'll get to that, but like I said in my letters, my job here is to get out of the way. This song's like a new baby—perfect and fragile. You two should talk and figure out how you'll help it grow."

After he'd left, Ashley nodded toward the piano. "Can you please play that opening again?"

Georgia did it, her face hot, Ashley's thigh pressing into hers. They couldn't be any closer, and she was grateful Ashley had joined her on the stool without bothering to pull up a chair. Her fingers found every note with joy because of how much she'd missed this feeling. The sound struck something deep inside her, and she knew Ashley could feel it, too.

Ashley stopped her, gently holding her wrist.

"That's so interesting. You expect the next bar to be this," Ashley said, demonstrating. "But when you do *that*, it's so much more satisfying. How did you think of that?"

"I don't know. That's the part I found myself humming the other day. It took me a while to find it on here. I'm so glad you like it."

"What do you mean? Find it on here?"

Since they'd begun talking about this project, she'd known there were many things about herself she wouldn't be able to mask. She hoped their different approaches to writing wouldn't be a problem.

"I taught myself to play, and I only go by what sounds good in my head. I hear the music inside," she said, tapping her forehead. "Then I test notes against what I can hear. I don't know what they're called, which key it is, or anything."

"Really? So, none of those changes were planned because you knew they broke the rules? It was instinctive?"

"That's right," she said, laughing nervously.

"Don't be embarrassed. Do you have any idea how much I envy you? Mom started sending me to piano lessons when I was seven. I have all the technical skills in the world, but sometimes that doesn't feel like enough."

"I wish I had those skills. I've tried learning to read music as an adult, but it felt like another language. I just couldn't do it."

"You don't have to worry about it. I love this song. Do you have a melody?" she said, tinkering around with the keys. Ashley smelled so good that Georgia wanted to bury her face in her hair. She loved this—sitting closely together, messing around with her song. She'd been so worried about Johnny and Judy returning, but now it felt like everything would be okay. They'd still have these moments.

"Not yet. I'm not exactly sure what it's about. I just knew the mood I wanted."

"And what mood is that? I know how it makes me feel, but I want to hear your perspective."

Georgia played as she spoke, going through the shades of feeling. "Hopefully, it's exactly what you're imagining. I was thinking about us being out here, away from our lives. It's nervous and excited. Like you're saying, it's the unexpected fitting together better than you think it would or could."

Georgia watched her profile, loving how Ashley was absorbed in something she'd made. It was a way of connecting them, passing thoughts back and forth, a substitution for what she truly wanted. Touch.

"You know exactly what it's about, then."

"Well, yeah, I guess. But there aren't any lyrics."

"Play the opening again?"

She could feel Ashley watching her hands as they moved over the keys. Ashley asked her to play the song repeatedly. After a while, she hummed, adding the beginning of a melody over the chorus. Georgia liked it so much she squealed. "That's it!"

Ashley jokingly put a hand over her mouth. "Calm down. It's just a thought."

Georgia tugged her hand away. "I can't help it. I'm a screamer."

She hadn't meant it to sound dirty, but they both knew it did. Neither of them seemed to be able to help themselves when it came to innuendo. Ashley looked away from her and down at the keys, playing a few notes and smirking. "Really. So, you don't have any lyrics for this song? Or any ideas?"

"Not yet, no. Would you like to write some?"

"Why don't we try and write them together?"

"I'd like that."

Ashley paused, taking her hands from the keys and meeting her eye. "We haven't told Johnny about the plan for the album. We should pitch the idea to him, don't you think?"

Georgia squirmed on the piano stool. It had taken all her courage to play him this song, and telling him about the idea was even more nerve-racking. She was taking the lead in this project more than she'd ever imagined she would—how strange to do that at a time when her confidence was at its lowest.

"You really think it's a good idea? You weren't just humoring me?" Georgia asked.

"Are you joking? Now that you've suggested it, I can't imagine us doing anything else."

Georgia grinned and played the opening notes of their new song again, with more power this time, humming Ashley's melody. "Is that it?"

Ashley leaned into her, nudging with her shoulder. "See, you're so talented. I only just came up with that, and you've already memorized it."

"That should tell you how catchy it is."

"I see this as the opening track. It sets the scene for everything that comes afterward."

"And what is it about? Being out here at the ranch? Maybe even our first meeting?" Georgia asked, remembering that day at The Chop. She'd never forget what it was like to see Ashley's face in person for the first time. It stirred such complicated emotions. What she'd felt before that day was almost hatred, but everything changed as soon as Ashley's beauty—inside and out—was before her.

"Yes. A fictionalized version, of course."

"Of course."

Ashley played the phrases leading up to a key change and paused. "This is where we each realize that the other person is not what we thought they were."

Georgia closed her eyes, the song unfolding in her mind like it always had in outline. It was like a painting with out-of-focus colors. No words came to her at all, only feelings.

Ashley stood and paced, putting her hands on her head. "This song is like a door or a gateway. Do you know how, in dream symbolism, doors are like the gateway to a change or a transformation? The opening track is us meeting and passing through into something different."

"Transformation. I like that," Georgia said, loving seeing how swept away Ashley was. She loved the idea, too, because wasn't that what Ashley had been doing for her since they met? Transforming her concept of herself as an artist, altering her expectations of what she could be.

Ashley sat beside her again, playing the opening notes and trying a lyric. She sang it again, and a line that rhymed popped into Georgia's head. Without thinking about it, she sang it.

Ashley clapped. "Yes, that's perfect."

Georgia paused to grab her notebook, and they were on their way. They traded lines back and forth, finishing one another's sentences. The song's structure remained unchanged, but they tweaked the lyrics to fit better. Later, Georgia knew she'd have trouble remembering who wrote what because they were so in sync. Sometimes, Ashley would say a word or a phrase the moment after Georgia thought of it, but before she could say it aloud. It came so easily, and they were so absorbed in their task that when she looked at her watch, she was shocked to discover a couple of hours had passed.

They'd filled out the lyrics for the whole song, including a killer bridge. Georgia read over her notes and crossed out a line, replacing it with one she thought was better. She paused with her pen over the page. "Sorry, is that okay? I think this captures what we mean more fully."

Ashley read it over and smiled. "No, that's better. I see."

They sat quietly, reading over the words together. Georgia took the notebook and placed it on the piano's music shelf. "Should we give it a run-through?"

"Go ahead. You sing the first verse, and I'll do the second?"

"Yep. And let's join in together on the chorus."

They stopped and laughed when Georgia made a mistake, but it went smoothly when she played it again. It felt so good, and she noticed they were both throwing everything at it vocally, playing off one another like they'd done this a thousand times. Their voices sounded good together. Great, even.

When they finished, they sat quietly for a moment, stunned. How had that been so easy? She'd never felt this way when collaborating.

"This is it. It's done," Ashley said, grabbing her shoulder excitedly.

"Are you sure? Let's let it marinate a little. It's a good start, but sometimes you can't trust the first version. We should give it some distance and see what we think after a day or two."

Ashley shook her head. "C'mon. You know how good that was. Don't you?"

Georgia laughed, tears standing in her eyes. God, this was wonderful. "You're right. Let's get Johnny so we can play it for him."

CHAPTER TWENTY-FIVE

Ashley was confident their first time together at the piano was a fluke. They'd struck gold immediately—she'd been working at this long enough to know how unusual that was. She'd rarely cowritten, but she'd spoken with many people who had. Lightning didn't strike twice. They were sure to hit bumps in the road, have disagreements, and have long days when they spun their wheels and got nowhere.

After the next two weeks in which each day was as fruitful and rewarding as the last, she admitted to herself that she'd been wrong. The first day was the norm, not the exception. She'd never experienced anything like it and wondered if she would again. She was used to holding her work close to her chest, protecting it while the record company tried to change it. She'd never imagined that she'd be so good at sharing the process with someone else. The ideas just kept coming.

Today before getting out of bed, she began furiously scribbling in her notebook. She'd been in the studio with Georgia since breakfast, figuring out the chorus of her new song. It had a chunky riff that came to her from nowhere, and Georgia loved it, asking her to play it over and over. The song was unfinished, but they were sure they had something special.

They played the opening for Johnny, who sat in his armchair and listened quietly with his eyes closed and his hand on his heart. When they were finished, his eyes snapped open. "Wonderful. So wonderful. What you were working on yesterday would flow nicely into this. That one's an epic, but this one could be strong and sharp."

"That's exactly what I thought," Ashley replied.

"Great. Can you play the long one for me again? I've been thinking about it quite a lot."

Georgia moved to the piano, and Ashley picked up the guitar. They both loved country story songs, which inspired their approach to this song. They ran through the winding narrative, shooting one another a smile now and then.

When they were done, Ashley put the guitar back on its stand. "We think it could use another verse or even two. It'd make for a long track, but it works."

"The first three verses are Ashley's, so I'd have four, five, and six. We might alternate—we're not sure yet."

"But we're writing each other's verses to play with what we imagine the other person is thinking. We thought that'd be cool," Ashley said.

Johnny laughed. "Each of you writing as the other person? That's an interesting concept."

"We're having a lot of fun with it," Georgia said.

Ashley was surprised at how much Georgia enjoyed making fun of herself—she could be cutting in a funny way. It took Ashley a while to get into the spirit, but she liked writing her verses once she did. "So, is there anything you'd change with this one? Anything you think we should add?"

Johnny waved a hand in the air. "Like everything you're doing, this is coming along beautifully. As for adding things, I can hear strings. Nothing too dramatic or overpowering. What do you think?"

They looked at one another. The synergy was incredible—they'd talked about that earlier this morning. Georgia nodded. "That sounds wonderful."

He put his fingers on his temples. "Gosh, I can hear it. I'll get working on the arrangements this afternoon. I knew a few guys we can bring in to play."

Ashley was grateful that they were far away from Splash's meddling. Using strings was a departure for both of them, and she could imagine the agonizing meetings it would lead to if they were in New York. They'd have stupid discussions about marketability and have to fight, putting forward different cuts. The guys at Splash only trusted them enough to go off on their own because of Johnny, but at least they were free.

Johnny clapped his hands together once. "This is an amazing thing to witness. Thanks for letting me be a part of it."

"Thank you for creating an environment where we can do it," Ashley replied.

"Taking a break is also important when you're working so much. You're headed to LA next week, aren't you, Ashley?"

She nodded, heart sinking at the thought of interrupting their work. She'd been thinking again about blowing off The Vanguards, but her work ethic extended to industry events. She'd made a commitment, and she wanted to follow through. If she weren't up for such a big award, she'd have called her team and told them to cancel weeks ago. "Unfortunately. I'll be back as soon as I can."

"That's not really a break, is it? We should do something before then. Do you both like steak?"

Georgia nodded. "I love it. A steak dinner sounds wonderful. How can I help?"

"No, no. We'll go out. As much as I love my place, I never wanted you two to be cooped up here. Let's shake out the cobwebs. There's a steak house in town with a private room. The owner is a great friend of mine. I'll call them and give them a heads-up we're coming, and they'll sneak us in. What do you say?"

"Sounds great to me."

"Perfect. We'll go this evening if they can accommodate us."

Ashley took extra time over her outfit, though she didn't have much in her suitcase from which to choose. Caring about what she wore was foreign—she'd always hated accumulating junk, a feeling that extended to clothing. Most of the clothes she had for events were borrowed. Luckily, she'd packed her one good Armani suit. It had a double-breasted blazer, and it was in a checked pattern. She wore the preppy number semi-ironically, but it was the best thing she had. She'd worn the pants the first time she met Georgia and noticed how she stared at them.

When she walked into the living room, three heads turned to look at her, and she was pleased she wasn't the only person who'd dressed up. Judy wore an elegant white dress, Johnny wore neatly pressed trousers, and Georgia was dressed in a green dress that made her eyes glitter. The neckline wasn't low but showed just the right amount of cleavage. She looked spectacular.

"Look at us, all gussied up." Johnny smiled.

"You both look beautiful," Judy said. "You're going to love this place. They do some of the best food in the region, and that's saying something because Taos is a foodie's paradise."

In the back seat, Ashley stared across at Georgia, illuminated by lights as they passed other cars. She looked like a 1940s movie star, her hair falling in waves. Judy and Johnny talked quietly in the front seat, but back here, they weren't saying a word. Ashley wished she could touch Georgia's hair. They'd been working so hard, but this undercurrent of desire was always with her. It grew even stronger when it was quiet like this, with no distractions.

"What is it?" Georgia said softly.

"I like how you've done your hair. It's really pretty."

"Thanks. I like your suit," she replied, reaching over and smoothing her hand over a lapel high enough to be perfectly appropriate. It still made her weak-kneed.

Judy drove them to the restaurant's back entrance and parked. Johnny got out of the car first and checked to see if anybody was around. He ushered them out and put his arms around them, guiding them toward the door. A tall, gray-haired man with a long beard waited, holding the door open. He closed it behind them, and they quickly followed him upstairs into a separate dining room. It had a large table in the middle with rustic, handmade-looking chairs and a white tablecloth. The lights were dim, and candles in holders flickered on the table.

The bearded man smiled at them, and everyone relaxed now that they were inside. Ashley always felt ridiculous when she had to hide. All this fuss over ordinary people like them doing nothing more exciting than having dinner. If she thought about it too much, it drove her crazy.

"I think I got you in here without being seen."

"Thanks," Ashley said, shaking his hand.

"Pleased to meet you both. I'm Eugene."

"Thanks for getting us in here. I'm looking forward to a good steak dinner. Johnny and Judy speak highly of your food," Georgia said.

He spread his arms wide. "You've come to the right place. You're about to eat one of the best meals you ever had."

Forty-five minutes later, Ashley was beginning to think he wasn't exaggerating. After an appetizer of grilled lobster tail served over chorizo, Eugene placed her entrée before her. It was a ribeye steak with a creamy mushroom sauce and fluffy mashed potatoes, and it was heaven.

"Wow," she said, turning to Georgia. They'd both ordered their steaks medium rare, and Georgia looked like she loved it just as much as she did. The meat was tender, the flavors hitting the pleasure center in Ashley's brain like a drug.

"This is one of the best steaks I've ever had," Georgia said, leaning closer. Ashley nudged her with a shoulder, loving their shared private moments.

Eugene joined them at their table, slapping Johnny on the back and complimenting Judy on how well she looked. Another staff member—a young woman with short curly hair—walked around the table to refill their wineglasses.

"How's the food? Is everything okay here?" she asked, standing across from them. It was hard to miss how she eyeballed them, still trying to act unconcerned about having all these big celebrities in one room. She must have been briefed about Georgia and Ashley being here together, but it still looked like she couldn't believe her eyes.

"Perfect. We were talking about how incredible the food is," Georgia said, smiling sweetly at her. "Thank you so much. The service has been wonderful, too."

When she was gone, Ashley raised her eyebrows.

Georgia shook her head, laughing. "Did I lay it on too thick? I'm always extra friendly to strangers like that. I don't want to give them a reason to call me a bitch as soon as they leave the room."

"I don't know how anyone could think that of you. You're so nice."

Georgia threw her head back and laughed. "*Nice.* Oh, how quickly you've forgotten. You thought I was a bitch. Admit it."

"You thought I was a bitch, too."

"Guilty as charged. Anyway, this is fun. More than fun. I'll remember this time as the best of my life."

"I know what you mean. Even the food tastes better. Everything about our time out here has been magical."

Was she being too intense? Georgia stared at her for a long beat. Maybe it was something about how she'd said "our" like they were *we*—a couple. Georgia took a sip of her wine. "Making music, relaxing, and spending time with great people. It's beautiful. For the first time in such a long time, I feel like I'm fulfilling my purpose. I feel like an artist again. I wish it could be like this more."

"It could be," Ashley blurted out.

She must be drunk. What was she saying—that they could stay here forever? It was a dream, an unrealistic one. Still, after their time together, returning to New York and going on as she had been was the loneliest thing she could imagine. Given how independent she was, it took a lot to admit that she dreaded not seeing Georgia daily. They weren't even in a relationship, yet she couldn't bear the thought of being apart. Every night, she lay in bed and hated the distance between them. Down the hall was like another country.

It was insane to think like this.

Georgia's green eyes were locked on hers, the room falling away. In the background, she heard the others laughing and talking, but she only wanted to look at Georgia. To have this moment and never let it go.

"You're right. It's beautiful. That's all I mean. I don't know," Ashley said.

Ashley broke eye contact, her nerve failing her. Sometimes, she wondered if being away from home and her friends had robbed her of all perspective. Aaron told her to go with her feelings for Georgia, but surely, if he knew how much she was losing herself, he'd tell her to pump the brakes. They were having a wonderful time out here. Still, it wasn't real life.

"No, what did you mean it could be?" Georgia asked, leaning closer to her again, enveloping her in those beautiful scents.

"Nothing. I meant that life could stay like this, even when we're back in New York—at least a little. We could play our music for one another and give each other notes. Things like that."

She wanted Georgia to protest, to say they would do so much more than that. This blissful time at the ranch wouldn't end—it was all beginning.

Instead, Georgia returned to her meal, taking the last mouthful of steak. "Sure. That'd be great. Excuse me, Eugene? This is incredible. I can't wait to see the dessert menu."

"Me neither," Ashley said, forcing a smile. She was being such a fool.

CHAPTER TWENTY-SIX

The following day, Ashley woke with so many ideas racing through her mind. She was eager to catch one and put it on paper. Like all nights since their arrival at Celio Ranch, it was full of dreams of red-haired beauty and curves so luscious she wanted to taste them. She'd felt like this only a few times—a creative force so powerful, so crush-driven, it made her want to crawl out of her skin.

She had breakfast with everyone on the deck, her mind only half on her meal. They talked about the weather and Willa and how good their meal had been the night before. Afterward, Ashley stood and collected empty plates. "Thanks, guys. That was delicious, as always. I feel inspired today, so I'll head to the studio right away."

"Wonderful," Johnny said, putting his hands on the table with his palms resting up. By now, Ashley knew he believed writing music was mystical. That inspiration came from the sky. That if you were open enough, you could put your hand into that force and pull it toward you, gather its threads, and let it carry you along. She didn't know if she believed that, but whatever the muse was, it was with her today.

"Would you like company? I feel like working too, but I won't be offended if you'd like some time alone."

Georgia was in her pink dress, and Ashley felt the hot flash of her dreams returning as she looked at her. She couldn't imagine wanting to be alone while Georgia was within reach, and she shook her head. "Not at all. I've got an idea that could go along with that new piece we explored yesterday."

"Yay!"

In the studio, Ashley picked up the Fender guitar she loved. It was a relief to have something to do with her hands. She strummed the chords they'd worked out yesterday. "I was thinking about this one when I woke up. It could be a really simple thing about running away. Living in a little bubble somewhere where nothing can touch you."

Georgia put a finger under her chin. "Hmm. What could have possibly inspired such an idea?"

"Ha. I guess it just came to me from thin air. Johnny's magic."

Ashley played, letting images and thoughts float through her mind. Georgia felt her way along at the piano, trying different phrases to complement her chords. She stopped playing for a moment. "Hey, do you think we'll ever tour this record?"

"Weird that I hadn't really thought about that. Would you want to?"

"Of course. It'd be fun, don't you think?"

"I do think. Absolutely."

"It'd be a huge tour. We could put on an amazing show."

The album probably wouldn't come out for a year, and Ashley wondered what kind of relationship she'd have with Georgia by then. She could picture them sharing hotel suites and airplanes, joking and talking, or sharing satisfying silences. Touring always made her feel lonely, even when she was close to her band. She'd toured with the same musicians for years, but still, there was a sense of disconnection when you were on the road. Somehow, she was sure she could never be lonely with Georgia, even if they were only friends.

Georgia searched her face. "What are you thinking? You look all wistful."

"Nothing. This is my work face."

"Then tell me what you're working on in that mind of yours."

"Maybe we could work in that line you said the first morning we were here. It could fit well in a song like this."

Georgia frowned, looking so cute that Ashley wanted to go over and touch her face to smooth her brow. "I can't remember what I said a few weeks ago, I'm afraid. Remind me?"

"Something about not growing tired of beauty. I think with this song, I could, I mean Ashley the character…" She trailed off. Sometimes, while writing, they talked about themselves in the third person. They treated the album versions of themselves as characters, and it was always a little awkward, but she didn't know how else to do it.

"It's okay. You can say you. I'll know what you mean," Georgia said gently.

"I think that's what Ashley would think about after getting to know Georgia. She'd want to pick her up and take her away from everything. And the idea of not tiring of the beauty—it's the landscape, of course, but it's the person, too."

"That's a pretty idea."

Their eyes locked, and you could hear a pin drop. The tension between them was so thick that Ashley was afraid to move, but she kept picturing herself getting up and crossing the room to the piano. She imagined putting her hand on Georgia's face, leaning down to press her lips to her soft skin. Georgia's green eyes made her feel like she was drowning.

Ashley jumped at the sound of the door opening, then slowly put the guitar down. Judy stood with Johnny at her side. They looked ashen, holding on to one another.

"Sorry to interrupt," Johnny said.

Ashley stood. "That's okay. What's happened? Is your sister all right?"

"It's not that. We're not exactly sure, but something's going on. Judy was just in town, visiting some friends and picking up groceries. And when she got back, well, you tell them, sweetheart."

"There are photographers out front, trying to get a look over the fence with their long lenses. They know you're here."

Georgia put a hand over her mouth. "How did they find out?"

"It can't have been Eugene. I trust him. Someone must've seen us all coming or going from the restaurant, though I can't imagine how when we were so careful."

"Is there any chance they don't know we're here? Any chance they're here for some other reason we haven't thought of?" Ashley said. They were talking about running away only moments ago. She couldn't bear the thought of anyone invading their sanctuary. She wanted everything to stay the same as it was right now, pure and perfect.

Georgia put a hand on Ashley's shoulder. "It has to be us."

"I'm very sorry, my friends. I know your anonymity here was important to you both," Johnny said.

It made Ashley want to cry that Johnny was bowing in apology. It wasn't his fault. For years, she'd felt hunted. So much of her life shrank when she grew famous—it gave so much, but nobody ever understood how much it took away. She had money and influence but couldn't spend time with friends without interruption. People said whatever they wanted about you and printed so many lies, and you were just supposed to keep your mouth shut and take it. She tried not to complain, but at times like these, she loathed it.

"You don't have to apologize. We're the ones who should apologize because those people are relentless. You won't get a moment's peace now that they know we're here."

Judy shook her head. "We don't care. Haven't you noticed this place is a fortress? We have high fences for a reason. People have sniffed around this compound ever since Johnny built it. Those photographers won't get anything good."

They stood in a circle quietly for a long moment, accepting that things would change.

Georgia sighed. "Okay. First, I'll get my phone out of my little safe and find out exactly what's happening."

"Mind if I come with you?" Ashley asked. She'd been itching to go and get her phone, but she wanted them to be together when they discovered whatever was going on.

"Of course not."

Johnny put an arm around his wife's shoulder. "We'll go out to the garden. Come talk to us when you're ready."

They walked down the hall toward Georgia's room. Ashley sat on the bed while Georgia went to the dresser and opened the safe, a clear container with a blue lid. She wondered how she could think about Georgia's legs at a time like this, but there they were, long and impossible to look away from. She supposed nobody could blame her—Georgia was famous for those legs. People wrote stupid articles speculating she'd insured them for a million dollars.

Georgia looked pale as she cradled her phone in her hands. "Are we sure we even want to know? Won't it only make us angry?"

Ashley shrugged. "I'm already angry. I don't think I can stop myself, anyway. Can you?"

"I guess not. I'll take it off airplane mode."

Before she opened her browser, the phone pinged with a flurry of messages. "Here. My friend Rachel has texted them."

The photos were fuzzy, but Ashley could immediately tell they'd been taken across the table in the private dining room the previous evening. Candles flickered around Ashley and Georgia, sitting with their heads close together. There was no mistaking that it was them.

"It had to be the server. The woman with the short hair," Ashley said. Aside from Eugene, she was the only person who had entered the room.

"Wow. Eugene and Johnny seem like good friends, so he'll be pissed that he trusted her. I guess she doesn't care too much about her job."

"She probably sold those photos for a fortune."

Ashley learned long ago that some people didn't even need money to do crappy things like this. It was enough for them to increase their social media following and have a taste of celebrity.

Georgia typed a message, then tossed the phone on the bed. "Well. Here we go. I guess there won't be any more dinners. The cat is truly out of the bag. Everyone will know what we're doing out here. Why else would we be here together?"

"You don't want to see what they're saying about us?"

"I thought you weren't even sure you wanted to look at it?" Georgia said.

"I thought I didn't, but I guess I have some morbid curiosity. Can you imagine what it's like online right now? It must be a feeding frenzy."

"Absolutely. You can look if you want."

"I'll do it later on my own phone. I'm sure I've got a few texts to answer, too."

Georgia shifted back on the bed and leaned against the wall. Ashley followed her lead, trying not to think about the fact they were in her bedroom. Aside from Johnny and Judy's quarters, it was the one part of the house she hadn't thoroughly explored. It smelled like Georgia's hair, and she'd added lots of personal touches to the space even in the short time they'd been here.

Ashley pointed to a row of rocks on the nightstand. "What's that about?"

"Things I've picked up while we were walking. I'll take them home with me."

She must've been squirreling them away in her pockets when they were walking the grounds—Ashley hadn't even noticed. "Why?"

"They're a little piece of this place. I like taking souvenirs unless it's a national park or something, and you're not allowed to."

"Do you have one from that day at the gorge?"

"Of course," Georgia said, leaning over and picking up a long, pointed black rock. "See? Now I'll always remember where I got it."

"You're a strange one," she said affectionately. "So, what do we do now? Flying under the radar was important to both of us, but it seemed even more important for you. What do you think?"

"We'll have to be careful about going out. And we should have security to stop anyone from jumping the fence, which I'm sure they'll try sooner rather than later if they haven't already. I'll call Nicky and see about getting that arranged right away. We should try and get Splash to pay for it."

"Totally. I'd love it to come out of their pockets. They'd be loving this."

"Easy. We'll threaten to pack it in and go home if it's not arranged right away."

Ashley felt that her heart might stop with those words. From the corner of her eye, she could see the lovely curve of Georgia's leg, and fought the urge to put a hand on her knee. "But you don't mean that literally, do you? It's an empty threat?"

Georgia's eyes were wide as she stared back at her. "How could I want to do that? Is that what you want?"

"I don't want to. I'm just scared that you might."

Georgia picked up one of her pillows and threw it. "You're insane. I always wanted to keep this to ourselves, but we've come so far. I won't let a little publicity get in the way."

Ashley tossed the pillow back and then tried to relax against the wall. She'd never lost the fear that gripped her before they arrived, that Georgia didn't want this as much as she did. She'd never been so afraid to lose something. It was precious and rare, and as she looked into Georgia's eyes, she felt calmer.

"I know I was reluctant in the beginning. I'm all in now, you know that, right?" Georgia asked, hand close beside hers on the quilt. An inch closer, and they'd be touching.

"Thanks for saying that."

She could feel a lump in her throat, the emotion making her reckless. She was about to say too much, that she didn't know what she'd do without this. She was interrupted when Georgia's phone pinged again, many times in a row.

Georgia sighed. "Okay, so maybe not a little publicity. Maybe a lot of publicity, but we'll just have to deal with it."

Ashley rose from the bed, knowing she had to leave the room. Pushing down her emotions in Georgia's presence was becoming too difficult to bear.

CHAPTER TWENTY-SEVEN

The next morning, Ashley sat quietly with Johnny on the back deck, looking at the gardens. She'd slept better than expected, given that she'd spent all afternoon the day before on her phone trying to do damage control. They hadn't seen much of each other that night because Judy and Johnny had gone into town to see Eugene.

It was exhausting after not having to worry about anything for weeks. Aaron was her first call, followed by her manager. Later, she and Georgia called the Splash executives and put them on speaker. They made their demands through silent laughter, each playing the diva.

It gave her whiplash how much everything had changed since the previous day. Security guards already surrounded the compound, and the label was eager to give them everything they wanted. She was still on edge, waiting for a photographer to pop up at any moment.

"Did you sleep okay?" she asked Johnny.

He shook his head. "I'm frustrated that I'm responsible for all this. I took you to that restaurant, and they blew your cover. I feel like a heel."

"Oh, come on. It's not your fault. You didn't know they were going to do that. You couldn't have known."

"I still feel bad. Eugene feels terrible, too. And that girl gave her notice before he could fire her. Sent him a text message first thing yesterday as soon as the news broke. Nobody feels good about someone losing their job, either. I don't understand why people do things like that."

Ashley hated the way fame tangled everyone in its web—Eugene had done nothing but give them a fantastic night out. The server had probably made an impulsive decision or desperately needed the money, and she seemed young. Ashley had done a few stupid things herself when she was that age. She shook her head. "Please tell Eugene not to worry about it. It's not his fault, either. It's happened now, and we'll deal with whatever we need to deal with."

The back door opened, and Judy and Georgia emerged with coffee. Willa followed them, disappearing under the table to sit at Johnny's feet. Georgia looked radiant in a floral wrap dress, barefoot, with her hair tied back. Her cheek seemed so smooth and soft.

"What did I miss?" Georgia asked, settling into a chair at the table across from Ashley. There were dark circles under her eyes, and Ashley wanted to hug her, to make it all go away.

"Johnny checked in with security. There's a crowd out front like we expected, but nothing to worry about," Ashley replied.

She was curious about how things looked at the front of the compound, but there was no way she was going out there, even for a peek. It was easy to imagine the zoolike atmosphere. The fans didn't bother her—they sometimes clustered outside her apartment building and were mostly sweet and well-meaning. It was the photographers. They had no problem shouting rude things to get a reaction or following her down the street and entering her personal space.

Johnny ran a shaky hand through his hair. "I can assure you that this place is secure. It was built to keep people like that out.

The fences are high, and they go all the way around. Nobody's going to get in here without us knowing. I know this isn't what either of you wanted, but you can feel safe here."

"I'll keep going into town to get anything you need. I'll tell you something good about this town, people will do what they can to protect us. Everyone knows us around here, and they won't take kindly to these intruders trying to make trouble," Judy added.

"Thanks, both of you," said Ashley.

"So, where does this leave us? Have you had the chance to talk about how this affects your plans?" Johnny asked.

"We talked a lot yesterday. This won't slow us down, not at all. We've both been loving it here, and we don't want to let them get in the way," Georgia said confidently.

An easy smile crossed Johnny's face for the first time since they'd sat down. "Well, that's wonderful to hear."

"This doesn't change anything," Ashley said.

"Not at all. I'm rattled, but I don't want them to dictate anything about this time. I say we ignore the hell out of them and let security do their thing. Keep working to make a great album."

Johnny's smile grew even wider. "Fantastic!"

They laughed when Willa jumped out from under the table, disturbed by the noise. Johnny leaned over and ruffled her fur.

Ashley wasn't sure if this was the right time to discuss her plan, but she figured she should leap. Bringing it up when Johnny and Judy were here felt less threatening—less like asking Georgia on a date. "I've been thinking. I figured that now that it's all public, we might as well go all the way."

"Go all the way, how?" Georgia asked, her eyes widening slightly.

"I'd love to skip The Vanguards, but I agreed to go months ago. I will honor that commitment. I'm up for an award, and I'm already skipping a lot of the stuff that goes along with it. I don't want to look ungrateful."

"Sure, we all understand that," Georgia said. "It's no problem. You'll only need a few days off for it, right? No big deal."

"Closer to a week once you count travel time and all. I wondered if you wanted to come to LA for the ceremony with me."

Georgia reached down for Willa, avoiding Ashley's gaze. "I didn't get an invite this year. No surprises there."

"You'd come with me as my plus-one."

"I'm not sure I understand."

Judy stood with her coffee mug, nodding toward her husband. "Excuse us. We'll let you two work all this out while we start breakfast."

"I'll be in soon, honey. I haven't finished my coffee."

"I need your help," she said emphatically.

"Oh, sure. Of course," he said sheepishly, following Judy inside.

Georgia kept patting Willa, who'd curled up at her feet. "I don't understand why you're asking me. I always assumed you'd go back to LA by yourself, and I'd stay here. I don't mind waiting. I'm truly not in a rush."

"It'd be fun to get out on the road again. Think of all the ideas we could have while staring at the highway."

"Oh, that's why you're saying it'd be closer to a week. You've got to be kidding. Do you still think you're going to drive? Can't you picture all those guys chasing your car? That's madness."

"We could think of a way to give these guys the slip. I know we could."

"Okay, assuming we could manage that, I still don't understand why you want me to come. It's your nomination, and I appreciate you trying to include me, but it has nothing to do with me."

The only thing to do was lie. Ashley couldn't say what she was thinking. All that award-ceremony artifice drove her nuts, and she only wanted to face it with Georgia by her side. More importantly, she couldn't bear being away from her for so long. She missed her when she was down the hall, so she couldn't imagine putting so much distance between them. She shrugged. "We're getting so much amazing stuff done. I don't want to break our flow."

"Come now, you must be joking."

"Why?"

Georgia wasn't paying attention to Willa anymore. She was looking at Ashley like she'd sprouted an extra head. "You know why. It'd be a circus. If we went, we'd spend all our time dodging questions. We wouldn't be able to spend any time working. I don't have a dress, so I'd have to sort that out and deal with all the bullshit that comes along with going to these things. Nobody would care about your nomination or be talking about your album if I were there. I'd steal your thunder."

"I don't care much about awards, in case you haven't noticed. I mean, I like to win like anyone, but the rest of it? That's nothing."

"I care. People will say I'm trying to upstage you."

"Who cares what people say?"

Georgia's eyes narrowed. "I'd love not to care, but I'm not going to pretend I don't. Our situations are very different at this point in our careers."

She held up her hands. "Okay, I'm sorry. I understand where you're coming from. I can see why you'd be concerned about that."

"Thank you."

They were silent until Ashley couldn't sit still anymore and went to Willa, crouching down. She held her big, trusting face in her hands while Willa's tongue rolled out. "I'll miss you too, girl."

"Do you truly think it's worth me coming along? You think we could do something worthwhile in the car?"

Ashley didn't dare to look at her again. She kept playing around with the dog, trying to be cool. "Of course, we could. That's the great thing about writing, isn't it? That you can do it anywhere. We could record voice memos and flesh things out when we got back here."

"I could come with you, but not go to the awards show."

"Sure, if that's what you're most comfortable with."

"You sound unhappy about it."

Ashley sighed. "I'm sorry, I'm not unhappy. I don't want you to come if you don't want to come, but…"

"But?"

She was tired of dancing around the topic. She didn't have to declare love, but suddenly, she couldn't avoid saying what she wanted. "I'd like you to come. It'd be more fun with you there. I like the idea of facing the crowds with you—showing everyone that we're friends and don't care what anyone says about it. People will say a bunch of stupid stuff like they always do. But so what?"

Finally, she risked a look at Georgia, who was smiling down at her. "Okay."

"It's okay if you don't want to," she said, realizing she was putting too much pressure on her.

"Stop. I'll come. You're right, it'll be fun. We can make fun of it all. There are a few people I'd actually like to see, and with everyone else, I guess it'll be a cool way to show I'm not going anywhere."

Georgia must be rubbing off on her because Ashley clapped in excitement. "Yes! Road trip!"

"I still think you're crazy for wanting to drive."

"We'll come up with a cunning plan, don't worry."

They beamed at one another, and she understood that Georgia had always wanted to come and only wanted to be convinced. Her heart soared, and she wrapped her arms around Willa, feeling vaguely pathetic because she was hugging an animal when she wanted to be holding Georgia.

CHAPTER TWENTY-EIGHT

It was like something from a spy novel. Georgia wished they could drive out the front gates like ordinary people, but it was fun to fool the photographers. They enlisted help from Johnny and Judy's friends, who arranged decoy versions of them in wigs with coats over their faces, and brought in extra cars as red herrings. They drove to Eugene's house in the middle of the day in separate vehicles at different times, Georgia in one of the restaurant's refrigerated vans and Ashley in the trunk of an old Toyota RAV4.

They met in Eugene's garage, a large space with tools, mowers, and engine parts everywhere. Eugene leaned against the wall, waiting for them. He tipped each of their drivers while Ashley stretched. Georgia reached over and rubbed her shoulder, unable to help herself, knowing Ashley must've noticed by now that she kept looking for excuses to touch her.

"Are you okay? I feel like I got the good end of that deal, getting to stand up in the van," Georgia said.

"Don't be silly. It's not the first time I've hidden in the trunk of a car. It was pretty comfortable compared to some of my hiding spots."

Georgia smiled at her, turning to Eugene. "Thanks for organizing all of this. We really appreciate it."

His eyes twinkled under his spectacles. She suspected he enjoyed the spycraft as much as she did. "Least I can do. Let me show you your wheels to get to LA."

Eugene drew off a cover with a flourish to reveal a classic red Mustang, the polished chrome glinting under the lights. Ashley and Georgia shared a shocked look, and Ashley took the lead. "It's a beautiful car. I don't want to seem ungrateful, but isn't it a little conspicuous? I'm not sure a convertible is a good idea."

Eugene looked back and forth between them solemnly, then burst into laughter. "I was kidding. I just wanted to show you my favorite. I'm giving you the boring car."

He tossed them a set of keys and pointed to a dark-silver Toyota. It looked solid and steady with tinted windows. It would blend in on the road and give them some privacy.

"Perfect," Ashley replied, taking off her backpack. Like Georgia, she'd gathered some essentials, but they didn't need much. Designers would send them clothes, and they didn't plan to wear their own things on the way.

"The clothes you asked for are in the trunk if you want to take a look before you take off," Eugene said.

"Thanks, I'm sure it's all good," Ashley replied.

They were driving to LA disguised as Joanne and Christine, and they'd spent the last couple of days joking about their characters. Georgia told Ashley that Christine didn't wear black because she was worried it would depress her aura. Ashley said that Joanne hadn't figured out green was her color, so she couldn't lean on her whole shades of green thing.

Their teams were ecstatic about them appearing at the awards together, though their managers hated the idea of them risking the drive to LA. During a Zoom call on Ashley's cell, the teams soon understood they couldn't talk them out of it, so they bent over backward to ensure they had everything they needed. They'd couriered supplies to the compound, including wigs and costumes. They'd arranged for security to travel separately but close enough that they could swoop in if there were any problems. Georgia fretted about the trouble everyone was going to, but there was no other safe way to do this.

Ashley checked her phone, pushing back locks of hair from her dark-brown wig. "Security guards are saying they haven't clocked anyone following us here. I think the first part of the plan was a success."

Georgia never imagined that Ashley would look so good without her platinum hair. She was one of those people who could pull off any color, but Georgia feared she was the opposite. She wore a blond wig and dark contact lenses, and she was sure she looked weird. Still, her black sweat pants and white T-shirt were baggy and comfortable, and even with her nerves about the trip, she was thrilled to get back in the car with Ashley.

The warm smile on Ashley's lips told her she felt the same way. "You ready to have some fun?'

"Sure. And this time, it's not your car, so I get to drive however much I want," Georgia said, tipping her head toward Ashley. "She thinks she's a better driver than me."

Eugene hitched his thumbs into his belt, playing along. "Now, now, ladies. I've heard we might have a problem with you two engaging in some serious catfights. I hope I'm not doing the wrong thing by sending you out on the road together. I don't want any claw marks in this vehicle."

"We promise to behave," she said, and Eugene tossed her the keys.

Soon they'd passed the outskirts of town and were on their way to Phoenix, where they'd stay overnight. She wished she could feel as bold as Ashley, who insisted they'd be fine, just as she always had. People might know they were spending time together, but nobody would expect to see them at a cheap motel in another state, especially not in these clothes with different-colored hair.

Georgia checked the rearview mirror. "You really think nobody's following us?"

Ashley shrugged. "I'm pretty sure we slipped out without anyone seeing us. Let's just enjoy being on the road. I'm loving this."

"I still don't get how you can always be so chill about this stuff."

"I'm not. I have to work at it. I don't want them to spoil our good time."

Georgia couldn't stop staring at Ashley's profile, taking in the way the dark hair brought out her features. She had such a strong face, one of those women who could look handsome and beautiful at once. Feeling eyes on her, Ashley's dimple showed. "What are you looking at? It's the wig, isn't it?"

"Nothing. So, about these Vanguards. Tell me more about what you're hoping to get from us showing up together."

"I'm not sure how to answer that. I want to present a united front like I said before. I don't want to face everyone by myself. I hope you don't find that selfish."

"No. I can understand that. Don't you think everyone will assume we're faking it, though?"

"I'm not sure I care if they think that. I'll feel stronger with you by my side. That's what matters."

Georgia couldn't keep the smile from her face. "If I tried to put a line like that in a song, we'd say it was too cheesy."

Ashley laughed, then sang the line in a random tune. "I'll feel stronger with you by my side. *By my side.* Hey, that's not that bad. There are so many lyrics that sound cheesy if you examine them too much, but they still sound right."

"They sound right because you believe them."

They talked as the scenery slipped by, taking turns behind the wheel. Before long, Georgia stopped worrying about being spotted—she was having too much fun. She loved singing along to the radio with Ashley, giggling and chatting. It was like that wonderful day on the way to the ranch, only better because they knew one another more now. It made every moment feel exciting.

They stopped at a gas station, and Ashley went inside to get them coffee and snacks, throwing a bag of trail mix at her when she came outside. "Nobody's clocked us. Safe as houses."

They recorded voice memos on their phones of fragments and lines they wanted to use. Georgia was amazed at how the ideas flowed now, as if she'd pulled a stopper from her brain. It was hard to believe how hard she'd wrestled with writer's block. She held the phone before Ashley's mouth while she drove, watching her beautiful lips move. What they could create together was magic. "I can't believe we're doing this. We can even write on the road."

"I told you we could do it," Ashley said.

Georgia tucked her phone back in her purse. "Who are you most looking forward to seeing at The Vanguards? Ryan Worth?"

"He's a scream, sure. I'd love to hang out with him."

Georgia bit her fingernail, her thoughts darkening. Since they decided she was coming, she'd called Nicky to do some fishing. She'd called around town and confirmed what she'd feared—her ex-wife would be there. Her heart had sunk to the floor when she found out, but she refused to give up an experience she wanted because of Hayley. Hadn't she done enough of that? As nervous as she was about this event, being there with Ashley meant she'd get to do something she'd never done much of on these nights: have fun.

"Is something wrong?" Ashley asked.

"Nope, just thinking."

"Are you all right?"

Georgia sighed. She didn't know why she'd been keeping it to herself—she didn't want to seem dramatic, she supposed, but Ashley would find out eventually. She'd think it was strange if Georgia didn't tell her. "I'm okay, but I've been meaning to tell you Hayley will be at The Vanguards."

"Oh," Ashley said, keeping her eyes on the road. "How do you feel about seeing her?"

She'd told Ashley how they mainly spoke through their lawyers these days. They hadn't seen one another for months, and Hayley had moved on long ago with a succession of girlfriends. "I don't know how to feel about it. I'll try to rise above it. She'll have a date with her, of course. I won't be rude if I see her, but I'd prefer to avoid her as much as possible."

Ashley was quiet for a long time, and Georgia worried about how all this made her look. She wanted to be the kind of person with amicable breakups—one of those women who was so mature and functional that she had her ex-girlfriends around for tea. With

Hayley, that was never going to happen. "It won't ruin the night, I promise. I can handle it."

"I feel bad for putting you in this position. I wish I'd known."

"Would it have changed anything?" she said, fear creeping into her voice. She hated to think Ashley might not have invited her if she'd thought there might be drama.

"No, of course not. Not for me, anyway. I'd still want you to come." Ashley glanced over at her, then back at the road. "Actually, there's something I've never told you. Feels like as good a time as any to do it."

Something in her tone made Georgia sit up straighter. "What is it?"

"You remember how Hayley told you that story that I flirted with her in the bathroom?"

Immediately, Georgia felt a lump in her throat, the sense of betrayal like a punch in the stomach. Ashley was about to tell her that she *had* flirted with Georgia's ex-wife and lied about it. She seemed so convincing that first day, telling her she hadn't done it. "Yes. Of course, I remember."

"I didn't tell you everything. It's true that I didn't flirt with her, but I never told you that she was the one who came on to me."

"What do you mean? What happened?"

When she pushed the hair away from her face, Ashley's hand shook. "She was touching my arm and complimenting me. It was hard to mistake for anything else."

"Why haven't you told me this before?" she asked. Her temper was sheet lightning, flashing so fast, unstoppable.

"We'd just met when you asked me about it. I was uncomfortable."

"You've had plenty of time to tell me since then."

"I'm telling you now."

"Is there more? Did something happen between you?"

"What? No, of course not. It was brief, but it happened, so I thought I should be honest with you about it. If we're all in the same place, I'd feel strange if she and I know something you don't."

"I see."

Georgia faced away from her toward the window, not seeing the passing landscape. Instead, she saw Ashley as she was a couple of years ago, at the ceremony in her black sequined dress. Was Ashley wearing that dress when she laughed with her friends about it later that night? Did everyone gossip at the after-parties about Georgia's wife hitting on her rival? How juicy—everyone would have loved that.

"Georgia? Are you all right?"

"I'll be fine. Just give me some time, please."

She wished she could rewind to a few minutes before she knew this. She closed her eyes, sinking back further in the seat.

How could Ashley cause her so much happiness and then so much pain?

CHAPTER TWENTY-NINE

Georgia pulled into the car park of the Comfort Inn, rubbing her eyes before she unclipped her seat belt. Every movement sounded loud to Ashley because Georgia had barely spoken for hours. Ashley had looked forward to this trip like a kid going to a theme park. She'd imagined the intimacy of being on the road, mentally rehearsing their conversations. They'd pass snacks across the car and drive with the windows down. It'd be light and free and fun.

The first part of the day was exactly as she'd dreamed it, but things went sideways when she told Georgia about what happened with her ex-wife. She'd never intended to tell her, but then Hayley's name came up. Now that she knew she'd be at the awards, it felt weird not to say anything. She figured they knew one another better now. There was a lot of trust, so they could get through uncomfortable things and become stronger on the other side.

Instead, a storm had settled over Georgia, and Ashley wished she'd kept her mouth shut. She'd gotten everything so wrong when she imagined they'd end up laughing about it. Hayley's behavior was so brazen, so ridiculously out of line, there was nothing you could do *but* laugh. And if Georgia laughed, it would mean one of Ashley's greatest wishes was coming true. She was over her ex-wife and ready to move on.

Ashley tried to give her the space she'd asked for, though it wasn't easy when they were in the car together all afternoon. They'd spoken only about practicalities, like when to stop for gas. Ashley felt so lonely that she almost wished she'd come alone.

Georgia pulled the key from the ignition but didn't move another muscle. They stayed in the car, Ashley so fatigued that the short walk to reception seemed like a mile. "Should I not have said anything? Would you have preferred not to know that at all?"

"I understand why you felt you had to tell me," she replied flatly.

Ashley took a deep breath. It was so unfair to be punished for something she didn't do. It wasn't her fault they'd had so many problems in their marriage or that Hayley liked playing games. She was innocent, so why was she getting the silent treatment? Georgia should be saving her hostility for the person who deserved it.

"What are we going to do about rooms?" Ashley asked.

"What do you mean?"

She didn't want to say the next part, but she had to. "Security texted me before. They said that given we wanted a small detail and discretion, they recommended that we stay in one room."

"Why?"

"Because it'll be hard for them to arrange to have one of their guys next to us in multiple rooms without anyone getting suspicious."

"Oh. If we're trying to pass as a couple, we should stay in the same room, anyway."

"Maybe we say we want to spread out and try to get a double?"

"Sounds good," Georgia replied, yawning. Ashley watched her, wondering how she could be so cavalier. Didn't she feel awkward, too? Was Ashley the only one who'd just spent the last two hours feeling like hell?

They took their luggage from the trunk and walked silently to reception. Ashley did all the talking to the clerk, who barely pulled his eyes from the video playing on his phone. He impatiently tugged on a long silver earring while she asked if they could get a room with two queens.

"Sorry, ma'am. I can only give you a king or a queen. All our doubles are occupied."

She tried to catch Georgia's eye to make sure it was okay, but she was hunting through her purse. They had no choice, anyway. A king bed was so large they could comfortably share it without touching. "We'll take a king, please. Don't worry, honey, I've got it."

She gave the clerk her credit card, which was under an alias. She'd worked with the bank to secure a card with a fake name so that she could stay in hotels without giving herself away. She was sure Georgia's card didn't have Gigi Lark on it, but it was still safer to do it this way.

They let themselves into their ground-floor room, Ashley crinkling her nose at the cigarette smell even though they'd asked for a nonsmoking room. She usually loved staying in hotels. She found the predictability comforting—the white sheets, the coffee maker, and the soap and lotion in neat generic packaging. It wasn't easy to enjoy it tonight. She hoped things would look better in the morning and Georgia would shake off her bad mood. She wanted to go back to being them again.

"Thanks for taking care of the room. I'll pay you back for my half."

"Don't be silly. That's not necessary."

"I didn't think of my name being on the credit card. Georgia Lark, anyway."

"That's okay. Not sure he would've noticed it either way. He was pretty deep on his phone. I'll leave security's duress button over here, on the desk, okay?"

"Sure. Thanks. Would you mind if I took a shower?" she said, unzipping her case to take out her toiletry bag.

Ashley wondered how long Georgia could go without looking her in the eye. "Of course. Go ahead."

She sat on the bed and stared at the closed door, hearing the running water. She would have been thrilled at the thought of sharing a room a couple of days ago, but now she felt only emptiness. Her phone pinged, and security told her they had two guards posing as a couple checked into the next room. It all felt like such a silly farce. Nobody knew they were here.

Georgia emerged from the bathroom in her boxer shorts and shirt, rubbing lotion into her hands. She glanced at Ashley, then walked over to the chair next to where her phone was charging. She sat down and scrolled, crossing her long legs at the ankle. Ashley rolled her eyes as she walked into the bathroom, so sick of the silent treatment. She understood that Georgia was upset, but seeing her acting childish like this was disappointing.

She took a long, hot shower, thinking about how strange it was that they'd be in LA tomorrow. They'd rented a hotel suite for a couple of nights, on which the makeup artists and hairdressers would descend the following morning. She looked forward to seeing her manager, Pam, and getting a dose of her level-headedness.

Ashley toweled off and put on her pajamas, enjoying feeling clean after a long day on the road. She spent too long moisturizing, then flossing and brushing her teeth so she could have more time alone. Finally, she exited to find the room dark. Georgia had taken the side of the bed furthest away from the bathroom, leaving on the lamp on Ashley's nightstand. Her back was to Ashley, and she could tell from the light that she was looking at her phone.

Ashley slipped into bed, the clean sheets smooth against her legs. She picked up the Emma Cline paperback she'd left on the nightstand. "I'll read for a few minutes if you don't mind me having the light on?"

"Mmm-hmm," Georgia replied.

Ashley grimaced and tried to focus on her book. After a few minutes, she heard Georgia setting her phone on the nightstand. Next, she tightened the bedclothes around herself, like she was trying to create a barrier between them. Ashley set down her book and turned off her lamp, wondering how she could sleep when a ball of resentment lay beside her.

The moment stretched out. Ashley could hear her breathing. It made her heart ache to have her so close but so far away. How many nights had she dreamed of lying by her side like this? Yet it was a world from how she'd wanted it to be. She couldn't take it anymore. She rolled onto her side, her eyes adjusting to the darkness until she could see the shape of Georgia's body under the sheet.

"Georgia?"

She didn't answer, which only frustrated Ashley more. There was no way she was already asleep. "How long are you planning on freezing me out?"

She rolled onto her back. "I'm not freezing you out. I want to go to sleep, that's all. We've got a long day of driving tomorrow."

"If you've changed your mind about The Vanguards, that's fine. You can stay in the hotel, and I'll go alone."

"Is that what *you* want?"

"I don't know. Is it going to be like this the whole time? Because if it is, I'd rather go by myself."

A long, burning silence grew between them, pregnant with hurt and anger. Ashley wished she'd found a way for them to have separate rooms because being around Georgia felt intolerable. She didn't just want out of this hotel room—she wanted out of the whole project. She thought she'd put up with just about anything to have the chance to work with Johnny, but her emotions were too big. This was a side of Georgia she didn't want to know, and all she could focus on was the mean things Georgia had done over the years. This version of her had always been there, waiting to surface and strike.

Why not return to her solo album so she didn't have to worry about all this mess? It was going to be good. Good enough, anyway.

"Like I said, I just want to go to sleep. Can't we talk about this tomorrow?" Georgia finally said.

Ashley got out of bed. She couldn't be so close to her for another minute. She'd sleep on the floor or in a chair. Maybe she could even go outside and sleep in the car. No, that was stupid. She wondered if she could text security and ask them to arrange another room. It was later now, so maybe they could work something out.

"Where are you going?" Georgia said, sitting up.

"I don't know. Away."

"Where?"

"I don't know. I just need to get away from here," she said, crossing the room to turn on the light.

Georgia squinted, holding up an arm. "Jesus. Dramatic much?"

It only made her madder. "Victim blaming much?"

"Victim blaming? What does that mean?"

She crossed her arms. "It means that your ex-wife made an unwelcome advance toward me, and now you're blaming me for it."

"C'mon. That's *not* what I'm doing. I'm mad that you never told me. I thought we were friends."

"Yet, look at how you're reacting. You've barely spoken to me since I told you."

Georgia looked at her evenly, but Ashley could see how quickly her chest rose and fell. She was struggling to stay composed, too. "How did you think it would make me feel when you decided to tell me that?"

"Which is it? You wish I'd told you before, or I shouldn't have told you at all? You need to pick one," Ashley said, gesturing wildly.

"You're being mean."

"I'm not being mean. I'm being honest. You pretend you wear your heart on your sleeve and you're all emotional, but you're not. You're cold, so cold. You've been cold to me all afternoon, and it's not fair."

"All I said was that I wanted time to think! You completely sprung that on me. We're talking about my ex-wife. You could have a little understanding."

Ashley deflated in the long silence, the anger draining from her body and leaving only sadness behind. Tears pricked her eyes. It was true—she could hear it in her voice. She still had feelings for her ex-wife, and Ashley had never stood a chance. She needed to get away from Georgia before she started crying. She wanted to go somewhere and lick her wounds. She'd been so foolish to let herself develop feelings for this woman. The only way to overcome them was to get as far away from her as possible. Focus on herself and her work.

She was leaving, so what did it matter if she laid her cards on the table? Might as well. "I understand very well. You're so hung up on your ex-wife that you're happy to punish someone who truly cares about you. You care more about her than the person who's standing right in front of you."

In slow motion, Georgia rose and came toward her. It was like the recurring dream she'd been having since they met, in which Georgia looked at her intently as though she were the only person in the world. Her chest was still rapidly rising and falling, her breath loud. The energy in the room was changing, but she couldn't let herself believe it yet. Was Georgia about to tell her to go away? Would she admit that even after everything that had happened, she still loved her ex-wife?

No. This wasn't that. Georgia stared at Ashley's lips, then into her eyes. And like a dream brought to life, she put a hand on her face, fingers brushing against her cheek. "It's true, I'm very angry with her. But you think I'm jealous of you. I'm not. I'm envious that she got to do what I wish I could do right now, and she treated it like it was nothing."

Oh God. Ashley put her hands on Georgia's shoulders, the room spinning.

CHAPTER THIRTY

Georgia's hand shook as she touched Ashley's face, her fingers full of electricity. She'd always wanted to know what it felt like to brush her hand on her skin, to memorize each curve and line.

It was hard to believe she'd been so afraid of Ashley's anger only minutes ago. She was terrified that Ashley would walk out the door, and the moment to declare her feelings would pass. She'd already let so many of those moments slip through her fingers. There were obvious ones, like the night they almost kissed in the kitchen. Innumerable subtler moments felt like they could have turned. Every time they sat close at the piano or watched a movie on Johnny's leather sofas, it had felt possible that this might happen.

She kept looking at Ashley's lips, still afraid to make the first move. Her soft blond hair flowed over her shoulders, and her mouth looked like heaven. As her brown eyes stared into Georgia's, she felt like Ashley was the first person who had ever truly seen her.

They drew apart for a moment and smiled shyly at one another. Ashley laughed as the beat stretched out, and Georgia laughed too. "What's funny?"

"I was just thinking, you remember that day we went to the gorge? I really wished we were Joanna and Christine because I thought this was impossible."

Georgia brushed her hair back from her face. "I wished that, too."

"It was so funny to be jealous of those women we made up."

"I know. But I'm so glad we're not Joanne and Christine because real life is better. I can't believe I get to kiss Ashley Archer."

Ashley reached up and pulled her down for a kiss, fist moving into her hair. The kiss was like Ashley herself—no-nonsense and direct, the kiss of someone who knew exactly what she wanted. Her lips were so soft and warm, Georgia moaning as she opened her mouth. It was such a long time since she'd been kissed like this, and Ashley was making her weak at the knees.

Their tongues met, and Georgia's stomach filled with liquid heat. She'd always wanted to do so many things to her, but she couldn't move for a moment. She let herself be kissed, her heart racing.

Ashley pulled away and pressed their foreheads together. "Are you okay?"

Georgia struggled to catch her breath. Every moment Ashley wasn't kissing her felt like a waste of time. She nodded, but Ashley moved back a little.

"I need to make sure you want this?"

"Of course I do."

Ashley pushed hair behind her ear, and Georgia's heart twisted to see the vulnerability on her face. "I know this is a risk, in a way. After everything that's happened between us."

"And you don't care?"

"No."

"Exactly. Neither do I. I just want you," Ashley said, and the words broke whatever spell Georgia had fallen under. She leaned in and kissed Georgia again, who melted into it.

Ashley walked her backward toward the bed, and they tumbled onto it together. Ashley climbed on top of her, and Georgia put her hands on her back, feeling shifting muscles under the thin cotton of her shirt. Ashley's hot breath was in her ear, her lips insistent on her neck. Her hips jolted when Ashley licked her skin, gently weighing her down. Georgia pulled her still closer, and they kissed slowly and deeply.

She was shaking again, but it wasn't from nerves this time. It was that she was so turned on. Almost embarrassingly so, but with Ashley, she was sure there was no reason to feel that way. Ashley was kissing her hard, and she clasped their hands together, pinning her hands down on the mattress. She felt anchored by her and utterly safe to let go.

Ashley moved back and traced a finger over Georgia's cheek, then her lips.

"You're so gorgeous," she said, running her finger over the skin above her shirt.

Georgia pushed her back so there was space, pulled her shirt over her head, and threw it on the floor beside the bed. She could feel the flush on her neck and chest and wished for a second that she'd thought to switch the light off. Ashley stared, then ran the tips of her fingers over Georgia's breasts, making her shudder. Georgia grabbed the hem of Ashley's shirt, and they tugged it off together. All she wanted was to feel Ashley's skin on her own, to be as close as they could be.

Georgia took a moment to stare, drinking in Ashley's toned shoulders and perfect breasts. Then, she lay back, pulling Ashley on top of her again. It was everything she wanted—their skin brushing, sending goose bumps down her arms.

Ashley was between her legs, making her wetter by the second as she moved against her. She could hear quickened breath, their kisses growing in intensity. She wasn't sure whether this was the world's hottest make-out session or if it would grow into something more, and she didn't know how to ask. It went on and on, her hands on Ashley's back, Ashley's breasts brushing against her chest. She was beginning to think she could come just like this—she was so hot it burned.

Finally, she rolled Ashley onto her back. Ashley made a small noise of surprise and looked up at her, grinning. Georgia held herself up on her hands, her gaze trailing over Ashley's bare skin.

Something had shifted between them, and Ashley looked up at her seriously and nodded. Georgia quickly pulled Ashley's pajama bottoms down and stood up to shed her shorts.

Ashley propped herself up on an elbow and stared. "Did you know that you're a full-blown goddess?"

"Stop it."

"I'm serious. Now, please, come back here."

Georgia kissed her lips, then moved down, kissing her breasts. She heard Ashley's soft moan and felt Ashley's hands in her hair. She kissed her rib cage and her stomach, pressing her lips to her upper thigh. Ashley's smell was intoxicating, her legs falling apart as Georgia parted them with her hand and moved in between them. She looked up at Ashley again and saw those brown eyes looking down at her, her breath quick and shallow.

It might be the first time she'd seen Ashley looking self-conscious, making Georgia's heart twist. She kissed her inner thigh, then moved to her center, Ashley gasping and gently putting her hands on the back of her head. Georgia wanted to drown in the taste and smell of her—she'd never had anything so beautiful. She licked and kissed her until Ashley cried out, hips stuttering. She threw an elbow over her face, breathing hard as she came.

Georgia rested her head on Ashley's stomach, but only for a beat because Ashley was asking her to come to her. They lay side by side, facing one another, and Georgia thrilled at how sated she looked. She'd done that. Her eyes were clear and bright as they looked into hers.

Ashley kissed her slowly, but it soon gathered heat. She grabbed Georgia's thigh and pulled it over her hip, and they both sighed when Ashley's hand moved between her legs.

"You feel so good," Ashley said, rolling on top of her. Georgia arched up toward her, feeling like they could never get close enough.

Afterward, they lay on the mattress, Georgia in a sensual haze. Ashley had a leg slung over Georgia's hip, her face buried in her neck. She could feel it each time Ashley blinked, her eyelashes brushing her skin. She started to fall asleep, but Ashley's hand brushed up and down her ribs, and it made her shiver. "That feels nice."

"Can't believe that just happened. Nobody would believe it."

"I'm not sure I believe it."

Ashley briefly propped herself up, kissing her sweetly before dropping back down and nuzzling her neck. "Do you know what I'm realizing?"

"No, what is it?" she asked, trailing a hand over Ashley's arm. She was fascinated by how the tattooed skin felt under her fingers. It altered the smooth skin's texture, and she wanted to remember every part of it.

"I think I always had a little crush on you. I just never admitted it to myself."

Georgia laughed. "I think I was the same. I was a little too interested in what you were doing for it to be innocent, and I loved watching your music videos."

"I watched yours, too. It's pretty funny to think I was acting like a kid, pulling your hair or something to get your attention. Know what I mean?"

She nodded, kissing Ashley's temple. They'd been childish—there was no doubt about it. They were quiet for a while, Ashley's hand running over Georgia's stomach. She was so happy to be here, to finally be able to touch her. It had been causing her so much angst to want her that much.

"It's okay if you don't want to come to the event, you know. I wouldn't have pushed it so hard if I had known she was coming."

It was strange how the sting of Hayley's betrayal had dimmed so quickly, after feeling like she'd never get over it. She hadn't slept with anyone since, and she doubted that anyone else could've obliterated the memory of Hayley like Ashley just had. "I'll be okay. I don't want to talk to her, but I can't avoid her forever. I'll keep my distance and hope she does the same."

"If you're sure."

"I'm sure," she replied, rubbing Ashley's shoulder. She didn't know if it was the right time to discuss their relationship. She couldn't imagine going to sleep without doing so. She wanted to prove that she wouldn't be over-emotional or dramatic about this. She could be chill, for once. She hoped they'd do this again. Still, she didn't want to give the impression she expected anything more.

"I want to make sure you know I'll be discreet at The Vanguards. Nobody will know this happened."

"Of course. Same for me, I'll be careful. People are already losing it over us being seen together, and they'll go crazy when we show up together. They'd be insufferable if they knew about this."

Georgia squeezed Ashley's shoulder. It was like she'd been thinking—they couldn't be together. They'd both always known that, so there was no point being disappointed.

"Exactly. This was just for us."

CHAPTER THIRTY-ONE

They woke up tangled in the hotel sheets, bodies pressed together. They'd set the alarm early to drive the rest of the way to Los Angeles. Georgia wished they could stay here, just the two of them. Funny to think she'd ever doubted whether Ashley felt the same way. It was all out in the open now, and Ashley couldn't stop touching her, not that she was complaining.

"We don't actually have to leave this room, right?" Georgia asked, sighing when Ashley kissed her neck. Ashley's naked body sliding over hers made her moan, goose bumps rising on her skin.

"I wish we could stay here forever, too."

Ashley gave her one last kiss, then slipped out of bed and stretched fully naked. Georgia watched from the bed, eyeing her as she crossed to the bathroom.

Moments later, she heard Ashley calling her over the sound of running water. "Want to join me?"

She couldn't push back the sheets and fly in there fast enough. They kissed under the rushing water until she pushed Ashley against the tiles.

Georgia took the first leg of the journey. Neither of them had slept much, but she'd never felt this high, and Ashley smiled like a Cheshire cat as they drove along the highway. Georgia couldn't help admiring how Ashley looked in her wig, even though she'd been wearing it the day before.

"What are you smiling at?" Georgia asked.

"Nothing. I'm just happy you came with me."

"Me too," she said, reaching out until Ashley grabbed her hand. "You look hot with dark hair, by the way."

"Thanks. Feel the same about you as a blonde. But I love your red hair the best, of course. You're so gorgeous."

She smiled. Ashley had been complimenting her a lot, and it was even more special in the light of day, not caught in the heat of the moment. Georgia drove with one hand on the wheel, wishing they'd never get to LA. "Hey, you don't think we're going to jinx anything about our writing, are you?"

"How so?"

"You know how sportspeople are told they shouldn't have sex before a game, or like a boxing match, or whatever? Because it depletes their energy and shifts their focus. Maybe it could be like that."

"I'm not sure that's a real thing, my dear."

Georgia laughed at her dry tone. "You know what I mean. Like, there was probably some sexual tension between us that made us work so well together. We've changed the dynamic now."

"I thought you stopped being scared about writer's block. You've been so productive since those early days at Johnny's. You've had more ideas than me."

Georgia shrugged. "I know, I've surprised myself. Just a thought."

Ashley reached for her backpack and took out her leather-bound notebook. "Only one way to find out. I was thinking before about how we both love road music. Tom Petty, that Melissa Etheridge song, Bruce Springsteen. Why don't we write a road song?"

"I love it. There's something so American about road music. We can do something with that."

They recorded voice memos and jotted down lyrics, laughing and gently teasing one another. It didn't take long for Georgia to know nothing had changed. They were more in tune than ever, finishing one another's lines.

When the sun was dipping, they arrived in LA. Georgia had never considered living here—California wasn't her scene, and she couldn't imagine not being a New Yorker. Still, she enjoyed what she saw as they drove down tree-lined streets and passed the manicured lawns of mansions. The Four Seasons was Ashley's favorite hotel, and she'd arranged for them to have a luxury suite with two bedrooms. Georgia wondered if they'd still sleep in separate rooms as initially planned. She was trying to take things one step at a time.

They drove up to the iconic façade with its palm trees and chandeliers.

"I'm glad you picked this place. I stayed here once with someone years ago. It's wonderful."

"Who did you stay here with?" Ashley asked.

"Nobody important," she replied, and Ashley stared at her in a way that made her melt.

Ashley handed the keys to the valet, and the manager, Richard, met them in the lobby. He'd been tipped off about their arrival, and he greeted them warmly as though there was nothing unusual about them being here together. The rest of the staff were too discreet to stare at them in their wigs and costumes. Georgia was sure they were only recognized vaguely by passing guests. *Aren't you somebody important?*

They got to the suite's living room, Georgia tipping the porter. Ashley lay on the sofa when he left. "Great sofa. I'm not sure I'll ever get up."

Georgia hovered, unsure of how close she was allowed to be. They'd been so connected this morning and talked all day, but they hadn't discussed their next steps. If she were more confident, she'd climb onto the sofa right this minute and take Ashley in her arms. Now, she wondered how she'd been able to keep up a normal conversation in the car. The memory of last night suddenly felt so overwhelming.

Ashley looked up at her. "Are you hungry? How about room service?"

"I could murder a good meal," she replied, walking over to the desk and picking up the menu. She gave it to Ashley while she entered her room and unzipped her suitcase, calling out through the open door. "But first, I could do with a shower."

"Should I order a pizza?"

Georgia stood in the doorway, putting her hand on her stomach. "You know I love pizza, but I've got to squeeze into that dress tomorrow."

"Cheeseburger? Just kidding. I'll order salads and soup."

"And some truffle fries. Let's not deny ourselves truffle fries."

"Agreed," Ashley said, reaching for the phone.

Georgia took a long, hot shower. It was the first time she'd been alone all day, and she spent the time wondering whether they'd sleep in their separate beds. The signals were hard to read, even though Ashley had been sweet to her today. Still, maybe she wanted to get a good night's sleep and focus on the awards show. It would be a big day, so it was okay. She could wait.

She was toweling off when she heard a knock on the door over the bathroom fan. The food must've arrived. She was starving, so she quickly pulled on some sweats and a shirt and was about to open the door when she heard voices. The person delivering the food must be taking the opportunity to chat with Ashley, lingering over setting things up. She stayed behind the door, checking out her fingernails while she waited. She'd neglected them while they'd been staying at the ranch.

This was taking much longer than it should. She put her ear to the door, feeling ridiculous.

"I won't take up much more of your time, but I just wanted to say what a big fan I am."

Georgia rolled her eyes. She wasn't a diva, but they only wanted a quiet dinner, and they should be able to get that in the privacy of their room. Hotel staff usually understood that crossing this boundary wasn't okay.

"Thank you. That's kind of you. Okay, well…"

"For what it's worth, I think you're definitely going to win tomorrow night. I'm rooting for you."

"Thank you. Anyway," she replied, and Georgia heard impatience creeping into her tone. She wondered if she should call out and rescue her, but Ashley could handle herself, and she didn't want to worsen the situation.

"I was so annoyed when Gigi Lark beat you a couple of years ago. Your album was way better. I saw those stupid photoshopped photos of you together with that old producer guy, and I honestly can't believe anyone could believe they were real. As if you'd hang out with her. She's so fake."

Georgia couldn't help herself. She quickly grabbed the handle and opened the door, stepping out into the room.

"I don't..." Ashley said, turning around open-mouthed.

"Good evening," Georgia said in a bubbly tone.

Maybe she enjoyed the shock on the server's face a little too much. She was a woman in her late twenties with heavy eyeliner and hair pulled back into a bun. She gaped at Georgia, then looked at Ashley with pure panic. Georgia sensed she was desperate to reach for her phone to snap a photo to prove this was happening. Unlike the staff that had greeted them downstairs, she must not have been briefed.

"Excuse me," she said, backing away toward the door. "I'm sorry. I had no idea."

Ashley made eye contact with Georgia, trying not to laugh. "Just be a little more careful about what you assume about people, okay? Don't believe everything you read online."

"Don't worry. I'm not going to call the manager or tell anyone. You're fine," Georgia said.

"Thank you," she said, pushing her cart into the hall and closing the door behind her with one last look back at them.

Ashley smirked at her. "That was masterful. You couldn't help yourself, huh?"

"I couldn't. I just wanted to see the look on her face, and it was totally worth it. I hope you don't think that was mean?"

Ashley came closer, and Georgia's skin tingled with hope. "No, what she said was mean, and you had every right to do something about it. I don't blame you. In fact, I think it was cool."

"If Ashley Archer thinks I'm cool, I must be doing something right."

"You *are* cool. And trust me, I was about to say something to her myself. I'd never let anyone talk shit about you like that."

Georgia closed the distance between them and was rewarded when Ashley put her hands on her hips. It felt so good—she'd been missing those hands all day. She put her arms around Ashley's shoulders, looking down at her. Neither of them could stop smiling. "That's sweet. Thank you."

Ashley's eyelids fluttered closed, and heat gathered between Georgia's legs as Ashley tipped her head back. Georgia put a finger under her chin, raising her head a little more, drawing it out, and taking a moment to appreciate the full lips waiting for her. Georgia leaned down and kissed the skin under Ashley's eyes, then her cheek, hearing Ashley sigh as she got closer to her mouth. Finally, she kissed her lips, her hips jolting as Ashley pressed her body close. It was warm liquid and honey between them. Ashley grabbed her shoulders as they opened their mouths.

Ashley's fingers were at the hem of her shirt, pushing up and under to trail fingers over her stomach. Georgia shivered, kissing her harder. She gasped when Ashley's hands inched up further, palms cupping her breasts.

She kissed the shell of Ashley's ear while she rubbed a thumb over her nipple. "God, I want you."

Georgia reached down and put her hand between Ashley's legs until she panted into Georgia's mouth. "Fuck. Take me to bed?"

She didn't need to ask Georgia twice. She bent her knees, grabbed Ashley's thighs until they wrapped around her waist, and picked her up. Ashley giggled as she walked them into a room and toward the bed, their food growing cold as their moaning filled the space.

CHAPTER THIRTY-TWO

Ashley's heart thudded like a drum as they sat in the stretch limo. Georgia was beside her with her fingers around the stem of a champagne glass, but she wasn't drinking. Neither was Ashley—she didn't want to be even a little tipsy when dealing with all the reporters. Their publicists, Julia and Morrison, sat across from them, scrolling on their phones. Morrison chuckled at something on Instagram, holding his phone out to show Julia.

"Any leaks? Does anyone know?" Ashley asked. She'd been worried that the server might take her revenge by posting about their encounter somewhere. She didn't blame Georgia for standing up for herself, but it was risky. She still hoped to surprise everyone.

Julia shook her head. "Nope. Everyone's done what they're supposed to do. Not a peep."

Ashley leaned back against the seat, trying to slow her breath. Was this really her idea? She was typically low-key about everything but couldn't imagine being here without Georgia. She told herself to calm down because she could handle any drama with her grounding presence. Last night, after making love, she'd lain on Georgia's chest and listened to her heartbeat. Being with her like that made her forget about The Vanguards—made her forget about everything.

She looked at Georgia, thinking she looked more drive-you-crazy this afternoon than grounding. The hairdressers had parted her hair down the side and accentuated her natural waves. Her lips were painted red, and her green eyes looked more beautiful than ever under shimmering eyeshadow. And the dress—that dress. It gathered in at the waist and showed a tantalizing amount of cleavage. When she first spied Georgia in her gown, she'd wished so hard she wasn't surrounded by stylists. She wanted to peel it off her immediately.

"I like that color on you. Different from your usual green," Ashley said.

Georgia smoothed the sapphire-blue dress over her knees. "I asked for something different, but not too different. It's still a jewel-tone thing like my green."

"It suits you."

"Thank you. This suit is perfect on you," Georgia said, reaching over and rubbing the fabric between her fingers.

Ashley wore heels with her Saint Laurent suit, leaving the first few buttons of her white silk shirt undone. Stylists had helped her choose a gown months ago, but Georgia encouraged her to wear a suit. Georgia said she found her hot in a suit, so she was easily convinced. It was nice to feel so comfortable, so anchored.

Georgia brushed an imaginary piece of lint from the lapel of the jacket. When Ashley glanced at the publicists, Julia looked at her quizzically. She typed furiously on her phone with her thumbs. The text came through a moment later.

What is happening???

Ashley shook her head. She wouldn't get into it now, especially when she didn't know herself. They'd been having a wonderful, mind-blowingly sexy time together—but she had no idea if Georgia was serious about her.

The driver pulled up to the curb. Morrison and Julia were looking at their phones, getting the go-ahead from workers stationed on the ground to find the best moment to exit the vehicle. They wanted to ensure they stepped out of the car at a moment that would provide maximum impact. Ashley wished she was alone with Georgia. They'd spoken so much about this event, but there was a question she hadn't asked. It felt too important not to go for it.

She leaned over, the smell of Georgia's perfume overwhelming as she grew close. She loved watching Georgia cross her legs and stare at her lips like she couldn't help reacting to her, even when other people were around. "Is it okay if I hold your hand while we walk down the carpet? It'd send the right message."

"Of course. Please do."

Morrison's eyes had been glued to his phone, but he looked at them now. Ashley hadn't spoken to him much, but he seemed like a cool customer, one of those ruthless guys who lived and breathed the music industry. It was funny to think he'd probably been behind some of the meaner stories about her in the past, but he was all smiles at her now. "I love what you're doing. It's so clever. I wish I'd thought of it myself."

Georgia smiled tightly at him. "So. Is it showtime?"

He pointed at the door. "Sure is. Break a leg, ladies."

Ashley took a deep breath, preparing herself as if she were going onstage. She slid across the seat and took the hand of the attendant who helped her from the car, standing with her shoulders back. The crowd screamed when they spotted her, and she was aware of the buzzing from the journalists along the sidelines as they readied for her. Photographers were already yelling at her, trying to get her to turn so they could get their first shots. They could wait.

She leaned over to the attendant. "I'll take it from here, thanks."

He nodded and moved back. She stood before the open car door, blocking the view of Georgia, who grinned up at her. Ashley took her hand to help her from the car, and though she knew she must be imagining it, there was a moment of silence before the crowd roared. Georgia stood up to her full height and flipped her curls over her shoulder. They shared a secret smile, Georgia briefly looking down into Ashley's eyes. They turned toward the red carpet, took one another's hands, and stepped forward together.

A wall of cameras and microphones met them, and Ashley told herself to focus on one at a time. Julia and Morrison stood behind them, guiding them toward the more prominent outlets.

Their first stop was the host of a major YouTube channel. Dani Mills had long blond hair and thick lips, and she looked smaller than she was on screen.

She also looked like she couldn't believe her luck, getting to speak to them first. "You both look beautiful tonight. I'll ask what everyone's *dying* to know: What is going on with you two? Why are you here together?"

Georgia leaned toward the microphone, her eyes sparkling. Ashley was glad she was having fun with all this. "I'm here to support Ashley. She's made a wonderful album."

Dani waggled a finger. "Come on, ladies, you know what I'm asking. Everyone will be desperate to know how two of the biggest rivals in pop music ended up spending time together."

They'd rehearsed a few lines in the car on the way. It was Ashley's turn, so she leaned toward the mic. "I guess the takeaway is that you never know what's happening beneath the surface."

It was an annoyingly cryptic thing to say, and she knew it. They didn't want to seem like they were taunting the journalists, but they had to give them something. She was sure Georgia wanted to laugh as much as she did, but they kept their expressions neutral as Julia and Morrison moved them on to the next person.

It was a tall reporter with a square jaw, and his microphone had an NBC logo.

"It's a real shocker to see the two of you side by side. Folks speculated that those photos of you two having dinner were fake. You've proved them all wrong tonight."

"We knew the public would be surprised, but we haven't done this to be shocking. I just wanted Gigi to come with me tonight. It's an important night for me."

"Can you explain how your relationship has changed?"

Georgia shook her head, laughing to soften her words. "That's too complicated for a soundbite."

"Will you comment on the rumors? Were you with Johnny Rail because you're all working on one of his projects? How long have you been in New Mexico?"

This time, Ashley had to work harder to keep her expression neutral. She wanted to say that it wasn't *his*, it was *theirs*. Johnny would never want anyone to call it his project. "Thanks for the question, but no comment."

They moved on to the next reporter. The frenzy was expected, but its intensity was still tremendous. All the journalists waited for them, distracted from their own interviews by their presence. Maybe they knew they wouldn't get a scoop tonight—these red-carpet interviews were nothing if not predictable—but they all wanted something to titillate their audiences. Ashley descended a mental rabbit hole as Morrison and Julia guided them from one interview to the next. She tried to imagine how the reporters might react if they knew what was really happening.

The reporter was a tall woman who introduced herself as Lailah. "Gigi and Ashley, nobody ever thought they'd see you standing together like you are right now."

Ashley smiled, and in her head, she answered with the truth. "Standing together? You should've seen us last night. If you knew how many orgasms I've had in the last forty-eight hours, you'd wonder how I could even stand up."

She opened her mouth, but the daydream was so vivid that she couldn't speak. Georgia noticed her stammering and leaned forward. "Sometimes, life surprises you. But I'm very excited to be here. All the nominees have done great work, and I loved Ashley's latest album. I think it's her best work so far."

Ashley tried to focus, but her laughter broke through. She held the back of her wrist to her mouth, trying to compose herself. The more she tried to pull it together, the more she couldn't stop. She visualized Lailah's face if she said what she was thinking, the fake smile replaced with shock.

Lailah squinted at her, confused. "Are you all right?"

She pretended to cough, shaking her head. "Excuse me. A little nervous."

Julia leaned into her from behind with a bottle of Evian, but she waved it away. Georgia seemed to understand what was happening and squeezed her hand. "These nights always make you a little delirious."

Lailah nodded and changed course. "I'd love to hear about your clothes."

"Isn't Gigi's dress fantastic?" Ashley said.

Georgia stepped away and did a spin, putting a hand on her hip and winking at Ashley. It truly was so much more fun to have her here. They walked the rest of the gauntlet, stopping to whisper in one another's ears about the questions. Georgia put an arm around Ashley's shoulders as they stood before the cameras, flashes popping. There was a murmuring from the crowd, but Ashley didn't care. Who cared if people thought they were stunting? If they wanted a show, they'd get one. She turned her head and kissed Georgia's cheek. She wanted to kiss her lips, but she'd have to wait.

They were escorted to their seats. The organizers had had no idea Georgia was coming, but there was a seat with a place card that said, "Ashley Archer Plus-one." Georgia grabbed it, stuffing it in her clutch.

"Souvenir. You know I like to keep things," she said, smiling when she realized Ashley was watching.

Ashley pulled Georgia's chair out, not caring how many eyes she felt on her back.

"So chivalrous," Georgia said, folding her long legs under the table.

"You bring it out in me."

They sat, clasping hands under the table. Georgia bumped her with her shoulder. "Thanks for bringing me. This is a blast."

They locked eyes, and Ashley's stomach flipped at how those green eyes stared into her own. She had a flashback to two years ago—Georgia sitting beside her ex-wife, their heads close. She'd been jealous without knowing why. Now, she was the one lucky enough to sit by her side. Ashley reached over and brushed the hair from Georgia's cheek. "You're welcome. And we're just getting started."

CHAPTER THIRTY-THREE

These ceremonies usually held long periods of boredom, punctuated by terror as you waited to see if they would say your name. It was the first time Georgia had been to an awards show as a date instead of a nominee. Though the show hadn't started yet, she enjoyed herself more than expected. The ballroom slowly filled while everyone mingled, finding their places. Acquaintances she hadn't seen for months stopped by her table to say hello, and people she'd never met came over to introduce themselves.

Ryan Worth appeared behind her in his leather pants, red platform boots, and matching bow tie. He smirked at them, wagging his finger. "Ladies, ladies. Aren't you the talk of the town?"

Georgia rose from her seat to hug him, his smooth cheek sliding against hers. He whispered into her ear, "You little hussy. I knew something was going on that day I saw you at Splash."

She laughed as he pulled away, and he turned to Ashley, who rose to say hello.

"Hello there. Congratulations on your nomination, babes," Ryan said.

"Nice to see you again. And congratulations on yours."

"Seriously, you two, this is an iconic move. My hat's off to you."

"That means a lot, coming from you."

He gave them one of his cheeky grins and put his arms around them so they were all huddled together. "Come on, girls. I need to know what's going on here. Tell Uncle Ryan all about it. Are you having a thing, making a record, or both? Or are you just doing it to fuck with everybody? I swear, I hope it's the third one, you nasty little pair of bitches."

They giggled, Georgia shaking her head. "I'm not telling you anything."

"I knew you wouldn't, but you can't blame a boy for trying," he said, releasing them. "Whatever you're up to, I love it."

He kissed each of them on the forehead and strutted away. They were still watching him leave when their tablemates arrived, a trio of indie singers who'd formed a supergroup and recorded an album together. They hadn't met, so Georgia and Ashley shook their hands and introduced themselves.

Georgia felt eyes on her and looked over Ashley's shoulder. She locked eyes with her ex-wife, who stood at the table next to theirs. The strangeness was jarring—to think she'd once loved this woman. Hayley had cut her hair into a sleek bob, and the neckline of her red dress plunged almost to her waist. She wasn't quite smiling, looking as unsure as Georgia about how to behave.

How had their love turned into this? It was less than hatred, a surprising cool indifference. Georgia wasn't even in a relationship with Ashley, and their powerful connection made her union with Hayley feel like a shadow. Still, Hayley had been such a big part of her life. It was hard to remember now, but she had adored her.

Ashley realized she was looking at something and checked over her shoulder. "Oh. Are you okay? Damn them for seating her so close to us."

Georgia loved her in protective mode. It was too lovely for words. She held up the generic plus-one place card. "They didn't know I was coming, remember?"

"Oh, yeah. Right."

"Would it bother you if I went to say hello?"

"You don't have to ask my permission for anything."

"I know. But I'm asking anyway, would it bother you?"

Ashley spoke softly and looked into her eyes like they were the only two people here. "Maybe it would've, before the last couple of nights. But even if I were super jealous, I'd know you need to do what's right for you, and it's not my place to get involved. Go talk to her."

Georgia smiled down at her, wishing they weren't here so she could kiss her. She decided that people could think whatever they wanted and wrapped her arms around her. She could tell Ashley was surprised, but she hugged her back. They swayed in place, and Ashley whispered in her ear, "Go talk to her, and then come back to me."

"You couldn't keep me away," she whispered back. She couldn't wait until all this was over so they could be alone again.

She was unsteady as she approached Hayley, wishing they could speak privately. Still, it would only be brief. She hoped it would break the ice so she wouldn't have to spend her night wondering if they'd bump into one another. She wanted to be mature about this. Hayley's plus-one was the young model she'd been dating publicly for the last few months, Lexi Bacall. Fortunately, she stayed on the other side of the table, talking to a rapper at their table. They waved politely at one another before Georgia turned to Hayley.

She didn't know how to greet her. A hug felt too intimate, but it would be weird to shake hands. The problem was solved when Hayley air-kissed her. "It's wonderful to see you."

"Nice to see you, too," Georgia said.

"I won't lie. I'm shocked, although after I saw those photos of you two, I did wonder if something like this might happen."

Georgia shrugged, unwilling to give anything away. There was still some anger beneath the surface because of all those lies Hayley told, but she was surprised at how much had evaporated. It was a relief not to be so sad and angry anymore. She was healing, and it felt so good to look Hayley in the eye and know that they couldn't hurt one another anymore.

Hayley nodded over to where Ashley sat. "I'm not stupid, you know. I'm not as shocked as everyone else about this. I always thought there was something suspicious about how you talked about her."

"It was never like that."

"Well. Whatever's going on with you, I hope you're happy. I am with Lexi."

There were always so many questions about why Hayley acted the way she had after their divorce. For the first time, Georgia understood that asking was futile. There was nothing Hayley could do to her anymore, which was a peaceful, wonderful thing. She now understood that her ability to create had never left her. Her collaboration with Ashley and Johnny made her happier than she'd ever been. None of this would have happened if she'd stayed with Hayley—being brought so low had taken her to a higher level.

Maybe the cliché was true, and everything happened for a reason. Everything had led Georgia to Ashley.

"Thank you. I am happy. Have a wonderful night," Georgia said, then walked to their table without looking back.

Ashley put a hand on her shoulder. "Everything okay?"

"Everything's great."

Now, Georgia could relax and enjoy herself. A young R & B performer, Patti Grant, hosted the show—she was funny. Her jokes about Georgia and Ashley were kind and good-natured. Georgia tried to ignore how the cameras lingered on them. As the time for the announcement of Pop Album of the Year drew closer, Ashley grew quieter. Aware that audiences would try to read her lips, Georgia cupped a hand around her mouth. "Are you doing okay?"

"I'm not gonna win," she said, sliding a hand onto Georgia's thigh under the table. Georgia bit her lip, thinking she couldn't wait to get her alone in the hotel room later tonight.

"I'm not sure about that. You're a front-runner. Do you know what you'll say if you win?"

"Nope. This is one of the few things I can be reckless about. I haven't even thought about it. I think it's bad luck."

Georgia shook her head, thinking that she envied her. When she was up for awards, she agonized for days over her speech, memorizing it to seem sincere, like she was speaking off the cuff.

The Pop Album of the Year presenter was Vivian Black, a rap royalty artist. Georgia had always been a big fan and clapped enthusiastically when she walked onstage in a chain-mail dress and a mask. Georgia was almost as nervous as she'd be if she'd been nominated. She had a Vanguard, and Ashley should have one too.

"Each pop artist nominated tonight is a vanguard, an artist at the forefront of music. They innovate, creating music that is emblematic of our moment but that will live on for decades. It's my honor to present the Vanguard Pop Album of the Year," Vivian said, announcing the artist names while clips played on the giant screens. Georgia's stomach flipped as Ashley was projected. She grabbed Ashley's hand, not caring that it was on the table and everyone could see it this time.

"And the award goes to..." She opened the envelope theatrically and paused for what felt like an age. "*Pity Party* by Ashley Archer."

Ashley turned to Georgia, grinning. She wanted to grab and kiss her, but she settled for Ashley's hug. They pressed their foreheads together, and Georgia closed her eyes, savoring the moment. She'd had nothing to do with Ashley's album—they hadn't even met when she recorded it—but she felt so proud. And she loved being seen with her like this, their friendship out there for the world to see. When Ashley reached the stage, her hands were sore from clapping so loudly.

Vivian and Ashley hugged, and then Vivian bowed and handed her the award. Ashley sobered as she approached the microphone, waiting for the audience to quiet. "Thank you. I want to thank everyone on my team and the whole gang at Splash Records. It takes a village to make a record, and I appreciate every one of you. I'm very proud of this album, and it means a lot to me to have it recognized. But tonight, I'm looking toward the future. I don't know if I'll ever win another award like this."

They were so far apart—Ashley was up there on stage, and she was all the way down here. Yet, as Ashley looked down into the audience and their eyes met, Georgia could feel their connection through the crowd. Tears pricked her eyes because she knew before she heard the words. Ashley was going to speak about her.

"I don't know if I'll ever be up on a stage like this again, so there are things I want to say while I have the chance. I want to thank the people who are making my life better than it's ever been. I'm having the best experience of my life with Johnny Rail and Georgia Lark. Thanks for being my friends and collaborators. Working with you is the most fulfilling, special thing I've ever gotten to do, and I wake up grateful every morning."

She stepped away from the microphone, leaving a trail of applause and murmuring in her wake. Georgia clapped along, trying not to show how startled she was.

What the hell had Ashley just done, and why?

CHAPTER THIRTY-FOUR

"Can you tell us more about this project? Whose idea was this?" the journalist asked. It was the same NBC guy they'd met on the red carpet. Other reporters began yelling their questions before he could finish, and he shouted over the top of them. So many hands were in the air, but nobody waited to be called. Ashley felt like a teacher dealing with an unruly bunch of kids.

After a full minute of trying to cut through the noise, she held her hand over the microphone, leaning toward Julia. "I don't know what to say."

Julia was the calm and collected type, but even she looked rattled. "I don't know. I wish you'd told me you were planning on doing that."

Ashley knew she couldn't blame Julia for being frazzled, and she couldn't blame the reporters, either. Everyone had been speculating whether she and Georgia were working together, and she'd announced it before the world on live television. She still wasn't sure what compelled her to do that—especially when she hadn't discussed it with Johnny or Georgia. It was so out of character. Looking out from the stage, she couldn't see Georgia in all the bright lights. She could swear she could feel her, though—those green eyes seeing right through her. Was this why Ashley had been so eager for Georgia to join her? Was it some subconscious drive that made her do it?

The truth was that having everyone know felt good. Ashley wanted the world to know that she and Georgia were working together.

"You and Gigi have always been arch-enemies. Was that fake? Or is this a stunt? Which one is real?" a reporter asked.

"Is none of this real? Has this been a years-long performance art piece?" another one chimed in.

Ashley clutched her award statue, trying not to laugh, though it was out of nerves more than anything. It would be pointless to try to convince them that she could never be that calculating. She didn't want to try and explain—how could she even know where to begin? All she wanted was to return to the table and check in with Georgia to see how mad she was. Georgia had always been the main driver of the secrecy of their project, and she'd messed up by blurting it out and confirming what everyone only suspected.

Ashley held up a hand. "I'm sorry, but can we please keep the conversation to tonight's award? I'm not ready to talk about that."

Loud, angry conversations erupted between the reporters in the press pack. An older man with pale-blue eyes stood up. He spat his words in a heavy French accent. "Are you joking? You just announced that you're working with her. How can it be off-limits when you literally announced it ten minutes ago?"

Knowing she was about to make a room full of enemies, Ashley made eye contact with Julia again and shook her head. She backed away from the microphone.

Julia scowled at her but got up to face the crowd, forcing a smile. "Thank you so much for being here, but Ashley won't be answering any further questions."

Ashley was escorted back to her table. Her heart sank when she saw the empty seat next to hers. The show moved on, a heavy rock performance on the stage. The sound of dueling guitars grated on her. She felt dizzy—and she had no idea what to do.

She wondered if Georgia had walked out and returned to the hotel. If so, she couldn't blame her. Ashley reached for her clutch and pulled out her phone. Her tablemates stared at her, and the camera was probably on her, too. What did it matter? There were more important things.

Thank God. There was a message from Georgia. *Meet me in the bathroom. Left side of stage.*

She rushed across, ignoring Ryan, who tried to get her attention as she passed by his table. The area outside the bathrooms had chaise lounges and a television broadcasting the action from the awards. Nobody was there right now, but it was the perfect place to hang out and hide. The women's bathrooms were across from the sofas, but Ashley turned her head at a "Pssst." Georgia appeared around the door of one of the gender-neutral, single-cubicle bathrooms.

Perfect. Georgia crooked her finger, beckoning.

Ashley looked around and entered, quickly closing the door behind her. The large bathroom had a full-length mirror, an armchair in the corner, and a counter next to the sink for people to touch up their makeup. Georgia leaned against the wall with her hands on her hips, shaking her head. Her expression was hard to read, but the skin of her throat was red and blotchy. Ashley hated to think that she'd embarrassed her.

"You. What am I going to do with you?"

Ashley held up her hands, supplicating. She'd felt so brave while on the stage, but every moment since then had been terrifying. She wished they were anywhere but here. "I'm so sorry. I don't know what to say."

"Were you planning that the whole time? Is that why you brought me?"

"Honestly, no. Not consciously. It just came out. How mad are you?"

Georgia crossed her arms. "I'm not sure yet. I'm still too shocked. And it's not the easiest place to process something like this, with all the cameras on me."

"How can I fix this?"

"You can start by explaining yourself."

"I know I should've spoken to you first. It was out of line. I don't know what I was thinking."

"I'm going to need more of an explanation from you than that. You're the most self-possessed person I've ever met. I don't believe you lost control of yourself."

Ashley moved closer to her. If Georgia only knew—she'd been completely undone. She *had* lost control with this woman, and it was the best thing that had ever happened to her.

She swallowed hard, trying to bring herself back to Earth because Georgia was right. She deserved an explanation, and Ashley wasn't quite ready to lay it all on the line. "I was always completely on board with what you wanted when it came to keeping it all quiet. You know that, right? I just got up there, and I suddenly couldn't see the point of denying it anymore. Everyone knows something's going on. They knew as soon as they saw the photos."

"I'm not sure about that. Plenty of people thought those photos were fake, remember?"

"Yeah, but we weren't going to be able to keep it up. There's too much heat at Johnny's place. But of course, I get that it wasn't the right way to go about it. It wasn't my choice to make, and we should've decided together. Anyway, I wanted to say more than that, to tell you the truth."

Georgia softened at the thickness in her voice, pushing off the wall and stepping forward. They faced one another, threading their fingers together. "Okay. What did you want to say?"

"I wanted to say that we're more to one another than collaborators, but it was the closest I could get. Seeing as we haven't talked about it, I mean."

Georgia trailed her fingers down the side of her cheek and brushed her hair back from her face. "Why haven't we talked about it? We've had enough time alone the last couple of days."

"It's felt too new. Fragile," she said, and started laughing.

"What's funny?" Georgia asked, smiling along.

"I'm sorry, I can just see how ridiculous I'm being. You're right that I'm so controlled, usually. You bring something out in me because this is the worst possible time to talk about it. We're in the bathroom at the damn Vanguards. I should've brought it up last night like a normal person."

"It's okay. I could've, too. So let's talk about it. We're already here."

Ashley paused. So many questions and thoughts were running through her mind, and they all sounded too intense to say aloud. *Is it crazy to think that I'm falling in love with you? Could this ever work? Now that I've kissed you, I feel like I could never leave your side.*

"Are we dating? Do you want that?"

Her heart sank like a stone when Georgia cupped her hands around her face, shaking her head. "You must know how much I want to say yes. But can you imagine? What if things go wrong? It would be such a mess."

Tears sprang to her eyes. "That's not what I was hoping you'd say."

"I'm only trying to be realistic. I really like you, but our feelings have changed about one another a million times. What if this is just a fling brought on by being so close while we work together?"

"So, then we'd find out. The only way to know that is to try."

Ashley was so disappointed. She thought Georgia was brave, the kind of woman who threw herself into love with her whole heart. What did it mean that she'd married Hayley so quickly but wouldn't give Ashley a chance? Did she just not like Ashley enough?

She could take the easy road and wait until later to say how she felt. She could go through the rest of this night pretending none of it was a big deal. She could even play it cool and sleep with Georgia later tonight, acting like she could separate sex and her feelings. It was what she would have done a year ago, but the time at the ranch had changed her. She wanted to live in this moment, not later. She had to try one more time.

She wet her lips and stared into Georgia's eyes. No matter what happened, she had to show courage. She got down on her knees.

"What are you doing?"

"You know how in that song you mentioned, 'Remember,' I wrote about how we all need to live in the moment because we don't know how much time we have? I said that none of us can take tomorrow for granted."

"Yes. I know," Georgia said, pulling on Ashley's hands, trying to drag her back up.

"Just let me say this. Don't worry, I'm not proposing," she said, and they giggled, breaking the tension. She stopped laughing, pressing her face against Georgia's waist. Georgia brushed her hair with her hands so tenderly.

"I said that in the song, but I don't think I've ever truly lived that way. I've kept my emotions small, maybe because I was afraid. But you make me feel big feelings, maybe partly because you do, and I love that about you. I want to keep feeling them."

There was a long silence, and Ashley's heart clenched as tears rolled down Georgia's cheeks. She was worried it meant more rejection, but then she smiled through them. "Do you truly mean all of this?"

Ashley took her hand, kissed it reverently, then held her fingers as she looked up at her. "Maybe more than I've ever meant anything."

Georgia didn't answer. When she pulled at Ashley this time, she stood up and took Georgia's face in her hands. "What are you thinking?"

"What about the project? What if we mess it all up?"

Ashley shook her head. "We won't. But it's no longer the most important thing to me. You are."

Georgia threw her arms around Ashley's neck and held her tightly. Ashley closed her eyes, breathing in her intoxicating scent. It was such a relief not to hide it anymore. Georgia drew back, looking into her eyes. "What happens now?"

"Now? I mess up your makeup."

They laughed, holding on to one another like they might drown if they didn't.

CHAPTER THIRTY-FIVE

Georgia slowly opened her eyes and noticed how high the sun was. Ashley's Vanguard glinted on the dresser, thrown carelessly on it with their clutches and jewelry. They'd skipped the after-parties to return to their suite, then stayed up most of the night talking and making love. Together, they'd unstitched the tapestry of their past, laughing over how they'd each been interested in the other as soon as they met. Georgia confessed how much she'd spoken about it to Rachel, squealing when Ashley admitted she'd done the same with her friend Aaron.

"You'll meet him when we get back to New York."

"You'll meet Rachel and the others, too. They'll love you."

Georgia stretched her arms over her head, curling her toes. She rolled over and watched Ashley sleeping, the gentle breath making her chest rise and fall. Her full lips were slightly parted, and Georgia thought about kissing her awake. She should let her sleep. They had a long drive back to the ranch, and Georgia couldn't wait to get to work.

There was a lot to do—the attention on them would be even greater now. Everyone knew they'd come to The Vanguards together, so hiding in plain sight would be harder. She should text the security guys and warn them they'd need a secure place to stay en route. No more Comfort Inns or diner stops, not for a while. It would probably be wise to charter a private flight.

She picked up her phone from the nightstand, frowning at the texts on her screen from an unknown number. She hoped her cell number hadn't been leaked—it had happened before, and changing her number was annoying. The all-caps text caught her attention, so she opened the thread.

HELLO, IT'S JOHNNY RAIL HERE. I GOT A CELL PHONE SO I COULD TEXT YOU AND YOU COULD CALL ME ON IT. I CALLED SOMEONE AT THE RECORD COMPANY TO GET YOUR PHONE NUMBER.

Georgia sat up and said Ashley's name, but she didn't stir.

EUGENE CAME OVER AFTER THE AWARDS SHOW AND SHOWED ME A VIDEO CLIP OF ASHLEY'S SPEECH. I HAVE MADE ARRANGEMENTS. CALL THIS NUMBER AS SOON AS POSSIBLE. LOL.

Ashley had to see this. She shook her shoulder until she opened her eyes, blinking blearily at her. "What's going on?"

After Georgia explained everything, she checked her phone and saw that she had an identical string of messages. They put Georgia's cell on speaker and lay it on the bed between them. Before Georgia made the call, Ashley turned to her, biting her lip. "I'm sorry again about all the drama. I can't believe my actions have led to Johnny Rail getting a cell phone. That makes me feel very guilty."

"Is it so bad that you've pulled him into the twenty-first century? You know him. If he didn't want to, he wouldn't have."

"Maybe he felt like he didn't have a choice."

Georgia squeezed Ashley's hand, then leaned over to kiss her lips. "Don't worry. Let's wait and see what he has to say."

Judy picked up after a few rings. "Oh, I'm glad you called. Johnny's been pacing around all morning and driving me nuts. He's on the deck with Willa. Hold on, I'll get him."

When he said hello, his voice was so comically loud that Georgia laughed. They could hear Judy shushing him. "Good afternoon. Are you both doing okay?"

Ashley snatched the phone up from the bed. "I want to start by saying how sorry I am. I don't know what came over me."

"It's okay, my friend."

Ashley sighed, closing her eyes. Georgia trailed her fingers along her arm. She was being ridiculously hard on herself. "Thank you, Johnny. I know what I did wasn't okay. It was impulsive and stupid."

"Please don't worry. Life is too damn short for these kinds of conversations. I'm a solutions man."

"I'm so sorry you had to go out and get a phone. I know that must have been difficult for you."

"Actually, I do believe I'll keep it. It's so convenient. I texted my sister this morning, and she texted me right back. It's never too late to discover new things. I don't know what I was so afraid of."

Georgia smiled, shaking her head. His tone of genuine wonder was lovely, and it was great to see Ashley starting to relax against the pillows. One of her naked legs stuck out from under the sheets, and Georgia stared at it, telling herself she needed to focus on this conversation. Georgia leaned in closer to the phone. "What did you mean in your message when you said you'd made arrangements?"

"Someone's already tried to jump the fence this morning. Of course, you could come back here, and we could beef up the security, but I think the horse has bolted on being at the ranch. It seems just too difficult to work like this."

Ashley put her hand on her forehead. "God. I'm sorry again."

"Like I said, solutions man. I've lined up another place where we can write and record. Nobody will know. We'll go back into our little bubble and get this album done. Judy and Willa will come, and everything will be okay."

"That sounds amazing. Where?" Georgia asked.

"The good news is, you can stay in LA. You can go there tonight or whenever you're ready. You're going to be ladies of the canyon. What do you think?"

They grinned at one another, both knowing the Joni Mitchell reference and understanding that he meant Laurel Canyon in the Hollywood Hills. The neighborhood was famous for its 1970s scene when big stars gathered to party and create music. Given Johnny's history, it felt auspicious to go there.

"I think that sounds amazing. Where exactly are we going?"

"To my friend Carl Winter's place. He was a producer alongside me back in the day."

Georgia shook her head, eyes widening at Ashley. Carl Winter was almost as big a deal as Johnny himself. "I think we both know who he is."

"Great. Well, he won't be there. He's over at his place in France. But he's very happy for us to stay there and use his recording studio. We'll pack Willa up and get over there as soon as possible. Eugene will help us evade these vermin out the front of my house."

"That all sounds so good," Ashley replied. "Thank you so much for everything you've done."

"It's nothing. I'll text you the address when we get off the phone," he said gleefully. "And you let me know when you're coming."

"Amazing. One more thing. Why did you say lol at the end of your message?" Georgia asked. She'd almost forgotten about it, but she'd thought it was strange.

He paused. "Doesn't it mean lots of love?"

"Yes. That's exactly what it means," Georgia said, smiling.

They signed off, still holding hands. Georgia rolled to face Ashley, drawing the sheet higher over her breasts, loving how Ashley looked down at her body. "See? Everything's okay. There's a plan B, and nothing to worry about. We'll go to Laurel Canyon. Sounds pretty good to me."

"I still feel bad."

"Well, feeling bad never got anyone anywhere. It's done. I'm fine, Johnny's fine. Time to roll with it," she said, bopping Ashley's nose.

Georgia wasn't sure she'd ever felt this happy, and all she wanted to do was show it. In one night, her life had been altered beyond recognition. The pain haunting her since her divorce had faded. She could look her ex-wife in the eye without feeling troubled by all that had passed between them. She'd faced her demons, going to an event as part of an industry that had rejected her last album, and nothing terrible happened. People treated her exactly the same as they'd always done.

Most importantly, Ashley wanted her. After Hayley, her heart was scarred, and she'd wondered if she could still love as openly as she had before. It turned out that she could still use her whole heart—it had mended. Having Ashley feel the same way made everything right with the world. It made her feel like her old self again, albeit a little older and wiser.

"You're in a good mood," Ashley said, pillowing her head on her hands. She reached out a leg and tangled their feet together, her skin warm against Georgia's.

"So are you."

"I've just had the best nights of my life. And we're about to go on another grand adventure, even if I'll miss the ranch like crazy. Why wouldn't I be happy?"

"Ditto. So. How are we going to play this? Will we keep this between you and me and a few friends for a while?" Georgia asked, holding her breath. She had to remember that she and Ashley were very different people. Ashley was a more cautious, rational type—she liked that about her. Just because she was ready to shout it from the rooftops didn't mean Ashley would be on the same page.

"Is that what you want? To keep it super quiet for a while?"

Those brown eyes stared into her, so wise and warm that Georgia couldn't speak for a moment. How had she gotten this lucky? She traced her fingers over Ashley's jaw, down her shoulder. "I asked you first."

"I'm not going to call Splash or any media outlets or anything, but I'm sure about you. About us, I mean. I don't feel any need to hide it."

Georgia was so happy that she launched herself on top of Ashley and kissed her. Ashley laughed, wrapped her arms around Georgia, and kissed her back. Her mouth was so soft and sweet as it opened to Georgia, their tongues sliding against one another's until she could feel it in the pit of her belly. They broke apart, breathless.

"I take it that you don't want to hide it either?" Ashley asked.

"Nope. I'd be happy to tell Judy and Johnny we're seeing one another if you would be. We'll be staying at this house with them, and I don't want to have to sneak around."

"I'm with you. I have a feeling it'll make its way into the music, anyway. Might as well be upfront about it."

"I guess we know the ending of our album, don't we?"

Ashley looked up at her seriously. "Ashley and Georgia begin to fall for one another."

"Yay!"

Ashley laughed, with her hands on Georgia's hips. "You're so funny."

"I hope I'm not too much for you."

Ashley shook her head, holding her tight. "Trust me. You're just the right amount."

CHAPTER THIRTY-SIX

Ashley was sure she was in heaven, staying another night at The Four Seasons and cocooned in the magnificent suite with Georgia. They ordered room service, made love, and rested. They found unexpected joy in following Johnny's journey to LA as he texted them their progress. He messaged his observations of the airport lounge and the kind clerk at a car hire place. He sent photos of his food and Judy's feet. They laughed every time.

"Look at him," Georgia said, pointing to a selfie of Johnny holding a big milkshake. "You've utterly corrupted that man."

"You've corrupted me," Ashley replied, kissing her, drowning in the smell of her hair.

The last few days were beyond what she could have imagined. She'd known for a while now that she was more attracted to Georgia than she'd been to any other woman, but the way they fit together blew her mind. Being with her was easy, fun, and exciting. She wasn't afraid to ask Georgia anything, and Georgia always seemed to know exactly what Ashley wanted. Georgia threw her whole body and mind into her touch. She was so free, and it made Ashley free in return.

She lay with her head on Georgia's chest, trailing her fingers over her ribs. "I could stay here forever. We don't ever have to leave, do we?"

Georgia brushed her hair with a hand, and Ashley felt her rumbling laughter. "I can't see a good reason to, no. Although there is that pesky album to complete."

"We can do it from here. Record it on my phone."

When Johnny texted to tell them he'd arrived at Carl's place, they finally checked out. They'd sent Eugene's car back to him via a Splash intern and arranged to travel in an inconspicuous car with tinted windows. One of the security guys sat in the front seat, texting his colleagues in cars in front and behind them. Traveling around LA was much easier than a lot of places—it was full of people who were famous or good at looking like they could be. They held hands across the back seat, sharing a smile now and then as they passed over the winding Laurel Canyon streets.

They went through gates and up a long driveway, Georgia squeezing her hand as they approached the Spanish-style house. It was white with a terra-cotta roof, classic wooden shutters, and storybook stones lining a path up to it. It felt almost as secluded as the ranch, the overgrown gardens and high fences making the LA streets feel a million miles away. As they exited the car and stood together waiting, Willa ran up to them, panting. It made Ashley feel so at home that she could have cried with happiness.

"I missed you," Ashley said, bending down and letting Willa lick her face. Georgia's hand touched hers as she patted Willa.

Tears pricked her eyes when Judy and Johnny came out onto the lawn, clasping hands. The last few days had cracked her heart wide open. They'd become like family. It hurt to think of how lonely she'd been all these years without knowing it, but there was no need to regret a past that had led her here.

She embraced Judy and then Johnny while Georgia did the same, and soon, the four of them were huddled together, laughing. Judy reached over and brushed the tears from her eyes, then did the same to Georgia, tenderly rubbing her thumbs over their cheeks. "Are you girls okay? Why are you both crying?"

They made eye contact, and Georgia took the lead. "Everything's great. Just happy to be here. Let's talk inside?"

Johnny and Judy led them to a living room while their driver brought in their luggage. Johnny and Judy perched on one of the two large white sofas covered with throw pillows while they settled onto the other, a dark wooden coffee table between them. Willa lay next to the coffee table, looking up at them as if eager to participate in this conversation.

"Oh, congratulations on your award, Ashley," Johnny said.

"Thanks. And thanks again for organizing all of this. This place is wonderful."

"It's no problem. I'll show you the studio later. It's in a separate building out the back. It's a nice little space and has everything we'll need."

Ashley smiled to herself at how excited he was about everything. She hoped that would be how she'd be in forty years or so when she was his age—still in love with the work. Judy gazed at him affectionately with a hand on his knee, and Ashley flashed forward on that, too. Maybe it should scare her that she could already imagine growing old with Georgia, but it didn't.

Judy tilted her head as she looked across at them, squinting. "Is there something you two would like to discuss? You both look a little preoccupied. Am I imagining things?"

Johnny held his hands up. "Don't worry about anything. We can stay here as long as we need to, and really, Ashley, I'm not mad. In case you can't tell, I love my cell. I guess you can teach an old dog new tricks, after all. Ha ha."

Judy nudged him, and he fell quiet. Ashley watched Georgia's profile for a moment, admiring her full lips, sensitive features, and pale skin. It wasn't the right time to think about it, but she couldn't wait to touch her again. It was strange to discover that she could miss her when she was sitting right next to her. From now on, she would search for her in every room.

"Thank you for saying that, Johnny. But there is something else we need to discuss with you both. Only because we don't want to hide anything from you."

Judy covered her mouth, hiding a huge grin. Johnny was slower to understand, looking back and forth between them expectantly.

Georgia reached for Ashley's hand, and the corner of his mouth twitched up. "We weren't expecting it, but we've grown pretty close lately, as you might've noticed. We're dating."

"We're together," Ashley added.

Judy clapped and then jumped up to hug them both. "Oh, what a lovely thing. I could see it happening, and I'm so happy for you. You two go together."

Johnny cleared his throat, seeming to gather his thoughts. She hated it if they were making him feel uncomfortable. He'd never come across as uncomfortable with their sexuality, and she was sure he'd worked with plenty of gay musicians over the years. Yet, he was an older man, and maybe this was all strange for him. Ashley bit her tongue because, in the long beat that followed, she wanted to reassure him that nothing would go wrong. There would be no drama, and they wouldn't do anything to jeopardize their project.

He put a hand on his heart, a beatific smile crossing his lips. "I'm so proud to know you both. And now, I'm proud to have played a small part in bringing you together. This is wonderful."

Georgia shook her head. "I'm not sure if I'd call it a small part. We might never have met if you hadn't suggested we work together."

"Nonsense," he said, pointing between them. "Look at the two of you. You are so happy that it was clearly meant to be. I'm a big believer in fate, and I reckon I was probably only fate's instrument."

Georgia stood, reaching out a hand to Ashley. She took it, and Johnny got up as well. "I don't think I believe in fate, but whatever all this means, I'm just glad it's happened. Let's go look at this recording studio together. We've got work to do."

Ashley floated to the back door with Georgia's soft skin against her palm. She understood why Georgia wanted to pick up where they'd left off back at the ranch. She was sure she wanted to pour this love they were sharing into the music, to give expression to the wonder happening between them.

Ashley wanted that, too. She'd never been so happy. While Johnny and Judy walked ahead, she grabbed Georgia's face and kissed her, her heart taking flight.

CHAPTER THIRTY-SEVEN

Three Years Later

Ashley helped Georgia dismount her horse and stood close with her arms around her neck. They'd taken a dawn ride around the ranch trails, watching the sunrise over the mountains. The crisp morning air and the expansive blue sky made her feel calm and in control. She needed it this morning—not to relax, but to stay focused and present. She wanted to appreciate every moment of this day.

"I can't believe you wanted to take a ride this morning of all mornings," Georgia said, kissing her forehead. Ashley had leaped out of bed this morning, announcing she was in the mood for a ride. Georgia had thrown a pillow at her and groaned but agreed to join her.

They swayed in place together, Georgia murmuring into Ashley's ear, hands running over her back. Her touch had become familiar over the past few years, but it still made her swoon.

"Sorry I woke you up so early, but I couldn't think of a better way to start the day. Can you?"

"Oh, I don't know. I could think of one or two," she replied, grabbing Ashley's butt and laughing. "But it was a wonderful idea."

"You're insatiable. I think it's one of my favorite things about you."

They swung their clasped hands between them as they headed toward home. Their house coming into view always made Ashley smile, remembering the special time they'd spent getting it ready. First, they had the old house renovated and repainted in barn-style colors. They put in a deck, pool, and hot tub so that it would be like Johnny's place. They visited local refuges and adopted as many animals as possible.

Ashley had loved her apartment in New York but had never planned a home from the ground up like this. They'd maintained their solo careers—it was important to each of them to work on their own projects and release good work, but collaborating with Georgia was one of her favorite things. Whether it was designing this house or writing together, they were a dream team.

Her whole life with Georgia was like a dream.

They stood in their front yard for a moment, still holding hands. Willa ran toward them with her tail wagging, and they crouched down. "Oh, my god. There's a bow tie on her collar. Could she be any cuter?"

"Hey! What are you doing out here?" Rachel said, hand on her hip.

"Saying hi to our ring bearer," Georgia replied. "Doesn't she look like a pretty girl with her little bow tie?"

Rachel shook her head. "You're not supposed to see one another this morning. It's bad luck, I told you. You snuck back into your bedroom, didn't you?"

"Oh, no! We don't have anything borrowed or blue, either. I think we should call off the wedding. It's ruined," Ashley said.

She loved teasing Georgia's bestie. Before they'd even met, Ashley knew Rachel was the person in Georgia's life she most needed to impress. She was Georgia's most trusted friend and advisor, and it wouldn't bode well for their relationship if Rachel didn't like her. She knew she'd made it when she was invited to join the group chat. Eventually, she'd introduced Aaron, and he'd become part of it, too. Everyone called him the "token male friend," and he loved it. He and Mel acted like siblings these days.

Rachel slung an arm around each of them. "I'm the maid of honor. If I don't keep you two in line, who will? Sometimes, I think if you two had your way, you'd get married in your jeans, maybe even while you were still on the horses."

"Hey, that doesn't sound like a bad idea. It's not too late to change it up, is it?"

"Ha, ha. You should be nicer to me. I still haven't forgiven you for moving away from the city."

Ashley smiled. It had been a big decision, and they had kept Georgia's apartment for when they were in town. Their friends visited the ranch so often that it felt like they spent more time together than before. "I do appreciate you, I promise. And as the maid of honor, you understand how important it is for us to keep my strength up, so I'm going to get some breakfast."

"Me too. What are we having?" Georgia asked, and they started pulling Rachel toward the dining room.

"No. We'll bring breakfast to you while you start getting ready."

"Plenty of time," Ashley said, breaking free and running.

The dining and living areas were open-plan, and it felt like everyone she knew was here, crowded into every corner. They'd pulled chairs from all over the house to the long oak dining room table, already a twelve-seater. The Larks and the Archers were sitting close together down one end, deep in conversation. Their parents hadn't spent much time together—the Larks lived so far away in the UK—but everyone got along well when they did.

Ashley grabbed a coffee and a plate of eggs, cramming in next to Aaron. He'd been chatting to Mel, but he slapped a hand on her shoulder. "Good morning. On a scale of one to soiling yourself, how nervous are you?"

She considered for a moment, chewing. There had been butterflies in her stomach from the moment she awoke, but it was the good kind of nervous excitement. Marriage had never seemed important to her, not until recently. She'd never been the type of woman who dreamed about a wedding from when they were a little girl.

Georgia always joked about being way too young to be a divorcée, and she wasn't in a rush to get herself a second wife.

Yet one day, they'd been walking hand in hand on a secluded island beach, and Ashley had dropped to one knee. They already had a strong partnership akin to a marriage, but she could finally understand why people had weddings. She wanted to bring everyone they loved together and celebrate their joy. Georgia said yes before she'd finished asking.

She glanced across the table at Georgia, who now sat between her parents. She looked so fresh and radiant—and she couldn't wait to see her in her wedding dress. How had Ashley's life gotten this good?

"I'm definitely closer to a one than a ten. I'm so happy that everyone could make it. Except for them," she said, pointing to the sky. They'd been hearing choppers overhead since yesterday. It was annoying to have photographers trying so hard to nab something. They'd been stalked by the paparazzi from the beginning of their relationship, and they'd had to work hard at not letting it destroy them.

"Hope they enjoy their photos of your roof," Aaron said.

"And the tops of the marquees. Anyway, let's not talk about them. You asked if I'm nervous, but what about you? How do you feel about making your best man's speech?"

"Oh, I'm not nervous at all. It'll be witty and devastatingly clever but also sensitive and heartfelt. When I'm done, there won't be a dry eye in the house."

"You have no idea what you'll say, do you?"

"No. But I'm sure it'll still be all of the above."

She caught Georgia's eye, and they smiled across the table. She couldn't believe this woman was going to be her wife.

Despite Rachel's gentle teasing, they'd elected to have a nontraditional ceremony. They walked each other down the aisle, Ashley in a black dress she loved and Georgia in green. The large marquee had rows of chairs, with gold-colored balloons floating toward the ceiling and flowers lining the sides. A string orchestra played an instrumental version of their favorite song they'd written together.

Though Ashley genuinely hadn't been nervous, as they walked she was overwhelmed watching the faces of their loved ones. Many of them cried, smiling through tears. She made eye contact with as many people as possible—their parents, Johnny and Judy, Aaron, Mel, Rachel, and Eliza. She hadn't expected to feel so overcome. She clasped Georgia's hand, realizing she was crying as well. They reached the front and a wooden arch decorated with flowers. It meant a lot that Johnny had constructed the arch himself with timber from his ranch.

"Okay?" Georgia asked her, and Ashley nodded.

Eugene stepped forward in his suit pants and shirt, beard neatly trimmed. They loved the idea of being married by someone they knew, and he took his role very seriously. His voice shook at first, but then he smoothly and eloquently began his introduction.

Ashley had labored over her vows for weeks, reading them aloud to herself as she tried to find something true and worthy of a love she'd never even imagined. She thought about them in the shower, when she was out walking, and when she worked. It felt like a lot of pressure to distill everything she felt into a few short paragraphs. Now, she looked into Georgia's eyes, the rest of the room falling away. When she looked into that green, it all felt so easy again.

"It's hard to fathom that you and I were ever rivals. It's part of our history and something I can't regret because this was meant to be. I believe that I was always meant to love you. You make my life feel like a grand adventure. Walking by your side through the world is an honor I'm grateful for every day. Your love has made me grow, and I can't wait to grow with you for the rest of our lives."

Georgia smiled shakily and took a deep breath.

"You all know that I've been married before. When I met Ashley, I was fragile. I had a bruised heart, and the pain of love pressing on that bruise seemed too painful. But it didn't take long for everything to feel new. Since Ashley and I began together, I feel unbreakable. I've learned that it's what love feels like—like if I have this, I can always trust that my bruises will heal.

"I want to tell a story about what it's like to be with Ashley, though it's hard to choose a favorite. A few months ago, I was down about a new video I'd been working on, something not coming together the way I wanted. I came home in a bad mood, and Ashley was trying to cheer me up. Nobody knows this about me, but I can be quite dramatic."

The audience laughed knowingly for so long that Georgia clapped her hands together until they stopped.

"Ashley grabbed my hands and said, 'Sing with me.' I said I wasn't in the mood, but she persisted, knowing it would help. So she insisted we go down to this little hole-in-the-wall pub on Christopher Street, where they have karaoke nights. People were so happy to see us, and they begged us to sing some of our duets we'd recorded. One woman was so overcome that she was sobbing, so Ashley pulled her up on stage, too. It was one of those magical nights you never see coming, and that you'll never forget.

"We always say that I make her more spontaneous, and she grounds me. We make each other so happy. I know the rest of my life will have nights like that, whatever form they come in. I want Ashley to say, 'Sing with me' every time I'm sad, until our voices weaken with age and I can't hit the high notes anymore. I won't care. I love you, Ashley. Sing with me forever."

Bella Books
Happy Endings Live Here
P.O. Box 10543
Tallahassee, FL 32302
Phone: (800) 729-4992
BellaBooks.com

More Titles from Bella Books

Jones – Gerri Hill
978-1-64247-598-2 | 260 pages | Mystery
One weekend getaway, six friends, and a deadly secret that will wash away everything they thought they knew.

Merry Weihnachten – E. J. Noyes
978-1-64247-610-1 | 292 pages | Romance
Christmas traditions aren't the only things getting mixed up when these two hearts collide beneath the mistletoe.

Sweet Home Alabarden Park – TJ O'Shea
978-1-64247-570-8 | 362 pages | Romance
She came to restore a royal estate—she never expected to rebuild her heart.

Dr. Margaret Morgan – Christy Hadfield
978-1-64247-628-6 | 286 pages | Romance
Facing the professor on campus everyone hates is terrifying—but falling for her might be even worse.

Overtime – Tracey Richardson
978-1-64247-630-9 | 278 pages | Romance
A charming romance about second chances, found family, and scoring the goal that matters most.

The Big Guilt – Renée J. Lukas
978-1-64247-657-6 | 206 pages | Romance
What if the one who got away became the one you can't have?

www.ingramcontent.com/pod-product-compliance
Lightning Source LLC
Jackson TN
JSHW020823180725
87607JS00001B/2